NUNC!

NUNC!

A Novel

Quentin Letts

Illustrated by Jeremy Leasor

C

CONSTABLE

CONSTABLE

First published in Great Britain in 2025 by Constable

1 3 5 7 9 10 8 6 4 2

A CIP catalogue record for this book
is available from the British Library.

ISBN: 978-1-40872-284-8 (hardback)

Typeset in Baskerville by SX Composing DTP, Rayleigh, Essex
Printed and bound in Great Britain by Clays Ltd, Elcograf S.p.A.

Papers used by Constable are from well-managed forests
and other responsible sources.

MIX
Paper | Supporting
responsible forestry
FSC
www.fsc.org   FSC® C104740

Constable
An imprint of
Little, Brown Book Group
Carmelite House
50 Victoria Embankment
London EC4Y 0DZ

The authorised representative
in the EEA is
Hachette Ireland
8 Castlecourt Centre, Dublin 15,
D15 XTP3, Ireland
(email: info@hbgi.ie)

An Hachette UK Company
www.hachette.co.uk

www.littlebrown.co.uk

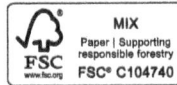

In memoriam Penny and Alexander

Da un grande ammiratore dei baffi e del genio di
Giovanni Guareschi

An English Town

THEY built things to last in ancient days and the cathedral town still had a stretch of its walls from Roman times. Luftwaffe bombers had failed to destroy it. So, more surprisingly, had post-war urban planners.

Alex Symons, an open-faced, corduroy-trousered Englishman, sixty-two years of age and on the cusp of corpulence, gazed at the wall through the car's rain-streaked windows. The Vauxhall's wipers whirred as the traffic waited for the lights to change. Anne would need to move into the right-hand lane but Symons resisted the urge to tell his wife how to drive. He no longer had the energy for that sort of thing.

His mind was on other things: this looming appointment with the specialist; and that Roman wall. Shoppers were scurrying past it without a thought, their capacity for wonder blunted, if it had ever existed, by a desire to escape the rain. Two thousand years those stones had stood. Grass withereth, flowers fadeth, luminous bone turns to dust,

1

but masons' stones endured. The one gap in the wall was where, in a burst of municipal energy in the seventies, a council bulldozer created a shortcut to the supermarket. Beside this pathway a sign, ordering cyclists to dismount, was now bent out of shape. It had been targeted by young vandals or, perhaps, the shade of a long-dead Roman builder affronted at modernity's cheek.

Red, amber, green. An Audi estate was slow to release its handbrake and by the time Anne persuaded a lorry driver to let her switch lanes they missed the light. This gave Symons more time to contemplate the Roman wall. Anne raised a hand to thank the lorry driver. Her eyes were still on the rear-view mirror as she said: 'I know you think I should have changed lane earlier.'

'I didn't breathe a word!' said Symons. Then, more soothingly: 'Thank you for driving.' It wasn't easy for either of them.

Right at Centurion Road, over a couple of mini round-abouts, then half a mile up the hill before you dipped left into the modern housing estate that had been built on former glebe lands. In ghostly acknowledgement of that, the roads had churchy names: Canon Crescent, Archdeacon's Dell, Temple View. The windscreen wipers continued their wheezy routine as Anne turned the steering wheel and brought the car into Jerusalem Row where the Sinai heart clinic was found. She parked opposite the pay-and-display.

'Five minutes early. Perfect. You wait here. Shouldn't take long.'

'I'll come in with you,' she said.

'No, I'll be fine on my own, poppet.' He didn't often call her that.

The clinic's porch was littered by a couple of old sweet wrappers and, though it was months since autumn's rot, a sycamore leaf as wide as a farmer's palm. Inside, Symons found the receptionist reading a celebrity magazine. When she deigned to acknowledge his arrival he gave his name and made some small talk about the weather. She suggested it would 'brighten later from the east'.

'Oh, good.'

'Simon, did you say?' She began tapping at her keyboard.

'Not quite. Symons with a y.'

The clinic's muggy air carried a tang of cleaning fluids. Lockdown-era edicts about social distancing lingered on the noticeboard. 'Are you our ten-past-eleven, Simon?'

'Yes. An appointment with Dr Gabriel. Symons is my surname.' From a speaker on the ceiling drifted a sentimental song. *Helping us to relax this Monday morning, that was Eva Cassidy with the immortal 'Danny Boy'* . . .

'Ah yes, here you are.' The receptionist settled into her patter. 'Fill in a form while you're waiting. The doctor's just with another patient. Take a seat and you won't have long.'

That was one way of putting it.

Presently a pensioner came wheezing down the corridor and was led away by a younger woman. 'That was the eleven-o'clock, Mrs Pepper – used to run the jewellery stall in the Buttermarket,' said the receptionist. She pressed a button to admit Symons to the corridor. 'I'll have your form if you've finished with it, Simon. Second on the right. No need to knock.' And yet he did knock. He was not sure why. A cheap, institutional door yelped on its hinges and there came a tired 'Enter'.

In Dr Gabriel's room a plastic chair stood at the angle left by Mrs Pepper. Symons noticed a yellow box of tissues on the desk. 'Thanks for coming,' said the doctor as she completed formalities from the previous appointment. She removed her glasses, rubbed an eye, refocused and smiled weakly. Symons knew he was unwell but forty-something, over-worked Dr Gabriel looked worse. If she wasn't careful, she'd be the first to peg it. A handbag lay open on the floor. Symons could see keys, mobile telephone, a tub of chewing gum, personal touches amid the bland carpet tiles. 'You've come alone?'

'My wife is outside in the car. She doesn't like surgeries.'

'Can't say I blame her.' A pause. 'Look, the tests are not encouraging. I had a discussion with your surgeon last night. The prognosis has worsened beyond any point where it makes sense to operate. At this stage there is only so much one can do. I wish I could be more encouraging.'

'I see.'

'Your general practitioner and other colleagues will devise a pain-management strategy and do their best to make you less uncomfortable. The EOL sector is pretty good these days. It's really out of my hands now. If this is any consolation, I doubt you will need to return here. Our part of the journey is complete.'

'EOL?'

The doctor summoned some softness. 'End of life. There is counselling available, for you and your family. People do often find that helpful. One patient's partner told me it was even joyful. That may seem an odd word but this can be a time of heightened emotion and affirmation. It can be surprisingly positive.'

'There's no chance of improvement?'

'One can never say never but we have tried everything.'

'I'm pretty fit.' Symons patted his gut.

'You could pass for a man ten years younger. Your diet has been reasonable. You have never smoked; your drinking has been slightly below average; and your notes show that you have maintained an active lifestyle. I wish more patients were so disciplined. But there is no justice, just genes. If we had caught it earlier, that might have made a difference.'

'You closed for lockdown.'

'Lockdown was unhelpful. Lockdown was an anomaly.'

'Jesus.'

The doctor looked away for a moment, as if contemplating a retort. Whatever it was, she thought better of it. 'A nurse will visit you at home and talk through palliative pathways. We are blessed in this county with an excellent hospice movement, despite funding challenges. I wanted you to know as soon as we were sure. I wanted to tell you in person.'

'Thank you for that. How many months?'

'Six, maybe.'

She gave him leaflets. The health service was enthusiastic about leaflets. They offered helpline numbers and support groups' email addresses. They explained what financial help the state offered patients below a certain income. Information on leaflets was of limited use, everyone knew, but the point was to be able to place something in a patient's fingers, something physical to clutch, to have to remember to take home. It lent the day shallow purpose. When people visited a doctor they expected to be given something: a blister-pack of pills, a next-appointment card or in extremis a leaflet. When the receptionist saw patients leave with nothing more than a leaflet, she knew it was bad, insofar as she cared.

Symons was in a daze. Tight in the chest, he walked down the corridor towards the reception area. The radio was playing 'Que Será, Será'. 'Will we have rainbows?' asked Doris Day before concluding that the future might not be ours to see. As he turned the handle of the outside door Symons heard the receptionist complain that her twenty-past-eleven was running late. The late twenty-past-eleven following the soon to be late Alex Symons.

Back outside, the early-April rain revived him a little. He splashed towards the car park. No rainbows were evident.

'Well?' asked Anne once he has settled himself in the passenger seat. She started the engine. It was easier to talk when the car was running.

'Not terribly good news, I'm afraid.'

'Another round of chemotherapy?'

'Chemo was an option for the first cancer but not now. I may have gone through that hell for nothing. They say there is no longer anything they can do. Shall we go? The ticket expires soon.'

'What do you mean, *no longer anything they can do*?'

'The doctor said I have run out of options. I am dying, apparently.'

'Oh, Alex.'

'Knew I should have gone private.'

'Oh, Alex.' She started to crumple.

'All they're interested in is getting rid of us. Let's go. Come on, don't worry about it.'

'You've been told that, and you want me not to worry?'

'Shall I drive? You're in no state.' Though he had not been up to it earlier he now felt strong enough to drive, despite his gout. There was something to bite into now, something to confront, and certainly no time to waste sitting in the wrong lane at road junctions. They changed seats in silence. In the drizzle.

Back home they had a row. Neither of them had much felt like lunch. He had taken more painkillers than was stipulated for a dose. Anne feared it could harm his kidneys. Trying to make light of it, he countered: 'That hardly matters now.'

'I'm going upstairs for a lie-down,' she said, colour on her cheeks.

A half-cut apple and sliver of ham remained on the plate where she had tried to eat. He picked it up and jettisoned the whole thing, plate included, in the bin. He slipped back into his coat, folded the newspaper into his pocket and hobbled round the block to Cloisters wine bar. Hock might help.

'Small or large?' asked Robin. Rob was a mate, probably his best, though the field of candidates for this title was admittedly small.

'Half-carafe. Probably shouldn't but what the hell.'

'Lunch menu? The kitchen has pretty much closed but I can probably get them to do you something. The lamb casserole's good.'

'Bloody lamb.' It was a running joke. Cloisters was known for its lamb and the chef cooked it pink. 'Just wine, thanks. Good and cold. I'll grab that table by the door. Can I borrow a pen? Might do the quick crossword.'

'Here. I'll bring the wine over.'

They had met as undergraduates at their college, St Luke's, and shared digs in their final terms. A few years later Rob came to stay for the weekend with Symons and his first wife – not long before she died, poor love – and they were walking back to the house after a few beers when Rob noticed 'For Sale' signs outside a derelict chapel near the cathedral. Symons didn't think Rob was serious when he announced, a week later, that he had made an offer on the place. It was swiftly accepted. With imagination and not too much capital Cloisters had quickly become a successful business. That felt like a lifetime ago.

The hock was cool and sharp. Symons made progress with the crossword and watched the late-lunchtime crowd: a few tourists, some hipsters with beards, a student being fattened up by his mum who was making a fuss about him being too thin. What a loud voice she had. A Range Rover stopped outside the bar and a county woman swept in amid clouds of scent and pink pashmina. She embraced a blazered man. Rob knew the woman – 'Good afternoon, Scilla' – and automatically brought her a large glass of vodka. A delivery boy, using his backside to open the door, arrived with two boxes of vegetables. He took them down to the cellars.

'That traffic warden's around, Ben,' said Rob.

'Won't be a moment,' shouted the boy. When Symons had first moved here you could park where you liked but the streets were now terrorised by a traffic warden called Keith. He was nicknamed 'Kruel Keith' because he seemed to take elaborate pleasure in dispensing penalties.

Hock and painkillers slowly worked their alchemy. Though the chest tightness eased, other problems did not. Where did one start with a pre-grieving wife? A Frenchman or American would declare his love with florid artistry but Symons was English. In thirty years he had never felt easy telling Anne she meant the world to him. If he agreed to see counsellors, they would only try to make him cry.

How could you analyse something so instinctive, and now painful, as love for your wife? Shrinks went through the motions. There would be rote routines and sing-song clichés and more leaflets. He didn't want that. He wanted to live. He wanted to drive his sporty Mazda down a country lane with sunlight glinting through the trees. He wanted to hit the ski slopes or sit by the fire with a whiskey for the autumn internationals. The doctor's answer to his question about the possibility of improvement – 'One can never say never' – was as blunt as these people got. Six months felt insufficient. Even at his most pessimistic he had hoped for a little more than that.

An hour or so passed and Rob talked him into having a sticky lemon cake to mop up the hock. Symons slipped a mouthful to Solly, Rob's spaniel. Solly had the best begging eyes in England.

'You spoil that eejit dog,' laughed Rob's wife, Nora, from the kitchen, flour in her hair and over her apron. There was more on her nose. Rob and Nora, dark-curled and from Donegal, had married late. Some best friends would have been jealous but all Symons felt was pleasure that his friend had married such a fine woman.

As the wine and drugs drifted through his body he flicked on his mobile and trawled cancer chat-groups for information about cardiac sarcoma. No one was terribly cheering. In time an email arrived from Josh. 'Hi, Dad. Any word on those test results? By the way, we've been to the hospital ourselves and we have news. Mia is pregnant! I think Mum guessed something last time we were down. Due date end of December. Could be a Yule baby.' The message ended with a kiss.

Bad news he could tolerate. Good news was too much.

His eyes began to swim and his chin pruned. Love for Josh overwhelmed him. It broke him to think of the boy's happiness being ruined by this cancer. Josh was so decent, always eager to do the right thing, trying to obey the rules. How could he make sense of something so random and hurtful?

Symons slipped out of Cloisters unnoticed. He did not want anyone to see that he was upset. Rob might merely conclude that Symons had drunk too much, which perhaps he had, but that was not the whole story. A shrewish wind blew and Symons raised the collar of his coat. Everything felt accentuated, sharpened, every smell and sound and sight. He was in the world yet apart from it, hovering over it. Most oddly he had never felt more alive, almost above life rather than in it. Was it the drink doing this or was it those pills? Or simply this surfeit of emotion?

As he was walking through the cathedral close a cassocked verger came out of the main entrance's wicket door and placed an advertising board on the pavement: 'Evensong 5.30 p.m.' That was in just over half an hour. A gust of choral voices leaked out through the doorway. Symons pushed on the small entrance and nearly tripped as he stepped over its lip. His gouty toe made its protests known but they were soon forgotten.

Churches have that same smell: polish, candle wax, flagstones, a suggestion of communion wine. Symons was not one to bob at the altar but that smell did at least persuade him to take his hands out of his coat pockets. The cathedral choir was practising in the stalls and it became apparent that the 'Magnificat' was causing problems. God had scattered the proud in the imagination of their hearts but the 'scattered' needed three syllables and a skittish rhythm. 'Maybe one more time if you don't mind,' said the choirmaster. The verse flowed better this time. 'Right, we'll just canter through the responses. Then the "Nunc", please.'

Symons took a pew to the back, by a pillar where he would be less obvious. After some hesitation he slid to his knees. Someone had gone to the trouble of embroidering these hassocks, after all, even if kneeling might exacerbate that gout in his right foot. What to pray? How to pray? Did prayer count if you only tried it when you were in a jam?

God, look after my wife. Have mercy on my son. Deliver the child safely. Josh will make a good father, better than me. Please, I'm barely coping.

It was no good. A toddler was wailing in the south transept, the gift-stall operator was packing away her wares and the choirmaster again interrupted the music to make further adjustments. Symons's prayers remained stubbornly earthbound. He lifted himself back on to the pew and eased the numbness from his right leg just as the organist embarked on the 'Nunc Dimittis'. 'Lord, now lettest thou thy servant depart in peace.' The men's voices soared, soldierly in unison. When the two parts split at 'and to be the glory of thy people Israel', the tenors went nuts.

And now, at last, Symons felt an inner surge. The trebles and altos entered at the Gloria and the piece acquired a stately sway. The choirmaster became so immersed in the music that his shoulders were rolling. To the organ's chords there was a thrust, a force, a richness beyond anything words could say. These musical phrases powered onwards, mocking stagnation, abandoning each brief settlement of harmony. Up at the altar the hard edges of the gleaming cross began to lose their definition and become fuzzier, giving way to an idea of different realities, a different age.

As in Cloisters earlier, Symons found his eyes brimming. Yet that was not the only explanation for this shifting perception, this blurring sense of transference. It was as if the ages were melting and he had surrendered to it. The imagination of his heart was unhooked.

Herod's Jerusalem

SIMEON'S eyebrows crinkled as he peered across Temple Square. Wrens could have nested in those brows. A warm, dusty breeze made a wind-chime tinkle at the top of Deuteronomy Street, between the saucepan stall and the barber's. The fading rays of another autumn day lent Huldah Gates a honey glow.

Simeon was testing this chair that young Benjamin had knocked up for him. Its wheels scrunched on the paving slabs. 'This should help you move around the square without pain,' the boy had said. 'Until your foot is better. See it as a short-term fix.' A temporary measure: didn't they say that about everything? Lean-to guttering in the alley by his landlady Noor's house had already been there fifteen years. The occupation had started as a 'special military operation' but the Romans were now rooted in Jerusalem's Antonia fortress, with no talk of any withdrawal.

Simeon tried a few half-revolutions, forward, reverse, a turn to the left. Benjamin had greased the wheels with plenty of lamb fat. Clambering into the contraption had not been easy and Simeon's knees were sticking up too high. The broomstick bumper would protect his right foot, the one with this damn gout, but Benjamin admitted that the pilot's low-slung position was not ideal. It was a first attempt. Future models could rectify design flaws.

Whoosh! After a push on the wheels Simeon was surprised how much ground he covered. A pigeon leapt out of the way. Each time Simeon pushed, the draught caught his wild hair. Benjamin had attached a rudimentary brake. It seemed to work. Here came Shlomo, chasing as the chair zoomed over the square's smooth flagstones.

'Woof!' went Shlomo.

'Woof!' replied Simeon. He gave another thrust and the dog tried to bite one of the wheels. 'You won't catch me,' laughed Simeon. In his excitement he forgot that near the top of the street there were four steps as it dropped towards Deuteronomy Square. Realising how fast he was approaching them, he pulled on the brake. It snapped in his hand. Another flaw for Benjamin to address in future models of his invention. As the chair sped past – more accurately under – the saucepan stall Simeon ducked but his left kneecap struck a clanking, clonking blow to two suspended frying pans. The chair's bumper clipped a revolving disc on which the barber's chair was fixed. The customer, mid-shave and in a semi-recumbent position, was sent swivelling and shaving soap blew off his chin. The barber turned back from strapping his blade to find he was staring at his customer's sandals.

Simeon threw the snapped brake lever overboard. Shlomo thought it was a stick and ran to retrieve it. In the low cockpit, his vision impeded by items of laundry from a washing line that he had collected en route, Simeon was starting to contemplate abandoning ship. Then he reached the steps and was assailed by terrible, tooth-loosening vibrations. He bore the experience with the stoicism that comes to a man in the throes of high-speed calamity. You simply don't have time to panic. To compound the problems there came a *crrrackkk* as one of the chair's wheels snapped in a pothole but the wheel did not immediately part company from its axle.

'Uh-oh,' said Simeon. The source of his dismay was not, as it happens, the wheel, or the wails from a mother who pulled her child from his vertiginous path. It was that Simeon saw he was hurtling towards Onesimus's fruit and veg' stall. Onesimus was Benjamin's father and he was one of Simeon's friends, albeit not an uncritical one. If there was one quality Onesimus had, it was a relish for order. No Jerusalem greengrocer was so proud of his street display. Onesimus spent hours arranging peaches in pyramids. Pears and apples were polished individually and presented their best angle to the buying public. No merchant in the old city took greater trouble creating a retail aesthetic with melons, marrows and pineapples in ziggurats. On this trajectory Simeon's wheelchair was going to hit the bullseye of twenty-one honeydews.

'Stampede!' Daft thing to say but it was all Simeon could think to cry as he hurtled towards the melons.

Onesimus was snipping a bunch of black grapes for Mrs Pappo, a silversmith's wife. His small-talk trailed when he heard 'Stampede!' and, looking up, he saw what was careening towards his display. The wheelchair winged Habib's dung barrow, with pongy consequences. It nearly flattened the poet Lysander who was crossing the street

15

with his head in the clouds. Sylvanus from the garrison raised a hand in an imperious 'Halt!' but Simeon, rattling past, gave the optio a helpless wave.

'You missed,' grunted Mrs Pappo. Onesimus had indeed just tried to cut the grapes from their stem but because his mind was elsewhere he very nearly trimmed one of her fingernails. Two seconds before impact the laws of physics reasserted their eternal truths and Simeon's right wheel flew off. The chair lurched away from Onesimus's display and Simeon instead ploughed into a compost heap of rotting husks and peel which built up during every week's fruit and veg' trading.

The silence was instant. 'I'm sorry?' said Onesimus.

'Missed,' repeated Mrs Pappo.

'Yes!' said Onesimus. 'Moses be praised, he missed!' And for the first time many could remember, the fastidious little greengrocer threw back his neck and guffawed. 'The mad maniac missed!' He lowered his scissors, seized Mrs Pappo's jowls and kissed her four times. Any nectarine treated thus would need to be discounted.

Reuben ran over from his tea stall in the square and started pulling the wheelchair out of the compost heap. Reuben was also laughing, as was Simeon. As for Mrs Pappo, she did enough blinking to suggest she had quite enjoyed being kissed by Onesimus.

'Are you all right?' Reuben asked his oldest friend.

'Seldom better,' roared Simeon. On his head was a cauliflower skullcap. The axle had left a scar on the street and the machine was a write-off; otherwise little damage, though Simeon did smell like a dustbin.

It did not take long for Kedar, the city's deputy warden, to materialise. He accused Simeon of damaging public property and being a public hazard. 'Is not the real danger,' reasoned Reuben, 'that Lysander may now write a ballad about his brush with death?'

'This is no time for facetiousness,' said Kedar, wrinkling his nose. Shlomo chose that moment to trot up with the retrieved brake handle in his mouth. He dropped it on the ground and barked, wishing the game to be repeated. The party was breaking up when a beautiful butterfly landed on Simeon's big toe. He was about to yowl when he realised it did not hurt at all.

Later, when the excitement was all but forgotten, a Roman cavalry turma clattered through Deuteronomy Square towards the Antonia fortress. In its midst was a centurion with a neck of steel and a face of determined crossness. Four horses pulled a cart containing bearded, bloodied prisoners. No one in the square said a word.

As for Simeon's wheelchair it was thrown next to the compost heap and stayed there for years, a testament to misplaced faith.

A Dog's Breakfast

WAYFARERS approaching Jerusalem were confronted by walls that seemed to stretch to the very ends of the Earth. Above the city hung a gauze of heat. The ground had been pounded to dust by the hundreds of hooves and feet that came daily. Jerusalem was all, and all was Jerusalem. In its seething centre sat Deuteronomy Square and it was here that Simeon and his friend Reuben gathered over their first teas of the day. Reuben glanced upwards.

'Hear that?'

'Nope.'

'Sounded like a cat. Yes, over there. Buzzard. Must have quite a view.' The bird was over Mount Moriah. Spotting prey on the rockface, it swooped. Within seconds the life was ripped out of an innocent shrew. Breakfast, and not a prutah to pay.

The streets and square contained little life at that hour. 'It's a slow morning, Simeon. I may not get rich today.'

'Who needs riches?'

'I do.'

'Relax. We've the cool of morning and the priests have yet to start their sacrifices. I'll take another cup of that tea if it's going.'

'You wouldn't prefer kykeon?'

'Come again?'

'Kykeon. A delicacy in Greece.'

'I'll stick with tea.'

Soon the city would swell with a din of sheep bells, hawkers and snake charmers' pipes. By midday smoke from the temple sacrifices would drift down and curl under every doorway until Jerusalem smelled like one vast kebab stand. By then Simeon would have limped to his pitch in Temple Square and lost himself for a few hours in the insistence of daily life. His job, though really it was more of a vocation, was to offer advice to visitors, to explain to them how the temple's customs and procedures worked, to suggest hotels and stables and restaurants and merchants who might meet their needs, and to watch the world's great, performative promenade. 'Life, Caleb, is a waiting game, a watching game, a way of passing the hours and nursing our woes until we are called.' And his apprentice, Caleb, who was a bright lad but not always industrious, would juggle pebbles or stamp on ants or whittle at sticks.

Deuteronomy Square was that amiable space just before the cobbles dropped towards Kidron and the houses became disreputable. Off one side of the square, Deuteronomy Street took pilgrims up to Temple Square. Even at this hour a few trinket-sellers were setting out their stalls. Water tinkled into a horse trough. Reuben's tea stall occupied the other side of the square. It was known for its mint tea, lemon koloochehs and a girth-broadening baklava. Customers sat on benches arranged under a bougainvillea. Two almond trees swayed in the morning breeze, pretty with white blossom. That was where Ezekiel sold his almonds but he had not yet arrived. In front of his stall was a spot where musicians could busk and children play leapfrog and Ibrahim the artist sometimes drew political cartoons in the dust. Street-sweeper Habib was doing his early rounds so at present everything was raked and tidy.

'Bloody money,' said Simeon.

'Money is our sure foundation and cornerstone,' said Reuben.

'Menachem the Essene rubs along all right without it.'

'Menachem the Essene survives on the charity of those who do have money. Fleas without a host soon die. Talking of which, have you seen Shlomo? I have some pastry scraps.'

'Shlomo doesn't need money.'

'Shlomo doesn't have to pay taxes. Without taxes Herod would have no army, Rome no empire and we'd still be in Babylon. Here he is. Shlomo!' Reuben whistled and the dog trotted over to accept the pastry scraps. Sparrows flittered around him stealing crumbs, worse than tax collectors.

Reuben's tea stall was one of the busier joints in town. Pharisees, Sadducees, Roman soldiers, none-of-the-aboves: all used it, even Menachem the Essene with his heron's gait and his 'Ah well, if you're sure you can spare it, that's frightfully kind' when someone filled his begging bowl. Essenes were holy men but with Menachem there was, perhaps, a lurking suspicion that he was not so much holy as indolent. Nature's scavengers had to work harder. Overhead the buzzard was back to its slow circuits, watching all, comprehending little. It saw the beginnings of the day, the new palace and Zerubbabel's ageing temple where a few priests were gathering yesterday's ashes. It saw women shake blankets on roof-tops and goatherds exhort their beasts up Hinnom Valley. At the four-towered Antonia fortress, Roman sentries changed guard. Smoke rose from breakfast fires. A few bleats and the occasional chink of hoe on stony soil reached the bird. Avian eyes saw all this and felt the rhythms of life yet the buzzard would never grasp the humanity of Jerusalem.

'Morning, Reuben.' First caller was Habib the sweep.

'Comrade Habib, *salaams*. May your broom blossom and your moons be many. Tea? Orange juice? *Kykeon?* You'll love kykeon. A Greek delicacy. Made with Pramnian wine.'

'Er, tea, please. But not for five minutes. I still have to tidy these gutters. Kedar always checks.'

Habib was the most conscientious of municipal employees yet the worst paid. To which Tambal would laugh: 'What is pay? We slaves know not of such things'. Here came Tambal now, head down, chuckling to himself, ambling with his long limbs and floppy sandals. Tambal was often an early taker for caramelised pistachios and apricot shortbread, for Tambal had a sweet tooth. To be accurate he had four sweet teeth. The rest had fallen out, rotted by the sugar canes he sucked. Tambal's owner was Zillah, who rose late and retired early, often with a different companion. Zillah had been married to more than one rich man – friends had lost count. Her third marriage was said to have lasted little longer than the hundred-and-nineteenth Psalm.

'I was expecting Jonah to be here,' said Tambal, ignoring a slap on his hand from Reuben as he pinched a still-warm pastry.

21

'As punishment for your thieving you can help me with this kykeon.' Reuben handed Tambal a mixing bowl and a clump of purple-headed plants. 'It's pennyroyal and I need the leaves taken off their stems.' Reuben returned to his stove, crushing roasted barley in a pestle and boiling it. This was added to wine and flavoured with goat's cheese and the pennyroyal. Reuben gave it a doubtful sniff and rubbed his hands on his apron in his distinctive way. A brush at his ankles told him Shlomo was interested. 'Here, Shlomo, try some kykeon.' The dog licked briefly at the cheesy mush of wine and barley. He soon crossed the square to lie in the sun.

'Are those your benches, Master Reuben?'

'Kedar! It's you.'

'Indeed.'

'My day is complete, yet the morning scarce begun.'

'No sarcasm, if you please.'

'You are just in time, deputy warden. I am brewing kykeon.'

'Eh?'

'Kykeon.'

'You shouldn't sneeze at the stove,' said Kedar, twitching. 'We have hygiene regulations.'

'Kykeon,' said Simeon. 'It's a Greek delicacy.'

'Greek?'

'Haven't you heard of it?'

'Of course I've heard of it. Everyone knows of kykeon.'

Kedar was tall and lean, his beard so neat that its hems might have been sewn by a Galilee fisherwoman. He had not one twitch but two. The first was a wriggle of the nose, the second a pouting of the lips, like a trumpeter between blasts.

'Want to try some?' asked Reuben.

Kedar recoiled from the pot's cheesy gusts. 'It's possibly a little early for me.'

'Smart people in Hellenic society take kykeon for breakfast,' said Simeon. 'Experts say it ignites the gastric processes, flushes the kidneys and stimulates the libido. Not that a man of your drive needs stimulating.'

'No, quite.' Kedar was not sure he knew the meaning of libido.

'Hellenic society is hardly your milieu, Simeon,' said Reuben with a scoffing tone.

'Not his milieu at all!' agreed Kedar, eager to show that he did understand that word. 'Though one day I could put in a word for you, Simeon. No garlic in it, is there? Well, perhaps just a small cup, then, Master Reuben. To ignite my gastric processes and my *libbido*.'

'Mrs Kedar won't know what's hit her,' offered Simeon.

'One kykeon coming up!' Reuben sank a ladle into the gluey pot. There was a sound of marsh suction as he lifted some steaming goo into a cup.

'How much do I owe you?' asked Kedar, making a show of reaching for coins.

As Reuben was tidying a dribble off the side of the cup he happened to look across the square. Shlomo had risen from his suntrap and was staggering about, dry-retching. 'Oh, I think we can allow this one on the house, Kedar. Now then, you mentioned my benches. Have we been forgetful again and placed them beyond our boundary?'

'I was going to say something, yes,' said Kedar, accepting the cup. 'On the house, you say? Very decent of you, Reuben. Very decent, indeed.'

'He's a good man,' said Simeon.

'Not having a kykeon yourself, Simeon?' asked Kedar, testing the bouquet of his brew and almost snapping his neck in the recoil.

'My palate is not sophisticated enough.'

'No. Well, thank you, Reuben. *Steeny yassas* and all that. And *efaristo*. Down in one!' With which he emptied the bolt of red kykeon into his mouth and chewed. To his credit he managed to swallow some.

'I'm still getting the hang of the recipe,' said Reuben. Kedar was unable to respond.

'He is savouring the taste,' said Simeon. 'There's a man who knows his kykeon.'

'I'll make sure the benches are moved back an inch,' said Reuben. 'Thank you for reminding me. See you later, Kedar.'

Deputy warden Kedar, cheeks bulging, departed in haste. Shlomo, meanwhile, was spectacularly sick under the trough. '*Steeny yassas!*' said Simeon and Reuben.

The Angel Feather

SIMEON'S days passed as days will: bursts of action amid stretches of inactive contemplation, when not even Caleb's youthful presence could stem the solitude. In Temple Square he answered the usual daily questions from pilgrims, took bookings for presentation ceremonies – when parents brought their newborn to be blessed – and recommended places to visit. 'There's a good fragrance store on Maccabees Street. Say Simeon sent you.' They did not need to know that the fragrance store was run by Simeon's young cousin Dan.

Roman soldiers were loitering. The authorities were on their mettle because the Zealots were active. Simeon saw a solemn little family arrive in the square and hesitate. Jethro the leper was swinging about on his crutch, bowing to women whose husbands told him to shoo. The more they said 'Shoo', the more Jethro persisted until eventually they gave him some baksheesh.

'Oh, hello, Simeon,' said a gloomy voice.

'Good morning, Lysander.'

'Is it?' asked the poet.

'Noon has not yet passed.'

'No, I meant is it good? Little positive that I can discern. But what do I know? I'm only an unpublished elegist.' Lysander was the son of a regional governor. He was in love with Zilla but Zilla had no interest in him, or his poetry.

'The satisfaction must be in the writing.'

'What's the point, if no one reads it?'

'God sees it.'

'God? God's busy. God has better things to do. God skim-reads and says it needs more work. Then he returns to his admin' or his lyre or whatever. Publishers are no better. I don't know why I bother.' The scar on Simeon's forehead was just starting to itch when he was saved by the family that had earlier entered the square.

'You'll have to excuse me, dear boy. I have clients to attend to.' He abandoned Lysander to help the visitors. They wanted to know about sacrifice procedures and where to buy turtle doves. The father offered Simeon a tip but Simeon noticed that the child wore no sandals. He declined the money and told the father to spend it on a cake for his daughter who was hiding behind her mother.

'Simeon, that was kind of you,' said Lysander when the family left. 'But that's the sort of man you are. A good soul. Unusual these days. I don't suppose you'd like to look at my latest ode.' Before Simeon could respond, Lysander continued: 'But no, of course you wouldn't. I shouldn't have asked. See you later, Simeon. If we're spared.'

As Lysander plodded away, Jethro the leper cried after him with an urgent tone. 'Mate, you've dropped something!'

Lysander looked down, for Lysander was tall and Jethro was roughly the height of a sheep. 'I don't think so,' said Lysander.

'Yes, look!' Jethro opened the palm of one hand, in the middle of which lay a blue ostrich feather.

'What is it?'

'It's your lightness of being, mate.' Jethro let the feather go. It dropped slowly and he was able to catch it before it touched the ground. 'You can have it if you like.'

'I don't think I'm ready for it,' said Lysander. 'It might break the camel's back.'

All this Simeon remembered that evening when he prayed in front of his own feather. Large, white, slightly damaged, it stood in the cracked jug on the windowsill in his bedroom. In early days his landlady Noor tried to throw it away. She called it a dust magnet and Simeon had to retrieve it from her rubbish pan, a little battered. He crossly told her it had been given to him by an angel. She'd pulled a face and asked: 'And what was her name?'

Simeon forgave her, of course. He worshipped Noor, even while paying rent to her. Now he mouthed his silent prayers to another great authority. Into those prayers we will not pry for they contained matters of a sorrowful nature and an author must not dabble in his subjects' souls. Simeon murmured his closing invocation: 'And please look after that family from the temple this morning. The little girl was a sweetie and she could do with some shoes.'

Did the feather's barbs stir? Simeon felt they did. That night, for once, he slept well and dreamed of his boyhood.

A Snake Strikes

THE barefoot boy checked for prying eyes before his flanks slid through the gap in the wall. Apparently the garden beyond belonged to Aretas, an important local man, but to teenagers one important local man was much the same as another. Simeon's father travelled, trading incense, and the boy went with him, learning to navigate by the night sky. His mother was dead and his aunts had youngsters of their own. Simeon helped pack and clean and occasionally picked up titbits of intelligence. It didn't cost much to feed him and he sang well. It was a clear, sweet, accurate voice. He would sing after supper, hands at his side, pushing forward his chin. His father would weep.

'Why are you crying, Dad? Aren't you happy?'

'I am, Simeon, but old people have wells of sadness. Your singing is beautiful. That draws my sadness bucket to the top.'

'That sounds odd.'

'Life is a little odd.'

They never stayed long in a place. Watch, witness, don't interfere: that was the code. Live and let live. They crossed territories and Simeon's father never complained about the authorities. Pay their demands and say 'Pax vobiscum'. You offered them a square of basbousa as a token of esteem. They seldom refused that.

Business took them from Gerrha in the south-east, where women glistened with scented oil and the grilled fish was succulent, to Antioch in the north. Father never lingered in Antioch. It was riddled with wanton Greeks and God would shake its pavements in disapproval. Petra was not so bad. Petra had red gorges and sooty falcons, fast and deadly. Simeon saw a falcon kill a plump oriole on the wing. The strike was instant. Thrilling. And arguably not so bad for the oriole, to die that fast.

For now Simeon just wanted to find the caracal. He had seen her tail dart through this gap. It was the time of day when adults rested from the mid-afternoon heat. Simeon stilled and listened, hoping to hear the wild cat's mews. Apart from a few crickets, the summer sun had silenced most creatures. The one thing moving was a column of ants marching up a pistachio tree. Other insects let them do their thing. It was never worth tangling with ants.

The gap in the wall brought Simeon into a spinney of mimosa, pine and bottlebrush trees. A medicinal scent betrayed eucalyptus, too, their branches swishing in the breeze. Twenty yards to the right was a clearing and beyond that a villa's verandah. No one was about. He had left his sandals the other side of the wall because bare feet were quieter. With sandals, eucalyptus leaves could make a racket.

'Meow . . .' The caracal's cry came from some sort of disused shrine covered in ivy. Simeon mimicked the call. Caracals were shy. The cat must have hurt her leg, for she kept licking it – when, that is, she was not cleaning two kittens. If Simeon could somehow seize one of those kittens, he would train it and become the most envied boy on the trade route.

The mother allowed Simeon to call to her. Slowly he reached into his pocket and withdrew a few lumps of cheese. He placed these on a flat stone and withdrew. The next three afternoons Simeon returned to the spinney. Each day his votive offering had disappeared. The crickets sang, the heat pulsed and the caracal allowed him to creep forward a few paces. It was on that fourth day, sliding through the wall, that Simeon heard the girl. She was walking near the verandah, singing, and she held a child of about five in her arms.

> *Hush little pumpkin cry no more*
> *Close those eyes and soon you'll snore*
> *Let your dreams rise to the skies*
> *Close those eyes and still your sighs.*

Maybe she thought he was a gardener. She raised her head in silent greeting and made a 'shush' sign with her lips and forefinger.

He asked: 'Would you like to see a caracal suckling her kittens?'

'A caracal? I've never seen one. Where is it?'

The child stirred. 'Shall we go and see the big cat?' the girl asked the child. He vouchsafed a solemn nod. They crouched at the stone where Simeon usually left his cheese. The child followed Simeon's arm as he pointed to the den where the caracal was tending her young. Something made her prick her ears.

'We'd better leave,' whispered Simeon. 'She's worried.' As they were standing, the reason for the caracal's restlessness became clear. A large viper was dangling from the bottlebrush tree just above them. It was near the girl's head. 'Don't move,' hissed Simeon. He picked up a stick from the spinney floor and was about to use it when the viper lunged. Simeon pushed the girl and child out of the way but in that movement the snake wrapped itself round his forehead, biting him. Simeon cursed. The snake moved at villainous speed towards the shrine, its belly cleaving to the earth. The caracal was equally swift, pouncing with paws and claws and teeth until the snake was dead in the dust. The caracal collected her kittens and fled, a streak of colour in the undergrowth. All that was left was one dead viper, two startled youngsters and an ecstatic five-year-old boy.

'Oh my God,' exclaimed the girl. 'Are you okay?'

'It got my forehead but I don't think it's too bad,' said Simeon, touching the wound with his fingertips. The snake's bite hurt like blazes. 'Are you all right?'

'We're fine. He's laughing!' The child's eyes put Simeon in mind of a hawk. 'But you'd better come inside and let someone see to that bite.'

'I shouldn't be here.'

'Why not?'

'I came through the wall. I've been watching the caracal for a few days. I was hoping to grab one of the kittens.'

'You're crazy. Aretas will have you thrashed.'

He again touched the bite. It had left a swelling welt. His father had told him vipers were bad but not deadly.

The sooner he got it under water, the better. 'There's a spring on the other side of the wall. I'd better go. Don't tell anyone.'

'You're shaking. You don't look steady.'

'I'll be okay, honestly.'

The girl said: 'I'd better take the little one back inside.'

'Is he yours?'

'No. He belongs to my master's daughter, Cypros. Her husband is out of town.'

'What's your name?'

'My name? Why?'

'I don't know.'

'I'm Hannah, from Samaria – well, my father was. He died.'

'I'm Simeon. My dad travels and I go with him. Mum died.'

'You saved us from that snake, Simeon.' She gently touched his sore forehead. She had the biggest eyes Simeon had ever seen. 'I've got to go. They'll be waking from their rest and will want to get ready for an event at court.'

When she reached the verandah she put the boy on his feet, turned her head back towards Simeon, and waved. She led the boy into the house saying: 'Come along, little Herod, let's go and get you dressed.'

Boaz Is Kept Busy

TALKING of painful heads, Jonah and his Pharisees were at Reuben's tea stall, singing. They loved these jamming sessions with lemon water, cake and mini sermons. Jonah sat at the top of the long table. Between songs he rubbed his face and patted his tummy and launched into another homily, be it on the rituals of worship or the decadence of Roman civic entertainments, from theatre to charioteering – 'No good will come of this indecent haste, this whipping of horse hide, this crazed jockeying for position and its attendant gambling!' Today he was telling his novices about the different types of Pharisee, from the fearful Pharisee scared of doing the wrong thing, to the shoulder Pharisee so proud of his goodness that he paraded it on his shoulder. The wait-a-little Pharisee always put off decent deeds until another day. 'Don't forget the bruised Pharisee,' shouted Reuben from his washing-up pots.

'In good time, Brother Reuben,' said Jonah.

The bruised Pharisee was so wary of lustful thoughts that he turned his gaze from any female form, and duly walked into a wall because the silly clot wasn't watching where he was going. This caused boisterous merriment and one lad jumped up to mime a bruised Pharisee walking into a wall. Everyone broke into a folk song about dancing round a grapevine. The rhythm started slowly and increased until the pulse was frenetic, hands being whacked on knees or table to keep it together. It ended with a great shout of delight.

Jonah went to buy more drinks. The tea stall was busy so he took the tray of cups to the counter. 'Ten lemon waters!'

'Are you okay carrying them back to the table?'

'Not a problem.'

'Would you and your friends care to read some of my poetry?' enquired Lysander, who liked to pounce on customers when they were at their most vulnerable. Lifting the tray of drinks, Jonah said: 'This is the season when we may read only holy Scripture.' At that point Lysander noticed a vision of loveliness drift into the square.

'Hey there, Tabitha.'

'Hey there, Lysander,' came the dreamy response.

'Morning, Tabitha!' echoed one of Jonah's lot.

'Hello, Daniel,' replied Tabitha the harpist, who, being blind, had a good memory for voices. The sunlight caught her honey-brown locks and her blue frock was ruffled by the wind. There was an enchanting sway to her movements. All the square was hypnotised.

CRASSSSSSH!

'Jonah's dropped the drinks.'

'Are you all right, Jonah?'

'He walked right into the tree.' So he had. Because he had been gawping at Tabitha.

'Cold towel for Jonah, please, Reuben. The rabbi has an egg on his forehead.'

All of which should have been enough for any morning but then Boaz the herald marched into the square and started to clear his throat. Boaz had two functions. The first was to be a vizier of the royal court, adorned in glorious robes. In this, Boaz was only partly successful, for he was plump and his uniform did not fit. His other duty was to be city crier, to bawl royal proclamations; and in this aspect of his work Boaz was perfect, for he had an extremely loud voice.

'OYEZ! OYEZ! OYEZ!' bawled Boaz, ringing a handbell. 'HEAR YE, PEOPLE OF JERUSALEM!' More clangs of handbell followed. Shlomo darted from under Simeon's table and fled. Simeon took some candle wax and moulded it into balls for his ears.

'If he shouts any louder, he'll burst out of that uniform,' offered Reuben. Boaz's tabard and belt were at least a size too small. It wasn't his tailor's fault. Boaz had a slow metabolism. He only had to look at a carp patty to put on a duella.

'Let me know when the siege is over,' said Simeon.

'OYEZ! His Greatness the King will make an announcement this evening from the palace balcony. All citizens should attend. It's a big one, folks. Worth attending.' The din ricocheted round Deuteronomy Square for some moments after Boaz had done a shaky about-turn and waddled back towards the palace.

Why did Herod want them? What was he going to announce? Jonah's table was sceptical. The Pharisees regarded Herod as a Gentile interloper. His love life was another source of discontentment, many wishing he had not split from 'the people's queen', the sainted Mariamne. Then there was griping about the drought, the price of olives and high taxes. Ibrahim the artist drew a picture of a Roman-helmeted snake eating a Judaean-looking shrew. It created quite a stir. By the time everyone had gathered in front of the royal palace there was a huff on, citizens muttering that they had better things to do at this time of day than listen to his nibs announcing another vanity-viaduct.

'OYEZ!' came a familiar cry. Spectators craned for a view of the palace balcony where the king was standing. He was not wearing the laurel garland and toga that some sceptics had predicted. Instead he wore his crown and gorgeously white robes that set off his tan. You could see how he had been a favourite of that man-eater Cleopatra. Herod handed a scroll to Boaz. The herald unrolled it, turned it the right way up (this always helped) and let rip:

'JERUSALEM! Nothing to me is more dear than this holy city. It is my privilege to serve as your king yet above us stands a king of kings, the only ruler of princes, and it is to His grace that we must bend our lives. To this course, my friends, I have been giving a great deal of thought and prayer . . .'

'Good grief, do you think he's about to abdicate?' said Zillah to her neighbour. She was watching from a dais put aside for Sadducees.

'Take another wife, more like.'

Near Simeon the conversation was more practical. 'Isn't that one of Zara's boys holding the royal regalia next to Boaz?'

'If so, he'll be deafened for days.'

Boaz took a gulp from a wineskin before he resumed: 'Generations ago, Solomon's temple was cruelly destroyed. Its substitute has started to look the worse for wear. Does the temple today reflect Judaea's greatness? We are the nation of Moses and Abraham. Our kingdom is prosperous. We've never had it so good. Let us show thanks by building a new temple, here in Jerusalem! Not just a temple. Let us build an entire mountain. Let us create the greatest building project ever seen. A world-beating house of worship! In Jerusalem!'

Boaz lowered his scroll and roared: 'THREE CHEERS FOR KING HEROD! HIP, HIP . . .' The crowd's response was more dutiful than enthusiastic.

Debate began as the spectators wandered home through jammed streets. Jonah's gang reassembled at the tea stall and this time there was no singing. After a huddle with other nationalists Jonah reported 'widespread suspicions the king has been put up to this by Rome' and a theory that the old temple would be destroyed. Herod would then 'discover' he had insufficient funds for a new one. It was a plot to rob Jerusalem of her temple and no doubt replace it with another decadent hippodrome. Hiram the stonemason was happier. A month earlier he had borrowed a small fortune to buy a quarry on Mount Hotzvim. That investment now looked timely. Hiram strode to Reuben's counter, slapped coins on the counter and ordered three platters of special chicken rice. 'And don't spare the nuts and raisins.'

For two days the city boiled with gossip. The Sanhedrin was at an impasse, Sadducees were delighted by the boost to growth, Pharisees sour about Herod's motives. How long would the project take? For how many years would the altars remain cold? How should Jerusalem observe its sacred responsibilities if there was no temple for twenty years? Did Herod – *who was not Jewish* – have the money even for phase one?

On the third day Boaz reappeared, rang his bell until its clacker whizzed off its moorings, and called another royal meeting. Once again, Deuteronomy Square made its way to the palace and awaited the news bulletin. 'OYEZ! OYEZ! OYEZ!' The third 'oyez' pinked a bit, for even a herald's voice can be over-used. Boaz worked a finger at his neck to loosen his collar. Herod, who was again on his balcony, nodded slowly as Boaz laid out the revised plan. It represented a significant concession: the king proposed that demolition work on the old temple would not begin until all materials for the new one had been bought and assembled outside Jerusalem. Not a stone of the current temple would be moved until the Sanhedrin's inspectors agreed that sufficient timber, marble, mortar and stone were in place for the glorious project. Carts, scaffolding and spoil sites would be open to public inspection. The new temple would rise faster than a vine. It would bring prosperity and glory to Jerusalem and become a wonder of the modern world. It would allow the king to prove his fealty to Judaism. But none of this, promised the king, would occur until the people were satisfied that he had the materials and the wherewithal to complete the project. Herod lifted the crown from his head and held it towards the crowd before he bowed to his subjects. 'Is he doing up his shoelaces?' murmured a wit. There will always be some who grumble about a king – any king – but his offer took them by surprise. It soon became apparent that most of the city, including Jonah's Pharisees, was ready to accept his compromise deal. If he could really assemble all the kit, so be it.

Scar Tissue

SIMEON, too, was prepared to believe the king's intentions with the temple. Yet as he stood in the crowd listening to Boaz he watched Herod closely and detected a hawk's glint in the royal gaze. As the king departed, disappearing with an impatient flick of his robes, he threw some command to Boaz and the herald instantly scampered after him. None of those who worked at the palace ever spoke adoringly of the king. It was more likely with fear.

'Come on, little Herod . . .' Simeon's forehead still throbbed and itched sometimes. There were days when, on hearing of Herod's brusqueness with slaves or his behaviour to his horses, he wondered if he should have let that snake do its damnedest. It was all so long ago . . .

By the time he had reached the lodgings in Petra he had been feeling feverish. Most of the household wanted to wait until Simeon's father returned but the chief groom insisted they cut out the poison immediately. With the wound so close to what passed for the boy's brain, waiting was unwise. The forehead had swollen alarmingly. A knife was heated in the kitchen fire, then plunged in water. They made Simeon lie on a table and drink arak before the wound was pierced. Simeon fainted, from pain or poison or arak, or all three. While he was unconscious the bite was criss-crossed and squeezed and sponged with hot water.

The next day he was lying in a shaded room, well below par, when someone arrived at his bedside. 'Aretas told me to bring peaches. He is grateful to you for saving his grandson.'

'Hannah.'

'How is the wound?'

'It'll heal.'

'It looks sore. But it looks fine, too.'

That was how it began. Trade took Simeon's father south to Aila and north to Zoara but the boy stayed in Petra to recuperate. He and Hannah became sweethearts. She started working for a family in Jerusalem. He saw her occasionally when trade took them there. His brow healed, the wound retreated. All that remained was this scar and its occasional itch.

Their marriage was not a big occasion. Her mother could not afford much and acquaintances on the incense route were dubious because the girl was a Samaritan. Only Simeon's father accepted her completely. The old man smiled and offered them dates and talked about the past, of his own wedding and his parents' wedding, back down the tunnel of time. At the modest wedding feast Simeon sang a love song to Hannah and the guests clasped hands to chests and said Simeon was wasted on the incense trade. He should become a cantor. But a cantor married to a

Samaritan would never find favour. The incense trade was not his thing – his stepbrother and he did not get on – so he joined the army. His father, no longer very strong, had shrugged. 'I can't lead his life for him. But it is bad luck on Hannah and his voice will be wasted.'

The morning after the wedding the old man left for Damascus. Simeon never saw him again. They said his heart just stopped. He had had a good life.

A Snakeless Charmer

ENOUGH of the glum past. Let me tell you about Shlomo. Shlomo the First. Shlomo the Great. Others followed but none quite compared.

He arrived one wary morning when Simeon was girding himself to visit Maccabees Street. His cousin Dan wanted advice on a business matter. It was never easy for Dan to get away from his fragrance shop so could Cousin Simeon please visit? Dan was a good sort and paid Simeon commission for temple visitors he sent to the fragrance shop. This money helped Simeon buy candles and silks for Noor. She reciprocated by sending treats to Dan and his family. Today there were some juicy pears to take. 'The children are so lovely,' said Noor. And Noor was right. Noor was always right, even when she was a little wrong. Lovely though Dan's no doubt were, Simeon found children difficult.

The other problem was the location of Cousin Dan's shop. It was in a narrow part of Maccabees Street where the snake charmer worked. Simeon's scar throbbed just thinking about it. The charmer – no man deserved that description less – had been quick to spot Simeon's fear of snakes. When Simeon approached, the charmer would whip the top off his straw box, give the cobra a prod and start blowing his pipe. The snake rose, swaying. The charmer would give it another couple of kicks to needle it, all the time playing on that damn pipe. Bystanders gathered and that only made it hard for anyone to squeeze past. The charmer, with much widening of eyes and tilting of head, would draw attention to Simeon's fear of snakes. The rougher sorts enjoyed such baiting. Only if Simeon gave the charmer money would he push the snake back into its basket.

'Maybe the snake chap won't be there today,' offered Reuben.

'He's always there,' said Simeon. 'He waits.'

'We all know most of those snakes have had their venom removed.'

'How do we know?'

'If it bit you, he'd be in trouble.'

'So would I.'

'You were so brave in the army but here you are, fretting about a tiny snake.'

'The small ones are the deadliest.'

While they were talking, a dog wandered up and said hello. Kedar and his constables tried to keep Jerusalem free of stray dogs but several still roamed the streets, cocking their legs and sniffing doorposts. Customers at the tea stall normally shouted at them but there was something likeable about this mutt. Simeon threw it some cheese rind. 'Good catch,' said Simeon. The dog licked its nose as the cheese went down the hatch.

'Sorry?' said Reuben.

'I was addressing our visitor.' The dog wagged its tail. 'Shalom,' said Simeon. The dog barked, just once, without excessive force.

'I've never seen him before,' said Reuben. 'Most of them I recognise. Handsome lad. Part pariah, part Pharaoh hound.' Now Reuben started woofing and saying shalom after a fashion. 'Shlom. Shlom.' The dog sneezed. Reuben sneezed back at it. The dog ambled to a nearby table and searched for scraps before returning to Simeon to sit neatly and stare at him with its brown eyes.

'He's limping a bit,' said Simeon. 'Here, boy. Let's have a look at you.'

The trouble was in one of the front legs. Simeon held out more cheese rind and the dog took it gently from his hand. He had a smooth, pale coat, sharp ears and a curling tail. Reuben inspected the problematic leg. In the left paw he found a length of twine attached to a small nail embedded in one of the pads. The dog must have stepped in a rabbit trap and bitten himself free. Reuben told Simeon to hold the animal while he fetched a blade. They soon had the problem removed. The dog stayed calm. Simeon could feel the thud of the dog's heart.

'You got any of that lamb fat left from yesterday's meatballs?'

'You spoil that eejit dog,' said Reuben.

'Poor lad. Soon have you right,' said Simeon.

The dog was glad to have the pin removed. A few scoops of lamb fat further helped morale.

'Shlom, shlom,' barked Reuben.

'We could call him Shlomo.'

'You'll be late to Maccabees Street at this rate.'

'I'm just going.'

The city had a buzz that morning. The past two months had been perfect for sun and rain, and vegetables were plentiful. Onesimus was doing a fine trade and even Ezekiel on the almond stall seemed half-cheerful. In Jerusalem's warren of streets, chickens were trussed like onions, merchants haggled, wrinkled ancients sat by the thoroughfares chewing khat leaves and an Essene in a loincloth predicted the imminence of the Messiah. Everywhere there was the smell of dung and incense and lunchtime cooking: garlic, bread, onions.

The snake charmer saw him fifteen paces away and leapt to action, grabbing his bulbous pipe. Simeon froze. A crowd of fools gathered round the snake basket and marvelled as the cobra swayed to the music. Its hood billowed like a Bedouin's headpiece. Simeon couldn't move. The snake charmer kicked the basket towards Simeon. The cobra was now making lunges at the pipe. The onlookers noticed Simeon's fear and jeered. Someone began clapping to the music. The snake's swaying acquired greater menace. Simeon sensed a ringing in his ears, blood racing through him, his brow starting to prickle. The entire scene started to rotate in his view, making him feel sick until . . . there came a barking. The spell was broken. Now there was a streak of fur towards the snake and the charmer dropped his pipe and reached for the top of the basket. Too late! In the kerfuffle the cobra escaped and slithered towards the crowd, to squeals from bystanders. The furry attacker, a dog, pounced on the snake, grabbed it by the neck and shook hard. The charmer tried to kick the dog but did not wish to expose his toes to too much danger.

'Damn dog! Stop it!' The crowd, having earlier cheered the snake, now rooted for the dog, hoping that the loose cobra would be despatched before it could bite any of them. And the snake was indeed a goner. The dog tossed its flaccid coil to one side and barked at it, once, without excessive force. Simeon had heard that bark before. By now the dog was a hero to all except the snake charmer, who was lifting the corpse of his snake with a distinctly cheesed-off expression. All Simeon could feel was relief. The snakeless charmer chased after the dog but without success, even though it still ran with a slight limp.

'Cousin Simeon, you look shaken.' Dan had come out of the shop to see what was going on. 'Come inside and have a seat. You just missed the girls.'

'I have some pears for you all,' said a dazed Simeon.

He stayed half an hour, answering Dan's questions about a sandalwood supplier in Berenice whom his father had once sprung from prison. Dan suggested he linger and say hello to the children but Simeon said he needed to get back to Deuteronomy Square. 'That snake charmer shouldn't trouble us for a while now,' said Dan as he showed Simeon to the door. 'Clever dog you've got.'

'He's not mine. He just arrived unannounced.'

'They do that,' said Dan.

Shlomo was waiting on the other side of the road. He trotted back through the city alongside Simeon. From that day the two of them were firm friends.

Gutter Instinct

THE king, to the annoyance of naysayers, soon managed to assemble all his supplies outside the city walls. Stone, marble and sand stood in vast piles, stretching down the Hinnom and Kidron valleys, enough to complete the project. A forest's worth of trees had been felled for scaffolding timber. Gravel, rock dust, ballast sand and sub-base were piled in mounds to rival anything knocked up by Imhotep. Ropes were coiled in all sizes and there were nails and hooks by the barnful. Halters for pack animals, panniers for camels, enough barrows to equip a multitude: these stood alongside pre-sculpted chapiters and column feet, faience tiles, paving slabs, plaster, brick, mortar and all colours of filling stone. The Sanhedrin was convened and agreement was reached: building on the new temple could begin. Herod acted immediately, ordering work to start the very next day. On Deuteronomy Square there was grudging respect for his executive despatch, despite the dust the project soon created.

One itchy morning Simeon and Reuben were massaging each other's prejudices over cups of mint tea when Onesimus emerged from a mound of persimmons. He was looking for his son Benjamin.

'Anyone seen that wretched boy? I wanted him here early to collect oranges from the valley. Third day in a row he's overslept.'

'Didn't we all oversleep at that age?' asked Simeon.

'He's a sluggard and I don't mind saying so,' averred Onesimus.

Reuben heard hooves. Moments later a mule came speeding round the corner. It was pulling a small cart on which sat Benjamin with his head of fair hair. The cart bounced and pitched and seemed certain to smash into the tea stall when Benjamin called 'Whoa!' and yanked on the reins. The mule stuck out its front hooves, braced its back quarters and sent up a cloud of dried mud. It stopped with inches to spare.

'And it's Javelin by a nose! Another first for the Jerusalem thunderbolt!' cried Benjamin as he jumped from his cart. The mule was grinning almost as widely as its master. And why not? A beautiful Jerusalem morning, an empty cart. You could raise some decent dust.

'You're late.'

'Hi, Dad. Yeah, sorry about that. There was trouble with Javelin's halter. But we're here now.' Benjamin fed Javelin a carrot.

'I told your mother to wake you. She's too soft. Some oranges need collecting from that barn just beyond Zelek's dairy. I paid for them two days ago so there'll be no trouble about money. I hope they haven't gone to someone else.'

'Righto.' Benjamin made a playful 'Tsssssh!' as he cracked an imagined whip. He was about to leave when he spotted the tray of lemon-scented koloochehs cooling on Reuben's counter. 'Those look good.'

'You want one?' Reuben prised a koloocheh from the tray.

'I haven't any money.'

'Away with you, before you drive your father round the bend.'

'Thanks, Uncle Reuben! Love ya.'

Benjamin roared 'Go!' at Javelin. He was still standing as the cart jolted off, heading towards Dung Gate and the Valley of Hinnom, where the oranges might or might not be awaiting their buyer. Benjamin's whoops were fading when a displeased Lemuel the architect marched up to Onesimus.

'Your idiotic delivery boy nearly hit my scaffolding,' complained Lemuel. 'He wants to be careful. I've a lot of men working there and we're on a tight schedule.' Lemuel was supervising the new Temple Mount's retaining walls and the scaffolding was already being raised.

'You leave my son alone,' snapped Onesimus. 'I won't hear a bad word said about him. He's a fine boy.'

'I say, those look good,' said Lemuel.

'You want one?' Reuben prised another koloocheh from the tray.

'I haven't any money.'

'I'll start a tab. I run a tight schedule on debts.'

It was elevenses by the time Benjamin headed back with his load of oranges. The scaffolders were having a break at the tea stall. Benjamin was just through the narrowed part of the street by the scaffolding when Javelin stopped.

'You can't stop there!' shouted Lemuel. Benjamin accepted this but the little mule would not budge. Benjamin jumped down and tried to bribe her with some celery. She wasn't buying it. Her legs were locked tight and she hee-hawed.

'You're causing a jam,' shouted Lemuel. Other carts were soon queuing in both directions. There was no way anyone could pass. Benjamin was sworn at. Javelin was called a stupid ass. Onesimus threw his eyes to the heavens and Lemuel said he would fetch Kedar. Things were reaching a climax of crossness when there was a dreadful crash and a section of scaffolding collapsed, narrowly missing the implacable Javelin. It transpired that a drain under the street had been dangerously weakened by the scaffolding. Mules have two qualities. The first is a refusal to budge once they have decided to stand firm. The second is an instinct for danger. Javelin had noticed the drain's weakness as she trotted over it. In the only way she knew, she gave everyone a warning of impending disaster.

Afterwards there was no more 'wretched boy' and 'stupid ass' and that night Javelin dined on the finest hay Jerusalem could provide.

A Remedy for Gout

ONESIMUS prided himself on his range of produce –
'Pips or peels? We sell it' – but the exception was garlic.
Shoom was so well established, it was pointless trying to
compete. Shoom toured the streets with bulbs of garlic
slung round her long neck. You could say she had a
monopoly but the people of Deuteronomy Square did not
see it like that. They simply thought: 'We buy our garlic
from Shoom.' They went through a lot of it.

Shoom was distantly related to Noor, though Noor
was vague about the family tree. Years earlier Shoom was
briefly married to a cousin of Noor. The poor chap did
not live long. Shoom's widow's weeds faded and were now
sky-blue rather than black. She was an ageless figure, and
in a way nameless. 'Shoom' is Hebrew for garlic. It was the
sales pitch she sang in her low voice.

Reuben did some research. Garlic was good for gout.
'Ask Shoom for garlic oil, Simeon. You could dip your big

toe in it like a piece of bread.' The gout was giving Simeon such gyp, he'd try anything.

'Yes, I have garlic oil,' said Shoom. 'Five-year-old vintage will be best. I will bring it tomorrow evening and apply it.' Simeon did not like the sound of anyone touching his toes but Shoom's oblong face brooked no resistance.

Treatment was administered on the roof terrace. There was a fair amount of whimpering before Shoom even touched Simeon's right foot. Noor told him to 'stop being such a baby' and Shoom just ignored his protests, setting to work on his toes, ankle and shin.

'I'm being ganged up on by you cousins,' wailed Simeon.

'I forgot we were cousins,' said Shoom. 'I miss him, you know. My husband. He was a proper man.'

'Unlike some,' added Noor quite unnecessarily.

Shoom may have had the purr of an actress but her hair was lank. Reuben said she reminded him of a kolos. Maybe so, but few antelopes exuded such calm. And Shoom had sympathetic hands. Despite Simeon's 'Oohs!' and 'Carefuls!', the application of garlic oil was not painful. Simeon even admitted it was quite soothing. The treatment was repeated five times in the first fortnight and it brought an improvement in the gout. The one drawback was that Simeon, from dawn to dusk, trailed a pong of garlic.

'You smell of toum,' said Reuben.

'I thought it was someone's shawarma,' said Jonah.

'I thought it was Shlomo,' confessed Noor. She suggested Simeon might want to start wearing patchouli to disguise the garlic. There was one benefit, mind you. Kedar could not abide the taste or smell of garlic. Simeon was left in peace by the little martinet.

'Not pleasant,' adjudged Kedar. 'Not pleasant at all. Mr High and Mighty Simeon brings increasing disrepute to our fine city and its streets. If it was left to me, I'd have no hesitation in drumming him and that garlic woman out of Jerusalem.'

Army Life

SIMEON and Reuben were playing mid-morning draughts when Calvus flopped down at the tea stall and started removing his helmet, sword and other impedimenta that made a Roman soldier's life such joy. Reuben, deep in thought about his next move, silently rose from the game, put on the kettle, fetched a cup and returned to the chequer board to take two of Simeon's pieces.

'Good move, Reuben,' said Calvus.

Simeon slowly lifted one of his front-line pieces and hopped over Reuben's remaining five chequers. It was a massacre.

'Oh,' said Calvus.

'I suppose you want tea,' grunted Reuben. Simeon began setting up another game.

'Wouldn't mind,' said the soldier. 'And a few ma'amoul, please. It's been a rotten night.'

'Was there trouble?'

'Not that I noticed. Hence the trouble. Centurion Lucilius did a barracks inspection at dawn and found evidence of intruders. They reckon it was town girls smuggled in by one of the lads. The quartermaster's stores were broken into and wine was spilled. An oil lamp was smashed in the bathhouse. Tiles are missing from the dorm roof. The centurion is blaming the sentries.'

'And you were on sentry duty?' asked Simeon.

'I was,' sighed Calvus. 'I wasn't asleep all the time.'

Reuben shovelled ma'amoul on to Calvus's plate. 'Five for the price of three,' he said, as ever rubbing his hands on his apron.

'A sentry's work is never done,' commiserated Simeon.

'Actually,' said Calvus, 'you're wrong there. My shift was meant to end at midnight but that oaf Flaccus recently chopped off his toe cutting firewood and he's in the sickbay. One measly toe and it's the life of Riley for Flaccus. I was told to do a double shift and after midnight my eyelids drooped. It's a new moon. The night was as dark as squid's ink. But now Centurion Lucilius says I'm the most useless legionary east of Brundisium. Hmmn, these are good. Any more?'

'Don't they feed you at the Antonia?'

'Not like this. Uh-oh!' Calvus, spraying crumbs, leapt to his feet, jammed on his helmet and started tightening his belt. Round the corner was coming a knot of soldiers marching to brisk drill commands – 'Left, right, left, right, squad . . . HALT!' A helmet topped by ostrich feathers wound through the ranks and emerged, as if through a hedge. 'And what have we here?' cried the helmet's diminutive occupant, bow-legged and brown as broiled meat.

'Ave, Centurion,' replied Calvus. He made to salute the centurion but forgot that he was still holding his cup. Hot tea flew everywhere. He hopped up and down. Lucilius watched with a leer. Under his arm he had tucked a knobbled, polished vine staff. 'Taking tea with the locals!'

'Would you care for a cup, Centurion?' enquired Simeon. 'I'm buying. And maybe some of Reuben's ma'amoul?'

'Roman soldiers have no time for tea and biscuits. A pot of posca after a day's hard march, maybe, but tea's for poets and politicians. Tea's for thee, not me.'

'Very good, sir, that rhymes,' said a tall goose of an optio. He was straightening his fingernails in the sunlight.

'I have always found posca a touch astringent,' offered Simeon reasonably.

'It's certainly not for foreigners,' barked Lucilius. 'Sylvanus, take a note.' This instruction was directed at the amiable optio. He glided forward half a pace and produced a wax writing tablet.

'Very good, sir,' he murmured. 'Dictate away.'

'Memo. Sentry Calvus found drinking tea with fresh Judaeans. Will present himself to wardroom before sundown shift for kit inspection.'

'Down in wax, sir.'

'Fresh?' said Reuben.

'We've been called worse things, Reub'.'

'Silence!' bawled Lucilius, whacking his vine staff on the tea stall bench and breaking it – the vine staff, not the bench.

'Oh dear, sir,' said Sylvanus, 'you've broken your stick.'

'Gimme another,' snapped Lucilius.

'Rotten luck,' continued Sylvanus. One of the soldiers

darted forward with a new vine staff. 'Will that be all the dictation for now, sir?'

'Aye,' grunted Lucilius, swishing the new vine staff through the air to test its weight. Sylvanus reversed half a pace and executed a stamp of his feet that could have raised a cloud of talcum powder had he not misjudged his position and stepped on a soldier's toe. The other man said: 'Ow!'

'So sorry.'

'Bloody fools,' growled Lucilius. 'Right, we must complete this patrol. Then pilum practice before lunch. And we all know what's for lunch, don't we?'

'Ham, Centurion!' said the platoon as one.

'Yes, indeedy.' He curled his lip at Simeon and Reuben. 'Platoon, quick march!' Off they stomped, shoulders squared, their caligae creating a rhythm that faded down the street. Reuben picked up the two discarded pieces of broken vine staff. They would do for firewood.

'Kit inspection at sundown,' said Calvus, chucking his helmet on the bench in despair. 'Bang goes my siesta.'

'He seems to have it in for you, Calvus,' said Simeon.

'The other sentries see how he treats me and dread to be in the same bracket. There is cruel logic to his methods.'

'What if we change that?'

'How?'

'By making him think you are good at your duties.'

'But I keep falling asleep. It's my bio-rhythms.'

'We can change that. Or at least we can change the centurion's opinion of that.'

A plan was devised. Simeon would dress as a 'town girl' and seek entry to the fortress while Calvus was at his sentry post. Simeon would make an owl's hoot and advance on the fortress gate where Calvus would accost him. Simeon would protest loudly and then run away, demonstrating that Calvus was superbly vigilant. Evidence of the failed intrusion would be left at the scene for Calvus to present to Lucilius. Simeon ran over the plan several times. It could not fail.

'You'll be the centurion's blue-eyed boy, Calvus. Remember: an owl's hoot not long before midnight, and make sure you whack me hard. I'll be wearing pillows on my head and shoulders.'

Dark night fell. Simeon was not the only person with a nocturnal adventure in mind. In a sparse barracks bedroom, Centurion Lucilius smeared charcoal on his face and hands and shins.

'Is this really necessary, sir?' asked Sylvanus.

'Don't be a wimp, man. We can't have sentries dozing. Calvus is a useless piece of meat. I can smell it in me nostrils. Okay, he passed his kit inspection but there's a vacant look in his eyes and a slouch in his shoulders. The man's a liability to his legion and I won't have it. Tight and taut. That's how we need to be.'

'It's a midweek evening in peacetime. The Zealots are taking a month off. The city's asleep. Calvus is popular with the lads.'

'I sometimes worry about you, Sylvanus. Worry about your attitude. You're not going soft, are you?'

Calvus was sitting in his sentry box, fighting the eternal battle against torpor, his mind filled with thoughts of ravioli, wine and hunting. He was chasing a boar through the forest and about to throw his spear at it when the tip sprouted fins and became a fat trout, diving into a pool.

59

Before it hit the water it took flight and became a hooting owl. This plot twist jolted his head into the air.

'Humppph?' he snorted. The hoot of an owl? Simeon's signal! Calvus jumped out of the sentry box. The night was damnably black and his head was foggy but were those footsteps ten yards away? 'What ho! Who goes there?' Simeon had told him to lay it on thick and make the challenge noisy enough to alert nearby sentries. 'Identify yourself,' roared Calvus, 'or prepare to die!' With that he took three paces, slashing his spear downwards. It hit nothing. Three more paces. Again he flashed his spear. The first two times it swished through the air. The third time it hit something solid, which gave a 'plongggg', followed by a string of oaths. Hit hard, hit often, Simeon had said, and don't worry about giving it a bit of what-for because he was going to be wearing plenty of pillows. That 'plongggg' was puzzling, because it didn't sound terribly pillow-like but never mind. Authenticity was essential. Calvus set about his victim with gusto. Victims plural would be more accurate, for his blows struck two people, one wailing in a high voice. Calvus should possibly have recognised it but by now his blood was up. Whack, whack, whack, thud, thud, thud. 'Intruders at the north-west tower!' he bawled. 'Sound the alarm!' Other sentries came running with drawn swords and a flaming torch. Calvus had expected Simeon to scarper by now, so had stopped for a breather. Gosh, that had been fun.

'Are you okay, Calvus?' asked the other sentries.

'Never been better! I sent him packing all right!'

From the ground nearby came groans. Simeon must have failed to make his escape.

'Quick, bring that torch,' shouted one of the sentries as an owl fluttered past in the torchlight. 'Holy Apollo! Are you all right, sir? It's the centurion. Properly bashed.'

All of which would have been seen and enjoyed by Simeon, had he only been lurking in the shadows, dressed as a woman. But it had been a long day, Noor's lamb casserole had been rich, a second glass of wine had been taken, and Simeon was still at home, asleep in his bed, his head full of dreams.

As for Calvus, he was called in next day by a dented Lucilius and praised for his alertness. 'As a reward,' said the centurion, 'I am giving you an extra week of sentry duty this month because you are so good at it.'

The Lamb of Dog

STEAM billowed inside the caldarium. By Rome stand-
ards the bathhouse was small. There were maybe six
bodies in the chamber but with all the vapour and darkness it was hard to be sure. The door opened and there
came a tapping.

'Simeon!'

'Shalom, Philippos. Where are you?'

'In the corner.'

'Which one?'

'Over here.'

An attendant dribbled water on hot coals. Moisture
dripped from the arched ceiling and the floor tiles were
splashy. Simeon could make out a huddle of bathers
speaking Latin. Philippos must be in the other direction.
Most bath customers were Roman or Greek with a few
Sadducees.

Simeon loved the eyeball-sweat of a good steam
followed by a dive into cold water. Reuben thought bathing

eccentric. 'You must feel like a hard-boiled egg afterwards.' It shook the inevitability out of a day and Simeon liked the anonymity of the steam room. Many people recognised Simeon from the temple entrance. In the steam, things were more opaque.

The heat worked into pores and lungs. To sit here half an hour, amid the hiss of water on hot coals, brought relief from the dirt of the day. There was no danger of being pestered by visitors or being subjected to young Caleb's chatter. No Kedar, either. Kedar might affect Roman airs but he was shy about sitting naked in the bathhouse. You couldn't be too careful, said Kedar. You never knew, said Kedar. Everyone just concluded that Kedar must be uncircumcised.

'I knew it was you from your stick,' murmured Philippos. Everyone murmured in the bathhouse.

'This bloody gout.'

'Everyone knows when you enter a dark room.'

'And when I leave. In Jerusalem that can have its advantages.' Herod's intelligence network created unease, particularly in the city's political class, but there was also pride in the level of snooping. Cyprus had its copper, Lesbos retsina, Jerusalem her spies. Friends exchanging confidences would tap their noses and say: 'Don't tell Amos.' Amos was Everyman and every next man might well be Amos. The one topic to beware was the king's marital life. No sane person talked about that, though lots had their thoughts.

'Tell me your latest,' said Philippos. 'It'll be good for my Aramaic.' They both knew there was nothing wrong with his Aramaic but nonetheless Simeon told Philippos about the previous day and the blessed lamb of dog . . .

On rainy days pilgrims stayed indoors and the sacrificial altars went unlit. With Temple Square deserted, Simeon and Caleb would drop in on shops, collecting half-forgotten commissions. Caleb would goof about in his wake, not learning as much as he would have done if he only stopped chattering for a moment. The boy had ants in his pants.

On this walk they reached the pool of Bethesda where Cephas the temple stockman was washing some sheep. The animals had been blessed and were due to have been sacrificed but the rain had forced a stay of execution. The sheep were jumpy. Maybe it was the new surroundings or the presence of Shlomo. Shlomo enjoyed a walk as much as the next man. He would trot alongside Simeon in proprietorial manner, a factor checking his estates. Spotting him, some of the sheep panicked. That made the others twitchy. Cephas shouted at Simeon for bringing that damn dog. Simeon firmly replied that Shlomo was a free agent and if Cephas had a problem he should talk directly to Shlomo.

Some sheep stood at one end of the pool, dropping dung everywhere. Others loitered at a distance chewing their cheeks and looking dithery. 'The one exception,' Simeon told Philippos as another ladle of water was added to the coals, 'was a black lamb that allowed me to scratch its head. It started bleating at Shlomo as if he were its mother. The dog soon started to wag his tail. He settled on the ground and the lamb did likewise. I told Caleb to help Cephas round up the sheep. We must have been there another ten minutes before the job was done. Shlomo and the lamb retired to a dry spot under a rosemary bush.

'The three of us – Caleb, Shlomo and I – departed for Tanners' Alley, where I had to see Elias the saddler about repairs to a satchel. When I came out of the shop, who should we see trotting down the lane towards us but the black lamb? It bleated at Shlomo and Shlomo barked back.'

'Dangerous territory for a sheep, the tanneries,' offered Philippos.

'We had more calls to make. The lamb followed us. The problem came when we returned to Deuteronomy Square and stopped at Reuben's. Shlomo and the lamb joined us under the table. Cephas appeared, asking if we'd seen his black lamb. I looked under the table but it had gone. So had Shlomo.'

'Where was it?' enquired Philippos.

'Other side of the square. Cephas gave chase. The lamb fled, only to reappear by the water trough. Cephas again pursued it but the lamb was too quick for him and ran through his legs. People started laughing. Cephas told them to help but no one did.'

'Why not?'

'Because they were enjoying the game and because once sheep have been blessed for the sacrifice and washed in the pool, you're not meant to touch them. Cephas fell over his crook and emitted some un-temple-like curses. The Pharisees were aghast. The lamb hid behind the washing-up basins, then in the bougainvillea, then near Jonah and his gang. Shlomo barked whenever Cephas was getting close. Both of them – Shlomo and the lamb – sprinted off in the direction of the theatre. It's surprising how fast a lamb can run. Reuben said they didn't return until evening, by which time Cephas had long returned to his sheep pen, saying the black lamb was blemished and would probably have been rejected anyway by the chief priest. This morning we found that the lamb had slept at the back of Onesimus's fruit stall. It couldn't be allowed to stay there, so Benjamin took it off in his cart and will give it to a shepherd friend in the hills off the Galilee road. He'll give it a life.'

'Won't Cephas hear what happened? Won't someone blab?'

'Undoubtedly.'

'And that won't be a problem?'

'Only for Cephas. He's meant to look after his stock. Who can he blame? Shlomo?'

'But the lamb had been blessed.'

'Indeed. And that is a problem for the priests, because they should have waited until they were sure the sacrifices were going to happen.'

'Why didn't they wait?'

'Because the one doing the blessing wanted to get away to his girlfriend in lower town. It's open to question if he even did the blessing at all.'

'So the high priest won't get to hear about it?'

'He'll get to hear about it all right,' said Simeon. 'What are spies for?'

'He'll be cross.'

'He'll be delighted.'

'I don't get it.'

'Dear heart,' said Simeon, 'it puts everyone else at a disadvantage. That suits the chief priest because they worry about their jobs. It's the time of year for the temple workers' annual pay deal. The chief priest can let it be known he won't make a fuss about the escaped lamb and the girlfriend in lower town if Cephas and the blessing priest accept a low settlement. That will help temple funds, which will please Herod, who will feel better disposed to the temple staff next time he visits.'

'So everyone gains?'

'And one black lamb gets to frolic in the hills off the Galilee road rather than being sacrificed in Jerusalem. All thanks to Shlomo. You could almost say it's a dog's life. Now how about a plunge in the cold pool? If no one's watching, I might even do a honeypot.'

'This is Jerusalem,' said Philippos. 'Someone's bound to be watching, surely.'

Isaac's Seat

ONE muggy afternoon Benjamin had to change a wheel in Deuteronomy Street. Javelin was watching her youthful master with an expression that said: 'I wouldn't have started from there if I was you.' Grunts and the occasional whack of tool rose from under the cart.

'Trouble?' asked Simeon.

'I hit a pothole,' said Benjamin's voice from the depths. 'The wheelwright near the Dung Gate had a spare. Should be okay once I have this shaft in place.' There came another flurry of smites followed by a curse as Benjamin hit his thumb.

Kedar and two constables arrived.

'This vehicle will need to be moved by nightfall,' said Kedar. Benjamin emerged with a smeared face and no shirt. Kedar frowned and said: 'Have some modesty, please.'

'I'll try to get the problem fixed, Mr Kedar, but it's proving uncooperative at present.'

'It's not the only one,' said Simeon.

'Hold your lip, Grandpa,' growled one of the constables.

'If this cart isn't shifted by dark it will be towed away, young man,' said Kedar. 'No obstruction is to be left in the street at night. People might walk into it and hurt themselves. Who knows when there is going to be an emergency and we have to evacuate the city in the dark?'

'There's the street-sweepers to think about tomorrow morning, too,' added the second goon.

'We seek to help small business owners,' said Kedar, 'but our leeway is limited. I have to tell you your cart may be subject to inspection and that might have implications.' Commercial vehicles licensed in the city now had to meet minimum safety requirements. Inspectors demanded bribes to pass carts as roadworthy.

'What a stinking rip-off,' said Simeon, scratching the itch on his forehead.

'There's no need to become abusive,' purred Kedar. 'Good day to you both. Towed vehicles, if not roadworthy, may be burned as temple kindling. Those are the regulations. They are set by the Sanhedrin, which I am sure we all respect.'

'They're getting worse,' said Simeon when Kedar and Co. had gone.

'They're always throwing their weight around with us younger lot. Give them a chance and they'd love to ban all wheels from the centre of Jerusalem.' Simeon had half an apple in his pocket. He fed it to Javelin and the mule nudged him by way of thanks.

Five more whacks of mallet pushed the new wheel home. Benjamin was relieved. 'I have to head past Mount Scopus tomorrow to collect onions.'

'Make sure you visit Isaac's Seat.'

'What's Isaac's Seat?'

And so it was arranged that Simeon would accompany Benjamin and show him his special place.

When next approaching Mount Scopus from Jerusalem you may notice, at the penultimate bend before the summit, the one with the twisted acacia and the memorial cairn, a tangled bluff two stone-throws to the left. Being hidden behind a thicket of brambles it is easily missed. Alight, tie your horse under the acacia and go and look. After that climb any mount will be grateful for a rest and the shade of an acacia on the slopes of Scopus is as close to heaven as a working mule can get. Approaching the bluff, watch your step for the ground underfoot becomes jagged and snakes can loiter in the quietest places, as Simeon knew only too well. Climb the old wall, beat aside the nettles, duck under the neglected fig tree and you will find a natural shelf of limestone that offers long views east and west. The rock is flat and wide. Your arrival may cause a commotion among the geckos and agamas who sunbathe there. Cucumber-shaped skink will dart for safety, mistaking you for an eagle. The eyesight of the skink is no better than that of a clerk. Soon you will have the place to yourself. The road is lost behind the vegetation. The only noise, aside from the chorus of crickets, will be an occasional puff of wind playing through the fig tree and fluting on the contours of the rock. You have found Isaac's Seat.

They left Jerusalem before rush-hour and bounced along, Javelin relishing the cool morning and the new wheel moving sweetly. They stopped for peaches and a lemon drink at a roadside stall. Simeon's treat. As they sat in the warming sun and the mule was given hay, the old man watched the boy's face, its blond fluff fringed by sunlight.

'You look sad, Uncle Simeon.'

'I'll survive.'

Simeon was indeed sad, for another boy who had not lived; but Benjamin was a great lad, much better than Simeon himself had been. Today's youngsters were impressive, though no one ever said so. They were kinder, more thoughtful, less vengeful. The world was going that way, despite the haters' worst efforts.

At the bend with the twisted acacia Simeon stepped down and cleared some weeds from the base of the cairn. Javelin was tethered and Simeon banished his memories for the walk across the crumbly hillside. The neglected fig was thick with fruit. They paused to pick a few and let Simeon retrieve his breath. Was this the branch where Hannah caught her shawl? Fig trees lasted many men's lifespans. They fruited for centuries while about them all sorts of destinies unfolded.

The thicket was more tangled than he recalled. A wall of clematis and dog rose had to be pulled aside. A partridge startled them by fluttering from its nest. Simeon felt a pumping in his heart. It was probably just the physical effort. In the undergrowth he saw a long-discarded cup and a broken sandal. Finally they could feel the sun's strength return and they were through the tangle of fronds and branches. And there was the perfect limestone shelf. Its surface seemed to writhe with skittering lizard-life. Then they had it to themselves.

'Amazing place,' said Benjamin.

Mount Moriah and the city lay below them to the west. Jerusalem's walls could have been a child's fort. That gleam of reflected light must be the gold cupola at Herod's palace. The temple workings were clear. Seen from this distance, man's ambition looked geometric. Herod's building drive was correcting the contours of nature and Simeon marvelled at the project's daring; yet he saw the pride in it all. Brambles would make short work of it if given a chance.

'How do you know about this place, Uncle Simeon?'

'I first came here as a boy when my father had business in Jerusalem,' said Simeon. 'I came here in my courting days, too.'

'It's hard to think of you being married.'

'It didn't last long, alas.'

He told Benjamin the legend that Isaac came here as a shepherd, though it was Moriah where Isaac was offered as a sacrifice by Abraham. God was merciful to Abraham. But Abraham, unlike some, had behaved properly. On the limestone shelf there were indentations and creases. Simeon could remember them from decades earlier. Had Isaac, too, seen them? Benjamin drank it all in. They turned now to the east, the light smoky over the farmland.

'I'm surprised the army haven't turned this into an observation point.'

'Maybe they don't know about it,' said Simeon. 'Herod's engineers would only want to wreck it. Are you an east or a west man, Benjamin?'

'What do you mean?'

'These days I prefer to look west. The sun is warmer, the shadows longer. To the east you have morning's hope, the cold wash of freshness, everything to come.'

'Can't we look both ways, Uncle Simeon?'

'Hard to do that simultaneously.'

When he and Hannah were here, did they look east

or west? Simeon was not sure. But other things he did remember: his back touching the flat stone, laughter rushing past her white teeth, tears as they contemplated impending separation. He had just learned of the posting to Galilee. Simeon had never before had a girl cry over him. He had not known he mattered. They raised their arms and yelled, for God to hear: 'I love youuuuuuuu!' They had lain under the skies, for God to see.

On the breeze came the bray of a mule. 'Javelin is bored,' said Benjamin.

'Your onions won't collect themselves. Time you went.'

'Aren't you coming with me?'

'You can collect me on your way back to Jerusalem.'

'Will you be okay on your own?'

'That's a question I've been asking myself a long time, Benjamin. I wouldn't mind an hour more here trying to work out the answer.' This place felt as holy as any temple.

Simeon waited until Benjamin was safely gone. Then, gazing westwards, a half-remembered tune flitted through his mind and he started talking. 'Beautiful child, it was like this. I was young. I thought I was unstoppable. I loved her, honestly and fully. There was no doubt about that, yet I betrayed her and I was not there when it mattered. That is why I am sad.'

Could he say he'd behave differently if given another chance? Was lust really a crime? In mitigation, your honour, my client was a young soldier full of animal drive. The accused accepts he was an obnoxious colt. But was God the judge here, or co-defendant? If God intended us to be chaste, why fill us to the brim with urges?

By the time Hannah knew she was pregnant Simeon was with his unit. Her employer in Jerusalem was not inclined to support her through the pregnancy so she wrote to Simeon to say she was returning to Samaria once the morning sickness passed. The Samaritan community in Jerusalem took her in without hesitation until she felt well enough to make the trip. She travelled in an escorted party, with guards to stave off trouble. At one of the stops a widow tied her ring to a thread and held it over Hannah's stomach to see which way the ring turned. She told her it was going to be a boy. The old woman was going to say more but checked herself and left it at that. Hannah's family had told Simeon all this later.

A raven cawed and a curious lizard emerged from a crack in the rock. It splayed its toes, puffed out its cheeks and absorbed the sunlight. Simeon envied the creature its stillness. A flurry of dust swirled, catching into an unexpected, rushing tunnel of old leaves and specks of dirt. Simeon shielded his eyes and pulled away from the force field as it continued, a light almost blinding him.

'Feeling sorry for yourself again, I see.'

Simeon blinked, cleaved to the dust and tried to gather his wits. 'Oh, it's you. I was hoping for God.'

'God's busy. God doesn't deal with selfish oafs. I mean, did you visit Hannah?'

'I sent money.'

'On the eve of battle, with a letter to say you didn't expect to live. How cheering for a mum-to-be.' Simeon shifted. This sun was roasting. How did the gecko bear it?

What should he have done? Desert? Turn up in Hannah's village with no money or prospects? Why must soldiers always feel guilty? The guilt of leaving home. The guilt of fighting alongside Rome. Killing was the least of it. Army life was smells, smoke, leather, horses, latrines, always latrines, and sweat, and the oil they smeared on their shields. Army life was male. Or was it? Anna. He had thought he could have it both ways.

'Anna was older than me. She knew the game.'

'Hannah was younger and she did not.'

'I loved them both.'

'You mistreated them both and your child died. Some game! Hannah died in agony, not knowing if you were on your way, not knowing if you cared. You were rolling in another's bed. You wrote a song for her and you only sang it to your lover.'

'All right! Stop my heart. Rip my gizzards. Take me instead of one of those dumb animals you have sacrificed.' The song, the song. It was scored on his innards for ever.

'Request blocked. Applicant still has no credible reparation plan. *Tch!*' A bang that made him start, a smell of singeing and of summer rain. And with that Simeon was again alone.

Benjamin and Javelin and a load of fat onions were waiting by the twisted acacia and the memorial cairn. The boy and his mule were tired and in no mood for talk. Nor was Simeon. Javelin plodded towards the setting sun, her young master at the reins, and beside him an old man who had learned that angels can bite like snakes.

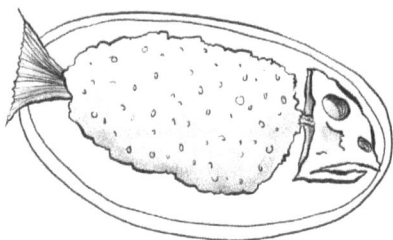

Tambal Tries Gefilte Fish

ZILLAH said Tambal was as expensive to keep as a carthorse but at least 'darling T' was not much of a drinker. 'He does eat, though.'

It was not just quantity. Tambal had come to love Roman and Hellenic delicacies: dormice stuffed with sugared pine kernels, snapper baked with quince, crayfish in plums, camel heels à la Apicius. Anything with goose fat or syrup found favour. He would sink his hands into cinnamon-roasted filberts and shovel them down his throat like locusts (a childhood favourite in Nubia). For elevenses it was chicken's brain boiled in narince or leftovers of pomegranate pot-roast crane. Lemony lovage tartlets flew down the chute before you could say 'Service!' Peach halves in cumin custard vanished in a trice. Peacock and apple rissoles, caramelised patina of jellyfish, muscat-jugged hare: Tambal found room for it all and would run a thumb round the bowl to secure the last of the goodness.

At Reuben's tea stall he was drawn to sticky cakes as a bee to hollyhocks. Zillah settled his tab without demur. Nor did she complain when he devoured rice puddings and star-anise jellies her cook created for toga parties. Half the Sanhedrin was seen around her lily ponds at these gatherings. Officers from the Antonia garrison attended, too, for Zillah's Greek chef had trained at Ephesus, cooking for the governor and once for Mark Antony and Cleopatra. He made them ostrich balls in apricot. Cleopatra asked for the recipe. Herod's palace tried to poach Zillah's cook – if poach was the verb – but he stayed put. Zillah was a generous employer and the king's granddaughter was said to meddle at the palace kitchens. Salome had strange gastronomic ideas. She could be trouble one day.

Zillah promised Tambal enough money, when she died, to return to Nubia and live in lordly fashion. She treated Tambal like the child she lacked; yet she refused to grant him his freedom until she died. 'I just like you as you are, darling boy, and don't see why we have to spoil everything.'

This did not stop Tambal dreaming. He missed Africa. Jonah, seeing this, said: 'Become Jewish and you could soon return home a free man.'

'That would be wonderful,' sighed the slave, 'but we have different gods. Anyway, your Jewish circumcision business . . .'

'Details, details,' said Jonah. 'Come to our Passover feast.'

Tambal had been born free and wished to die free. The Pharisee was certainly approachable and treated Tambal as an equal. That was more than the Romans did. Tambal remembered the afternoon he overdid it on sorb apples – he ate a whole bowl before they were stewed – and they fermented in his belly. A Roman patrol mistook him for a drunk. Tambal was thrown into a cell and was insulted despicably. He was released only when Zillah arrived to give the gaoler a piece of her mind. Tambal never forgot that afternoon in the cell. Jonah and his Pharisees were not like that at all. Tambal liked their attitude. He liked their clothes and ringlets. They enjoyed singing, didn't worry too much about table manners and their temple was impressive. Amazing animal sacrifices. Tambal was rather pro at that sort of thing. And so he accepted the invitation to the feast.

Zillah heard via Philippos – or was it Simeon? – that Jonah was trying to convert Tambal. Her immediate reaction was that it was a blasted cheek and she would tell Jonah to sling his hook. But was it wise to upset the Pharisees? Herod was not the force of old and her class was already being accused of Roman collaboration by hotter heads. Philippos – or was it Simeon? – suggested a more sinuous approach.

With Tambal having agreed to attend Jonah's Passover feast Zillah ordered her chef to take the day off. She went out to lunch. The household could fend for itself. Tambal, who could not cook, therefore went without breakfast and lunch. Zillah had given him so many chores that he had no opportunity to nip to Reuben's for buns.

The Passover feast was everything you expect of a Passover feast. The matzo was dry as a mouthful of sand. Green herbs were served in salt water. The horseradish was so hot that Tambal thought his mouth was alight. He knocked back the first of four goblets of wine. 'Endive,' said Jonah. Tambal inspected a limp plant, dipped it in the salt water, sucked it, and almost retched. He could have murdered some roast hippopotamus with elvers. That was the sort of fare he'd expected at a feast. As he downed another glass of wine, dried fruit came round. To the Nubian they looked like rabbit droppings. He was offered a miserable lump of lamb. Loosened by the seder wine, he sucked on the near-meatless shank and blew on a hole in the bone, wondering if it doubled as a whistle. He told Jonah you'd find more meat on a litter beetle.

'You eat beetles?' said Jonah.

'Don't you?' said Tambal.

'Not kosher!' cried Jonah.

Being unfamiliar with wine, Tambal failed to pace himself. Noticing that a senior rabbi had not touched his glass, Tambal said: 'Let me help you with that.' He gave the rabbi an enormous wink and drained it. The evening's proud host came round with minced carp moulded into a white blob.

'You never forget your first gefilte fish,' said Jonah with relish. Tambal gave it a sniff. It looked disgusting but he was almost howling with hunger, so scooped it up. Hole in one. Mistake. 'Pretty good, eh?' asked Jonah. Tambal's eyes watered. Somehow he managed to swallow. It tasted as if he had just eaten a mouthful of Nile mud. He rinsed back another goblet of wine and hung his tongue out to air.

When the moment arrived for Tambal's candidacy as a *ger* to be announced he had succumbed to hiccups and was having difficulty keeping one elbow on the table. He was escorted back to Zillah's house.

The next morning brought bright sunshine and bird-song. 'Morning!' sang Zillah. Tambal groaned. Zillah told her chef to rustle up breakfast. Its smells soon floated through the house. Tambal's gastric juices started running like the Euphrates after rain. The chef brought crisped bacon, sizzling sow's udders, roasted trotters and the most perfect boar's womb stuffed with leek and tarragon. Tambal was told that after breakfasting to his heart's content he could sleep all day.

'Did you enjoy that, darling T?' asked Zillah as his empty plates were cleared.

'You bet,' burped Tambal. 'I love pig!'

If the taste of freedom was gefilte fish, emancipation could wait.

Mrs Kedar's Moment

ONE blessedly unremarkable day Simeon was trying to interest Shlomo in a saucer of nearly sour milk. Shlomo gave it a sniff, sat and scratched one of his armpits.

'You spoil that dog,' said Reuben.

The morning passed slowly. Lysander drifted by, looking for something to rhyme with 'dystopia'. Kedar passed with a gang of workmen. 'I can't stop now! Important matters to attend to!' he shouted, though no one had said a sausage to him. Benjamin raced off to a fruit farm. Onesimus was doing a cantaloupes promotion and was running short. Deborah's 'Nice Juicy Melons' sign had created a sales frenzy.

Jerusalem's finest gossip, Ephraim, put down a half-finished cup of tea and asked Simeon: 'Who's the prettiest lady in Jerusalem?' Simeon pulled a 'Come off it' face but Ephraim added: 'Haven't you heard?'

'Heard what?'

'There's going to be a beauty contest. Orders of the king.'

Herod had commissioned a Greek sculptor to decorate the new theatre. There would be a statue of Aphrodite and this would be modelled on a local beauty. But who? 'Far be it from me to tell creative minds what to think,' said Herod. 'In this age of freedom of expression, our artist must choose the muse.'

The prospect of a beauty contest stirred a reasonable modicum of interest. Early money went on Tabitha but a competition is no fun without less-fancied runners. Tabitha, anyway, said she did not have time to enter the contest. Who, therefore, would be Aphrodite? Simeon loyally said Noor should enter. Noor tugged at her tea towel and blushed. 'Our late queen would have been a glorious symbol of love,' sighed Hiram the stonemason. Everyone shushed him. Beautiful, demure, savvy Queen Mariamne had been dead only a year, executed for being too popular. Speaking her name in Jerusalem's open air was not something to be done lightly, for the palace remained sensitive about the matter.

Zillah let it be known that she would not oppose her name going forward. This was good of her, for a lady of such class would not normally deign to enter a beauty pageant. Habib the street-sweeper said either of his two wives might attract favour in the paddock but it would be a job to persuade them to remove their veils. Benjamin thought the greatest beauty in Jerusalem was surely Javelin. Did love not make asses of us all?

'Now then, what's going on here?' demanded Kedar, back from his vital mission.

'Nothing to detain a man of your distinction,' said Reuben.

'We are discussing the king's latest excellent idea,' said Simeon.

Kedar, twitching a lot, said it was the first he had heard of the Aphrodite auditions. But the next day, when the palace published the contest's runners and riders, it was learned that Mrs Kedar would be chancing her arm.

Little was known about Kedar's wife. 'She may be ravishing,' said Simeon.

'If so, why have we never seen her?' asked Reuben.

'She more likely has a handlebar moustache, a wall eye and a backside like a Phoenician galley,' offered Ephraim.

The sculptor, shipped in from Mykonos at no little expense, was reputed to be the marble craftsman of the age. His concept was for Aphrodite to be depicted emerging from the waves in a chariot. Benjamin was dragooned into allowing his cart to be a model for the chariot. Off the boy drove to the artist's workshop. 'I had to stand there ages,' complained Benjamin. 'The artist said he was sketching my cart but he seemed keener on drinking assyrtiko and chatting. He got quite tipsy.'

Auditions took place. Zillah said it had been 'tremendous fun' and confirmed that the artist was a tilt merchant. They had got high as kites and maybe her top had slipped a little to allow him sight of her embonpoint. 'Greeks are such darling men and he was ravishing but not remotely heterosexual.' Deborah was given a basket of loquats by Onesimus to present to the sculptor as a bribe, though she was not to call it that. Noor fussed over her hair before she posed. She insisted she had no chance of winning but she and her girlfriends enjoyed preparing for the day. Of Mrs Kedar's audition, little was disclosed. Kedar exuded confidence but would not be drawn. Ephraim reported that Mrs Kedar's session lasted longer than those of her rivals. Over the workshop wall he heard the artist laugh and shout 'More!' while Mrs Kedar was sitting for him.

Art is a time-consuming mistress. She cannot be rushed. It was three months before the sculpture was ready. Fever ran high in Deuteronomy Square, not least when it was announced there was not one sculpture but three. Had the artist been so overcome by the beauty of Jerusalem's women that he had been unable to settle on just one goddess of love? Was it a three-way tie?

The king attended the unveiling ceremony with a husband's pride. 'Jerusalem will be pleased to note,' commanded Herod, 'that the goddess bears a striking resemblance to our new queen!' Indeed she did, right down to her snippety nose and a weakness in the chin, yet her naked torso was magnificent, the breasts and belly managing to be both slender and buoyant, almost ridiculously pert. It was greeted by polite applause and good-natured commiserations to Noor and Deborah, who accepted that it was always going to be tough competing against royalty. Zillah, on the VIPs' dais, extended magnanimous congratulations to the queen.

'Marble has never been more beautiful.'

'Too kaind, I'm sure,' replied the young queen, who was still a little starchy.

Zillah turned to a neighbour and hissed, triumphantly: 'I knew he wouldn't let me down. The torso. It's all me, darling! All me!'

Beside Aphrodite was a smaller statue of Cupid (naked, well endowed) on a dolphin. Cupid had Benjamin's face. The artist was accepting the applause when he spotted Benjamin in the throng and pointed at him, touching his own heart and blowing fervent kisses. Simeon suspected he had been drinking. Benjamin blushed the colour of Thracian wine.

'There's still one statue to go,' observed Reuben.

Before he removed the covers from the third piece, the king explained that it had been decided that a theatre so magnificent deserved statues to cover both poles of the dramatic arts. Comedy had to be counterbalanced by tragedy. Beauty existed not only in love but also, arguably, in life's more cruel extremes. 'We decided,' said Herod, who had a certain locus in this argument, 'that the theatre should be marked not only by a statue of Aphrodite and her helper Cupid, but also by Athena, goddess of war.'

Off came the covers and the crowd gasped. While hackneyed depictions of Athena cast her as creamy-cheeked and placid, here was a terrifying vision of balefulness. The face was stern with blazing eyes and bared teeth. And the chins! Onlookers stepped back, a child screamed, Shlomo howled. Some even fled, among them the city's deputy warden.

'Good grief,' said Ephraim. 'It's Mrs Kedar.'

The episode had two consequences. Unlike her husband, Mrs Kedar was rather chuffed by the statue. Among her acquaintances she was found to have grown a few inches in self-esteem. The Kedar children noticed a sunnier clime in the family courtyard between sunrise and dusk, when Mama was sovereign of their little kingdom. Now that she loved herself just a fraction more, her husband loved her a fraction less.

The other consequence came centuries later when the statue of Aphrodite was discovered by art historians. Its beauty was admired, its craftsmanship undiminished, yet its head was missing. Herod's wife had found that the statue's nose displeased her. When her son became tetrarch she arranged for an accident to happen in which Aphrodite was decapitated. But the torso, with its breasts and a belly button of irresistible sensuality, was left intact. Zillah's nudity, to this day, beguiles and bewitches.

The art historians concluded that land-locked Jerusalem was a great navel power.

The Little Devil

SIMEON was having a conversation in front of the feather. Well, conversation might be putting it too strongly. It was more a monologue. God was not answering back. There was nothing unusual in that.

'I watch and wait as instructed. For years I've done it. Nothing happens. I know I should be grateful to be spared and Reuben's fig bread is a consolation – you'll notice I'm now as fat as a pumpkin. But what good do I do? When will I be free? Come on, you promised.'

The feather did not stir. Simeon gave up and stepped on to the roof terrace to gaze at the stars and despair at man's toil and smudge. It was during this spell of revolting self-pity that he heard raised voices below in Deuteronomy Street – a shout of 'Stop that!' and 'Leave me alone.' Simeon peered over the edge and shouted: 'What's going on down there? Ho!'

'Go back to bed, old man,' shouted a familiar voice. 'Keep your nose out of it.'

Nothing was more certain to prick Simeon's curiosity. He grabbed his walking stick and a lantern and hurried downstairs, not bothering to don shoes or coat. He was dressed in his nightshirt with a blanket over his shoulders; with age one felt the chill more. By the time he was standing in Deuteronomy Street he had been beaten to it by Noor. 'They've hurt Ibrahim the artist,' she said.

'Who hurt him?'

'Kedar and his goons.'

Simeon's lantern found Ibrahim slumped nearby, surrounded by the tools of his trade: hammer, chisels, paint-stained rags. A cedar-wood carving was nearby. There was a bottle of cleaning fluid, a wine gourd and a pair of sandals. A rat scampered off with some dropped bread. Ibrahim's nose was bleeding and one of his hands had been cut. Simeon gathered the belongings and Noor fussed over the casualty.

'You do look a fright in that nightie,' she told Simeon.

'What's wrong with it?'

'No wonder the rat ran away.'

'Shlomo would have caught it in the old days.'

'These are the old days, nincompoop.' Simeon did not much notice this remark at the time but when he recalled it later, it puzzled him.

'I got there just as they were leaving,' said Noor.

'I wasn't doing anything wrong,' said Ibrahim. Noor held his head back to stem the flow of blood from his nose. If she did not loosen her grip a little, she would do him more damage than Kedar's men.

'Why did they do this?' repeated Noor.

'Because they can,' said Simeon. 'Herod should stop this.'

'It's not the king's fault.'

'He knows what Kedar is like.'

'Does he?'

'He most certainly does,' affirmed Simeon, intently.

Once his nose had stopped bleeding Ibrahim told them the story. He had been working late at Zillah's, sculpting a caprid backdrop for one of her garden shrines. He wouldn't normally work after dusk but Zillah wanted it finished for her next party. Zillah being Zillah, she had filled him with wine and they had chatted about Greek art and Ibrahim became heady with a sense that the world was becoming more equal. He left Zillah's in a happy mood. The sight of one of Kedar's night patrols would usually have been enough to have him hide in a doorway but he felt somehow protected by Zillah's patronage, so bade the constables a good evening. They beat him up.

'Why?'

'I told you,' said Simeon, 'because they can. And Zillah is hardly Kedar's favourite person in the world. Her grandeur annoys him.'

Through his bunged-up nose Ibrahim managed: 'They said the tools in my bag were dangerous weapons.'

'The power of art,' said Simeon. 'Your cartoons may have irritated important people.'

'And they said I had wine on my breath.'

'Kedar disapproves of too much booze,' said Noor.

'Kedar disapproves of everything,' said Simeon. 'He disapproves of Zillah. He disapproves of art. He disapproves of thought. That is why Herod tolerates him.'

'I thought the Romans might save me,' said Ibrahim. 'Two walked past en route to the Antonia. Kedar's men stopped kicking me. The Romans asked what the trouble seemed to be. I tried asking them for help but Kedar said I was a drunken Zealot and the Romans decided not to get involved.'

'At least they didn't harm your goat statue,' said Simeon. 'Here, I found it in the street alongside your belongings.'

The artist examined the figure. 'It's not a goat, actually,' he said. 'It was a little devil. I was going to give it to Zillah as a present – she likes imps and gargoyles – but it came out more malevolent than I had intended. Zillah was so kind that I didn't want to curse her house. I'll throw it away tomorrow.'

'Don't,' said Simeon. 'May I keep it?'

'If you like. But it worries me a little.'

The next morning Simeon walked to Kedar's house and rapped the pretentiously large knocker on its door. The servants were asleep. Kedar opened the door.

'I thought I told you last night to mind your own business.'

'I found this in the street. It was dropped by the artist. It might be important evidence.' He handed Kedar the little devil.

'What is it?'

'It looks like a goat charm of some sort. To bring you fortune.'

'It doesn't look terribly friendly.'

'They're quite valuable, I believe. I did not want to return it to the artist because plainly he is a scoundrel who deserved what was coming to him.'

'Indeed.' Kedar fingered the small object. 'Quite valuable, d'ye say? Well, you did the right thing for once, old man.'

So it was that the little devil came to lodge at Kedar's house. At first it appeared to bring Kedar good luck. As a mark of approval for his work in keeping the city streets shipshape he was promoted to captain of the guard at the new temple. The job brought more money and kudos. As captain of the guard he would supervise the daily ceremonial locking of the temple at the end of the day. Much jangling of keys was involved. Kedar now had operational liaison meetings with Roman commanders. Even the Sadducees would have to start acknowledging him in the street. Zillah, who had been told what happened to Ibrahim, became his sworn foe and told everyone he was a most unsuitable man to supervise the great temple. Her protests came too late. He had the job. Meanwhile Mrs Kedar had gone to see her cousins in Tyre and had not yet returned. Kedar was delighted. As, perhaps, was Mrs Kedar.

Each night Kedar would retire to his house, pour himself some wine from the priests' cellars, and thank the cedarwood goat figurine. He stroked its carved form. Sometimes, when none of his servants was watching, he would bow to it. The imp had brought him great fortune, just as that old fool Simeon had predicted. It had made Kedar the most important security officer in the city. It had put him on a level where he could ignore la-di-dah Zillah and her Romaphile friends. The goat would have them in time. The goat would also bring Herod his comeuppance. For had it not been the king who was responsible for the humiliating beauty competition? As Jonah sometimes whispered, Herod was not a proper king – nor even a proper Jew - and had only agreed to build the temple to court favour. Captain of the Guard Kedar would be able to issue orders to the senior members of the royal household. The king's writ did not run in the temple precincts, where Herod was accounted just another pilgrim. Maybe that was why he seldom visited the temple.

So wrapped up did Kedar become in that goat figurine that at the next Day of Atonement he put himself forward to take part in the ceremony of the two goats. 'If he really wants to, why not?' shrugged the high priest. The ceremony was a popular annual event and Kedar's duty would be to lead the second goat out of the temple, past large crowds, to the city's southern gate. There he would release the animal and let it run into the wild. The beast in question was a single-minded creature who did not take kindly to Kedar's yanking on its lead. The more the goat disobeyed, the crosser Kedar became.

'Is that Kedar's wife?' shouted a member of the crowd.

'Beard's not big enough.'

'No kidding.'

Kedar simmered. The high priest, from his ceremonial litter, smiled. It was good for the crowd to let off steam and Kedar might learn a lesson.

'If you can't bleat 'em, join 'em,' shouted another heckler.

'All right!' shouted Kedar. 'That's enough!'

'Oooh, someone's got his goat,' came the inevitable shout. It made Kedar turn round with such force that he nearly strangled the animal. The goat decided to tolerate no more. It pulled away from Kedar with such force that he dropped the leash. The goat rose on its hind legs, lowered its head and charged. Whack. Kedar scrambled to his feet. The goat again lowered its head and this time rammed Kedar in the groin. 'That must have hurt,' agreed the crowd.

One of the goat's horns caught Kedar's ceremonial tunic and ripped it, baring his backside. This won cheers from all sides. Soon Kedar was running out through the gates, heading in the direction of the Valley of Hinnom. Exit, pursued by a goat.

When Kedar finally returned home that night, having at long last evaded his crazed assailant, he seized hold of the little cedar-wood imp and threw it on the fire, a grin widening on its face as it was consumed by flames.

An Olive Branch

ONE blazing afternoon, when much of Jerusalem was snoozing, a self-important gathering formed in Deuteronomy Square to discuss municipal improvements as a wider part of the Temple Mount project. Lemuel was present to advise on architectural matters, Hiram was there in case anyone asked about masonry specifications and Kedar loitered near the back, swatting flies on his neck. Most people, if given a choice, kept their distance from Kedar but flies found him irresistible. Maybe he should have eaten more garlic. Kedar liked to be in on everything, particularly if Sadoc the Chief Sadducee was involved. There, indeed, sat Sadoc in the centre of the group, on an ornate chair under an awning held by two slaves.

'That's agreed, then,' said Sadoc. 'We will knock down this building, broaden the street, remove one of the almond trees and create a logical flow towards the new temple entrance. Thank you, gentlemen. Most satisfactory.' Sadoc allowed one of his slaves to step forward and pat his bald head with a cold towel. It was important to keep Sadoc's long, thin head cool because he was a man of immense brain. If it became cooked, Jerusalem would be in trouble. This was widely accepted.

Simeon watched from some nearby shade. He saw the pointing arms and nodding heads and said: 'Whatever it is, they're up to no good, my friend.' Shlomo, not being entirely sure what this meant, simultaneously wagged his tail and growled. This was called sitting on the fence. Some at the palace had made careers out of that sort of thing.

When sceptics forced Herod to agree not to start building until he had all his supplies, they thought it would gum up the project for years. As we have seen, he defied expectations and the project was now moving fast. In mere months Temple Mount had been cut and filled and buttressed and gabioned, an anthill of workers delving and sweating to create something to God and Herod's glory. Building labourer Og, who visited the tea stall most days with his brother Phut, kept the square abreast of the progress. Og was not exactly the most garrulous of souls but compared to Phut he was a positive parakeet. Both had vast, hairy hands, round shoulders and overhanging brows but Phut was utterly silent. If he could talk, he chose not to. No one made a thing of it. The time for that had been lost years ago. Not that it mattered. Who needs more talk in this world?

Meanwhile, Temple Mount rose and the bullock carts brought up flagstones and capstones and columns and architrave dressings and cornices from the dumps of supplies outside the city's gates. Jerusalem's energies seemed to be devoted to one cause and one cause alone, which was the new temple. All this activity appalled official Jerusalem's agents of inertia. The king was developing a reputation as a man who could get things done. No good could come of this. Yet Jerusalem's shops were full of construction workers and you never heard them say a bad word about the king. Few sounds are sweeter than that of a busy bazaar. Onesimus's fruit and veg' business was flying. At the tea stall Reuben saw record weekly takings. Being Reuben, he lowered his prices to let customers benefit from the greater profits. Onesimus did the opposite. 'It's boom time and no one is counting the small change,' he reasoned. Onesimus himself always counted his shekels, down to the last button and plum stone, but he was right that an air of infectious prosperity inhabited the city.

And yet, is prosperity merely to be measured in shekels? Happiness was interrupted after Kedar's goons pitched up in Deuteronomy Square and roped off the area near Ezekiel's almond trees. When Ezekiel turned up for work he was refused admittance to the cordoned-off area. 'Can't let you in there, chum. Not safe.'

'I work there.'

'Not today, pal.'

'What seems to be the trouble here?' asked Kedar.

'I need to set up my stall under the almond trees,' said Ezekiel.

'Singular,' said Kedar.

'Eh?'

'Tree. Singular. Almond tree. There's only going to be one of them. This one,' he gestured to the hapless victim, 'is being chopped down. Order of the environmental works committee.'

'I didn't know about this.'

'That,' said Kedar, 'is not my problem. It's all been properly decided. Site visit. Approved by Sadoc himself. Half that building on the corner is coming down, too. Its owner isn't too cheerful either but the common good takes priority.'

'Sadoc? His wife is one of my customers.'

'Well, that's nice,' said Kedar. 'Now if you don't mind, we must ask you to step back and allow my team to carry out the work safely. We wouldn't want the tree landing on you.'

An executioner arrived to do the task. 'Og, it's you!'

'Morning, Ezekiel. Yeah, sorry about this.' Og's oiled axe-blade glistened in the sunlight. 'I'll make it as painless as possible.' It was unusual for Og to be seen without his brother.

'Where's Phut?'

'He stayed at the depot. He likes trees.'

With each mighty blow, Ezekiel winced. Og was so strong that the sinews on his back seemed as thick as the almond tree's branches. As the tree toppled it seemed to sigh. Ezekiel could not watch the post-surgery tidy-up, branches being sawn into short lengths. The main trunk was towed away by a gang of slaves.

For the next few days Ezekiel was a sad sight as he traded listlessly beneath just the one almond tree. There was more light in the square, admittedly, and vehicular traffic (as Kedar called it) would in future flow more freely. Even so, the lone tree looked like a single tooth in a ravaged gum. Friends tried to raise Ezekiel's morale. Bildad brought lavender honey, Tambal showed him his Nubian knife (so sharp it could 'slice through human bone like cheese') and mimed what he would do to Kedar were he back home in

Africa. When Onesimus was not looking, Deborah gave Ezekiel a bag of cherries. Simeon told Noor to take Ezekiel some flowers. None of these gambits worked. Noor's flowers were not even found a vase of water. Ezekiel left them on his stall that night and by next morning they had been stolen by the crows. Noor did not mind, for her heart secretly lay elsewhere, but Simeon thought Ezekiel might have made more of an effort.

The Pharisees flirted with making a protest to Sadoc until Jonah came back from a meeting at the Hall of Hewn Stones and told his lads that there would no more talk of Ezekiel's tree. Civic improvements were not to be opposed. They were essential to the prosperity of the city and would allow the country to move forward in lockstep with the empire and modernity. Jonah invoked 'progress', a new word popular in certain quarters. 'Progress' meant change and change meant golden tomorrows. Simeon did not dislike Herod. Sometimes he felt rather proud of the king. Nor did he dislike Rome, for he had served with Roman soldiers and had a weakness for their macaroni. But he distrusted slogans.

'Are you a rabbi or a politician?' he asked.

'It must be possible to be both,' replied Jonah.

'So they've offered you a seat in the Sanhedrin.'

'Please,' said Jonah, 'your temper lets you down sometimes.'

Ezekiel, who had thought the Pharisees might be on his side, sank into a depression. Customers started to buy their almonds elsewhere. Soon he was having trouble replacing his stock.

'Do you have any of that lovely almond butter body lotion?' asked one of the upmarket ladies.

'No call for it these days, Lady Sadoc,' came the glum reply.

'What a pity.'

'Not much point any more, is there?'

'What do you mean?'

'Thou hast sore broken us in the place of dragons,' intoned Ezekiel. 'Our soul is bowed down to the dust. Our belly cleaveth unto the earth.'

'Oh dear. We are quite the Dismal Daniel today.'

'He gave up their cattle to the hail and their flocks to hot thunderbolts.'

'The Psalms can be so terribly gloomy.' She toyed with her topaz earrings and patted Ezekiel on the forearm.

Simeon let Lady Sadoc know it was nothing personal. Ezekiel had always found her charming. But maybe she could quietly let her husband know how the loss of the almond tree had dented public morale. Lady Sadoc was not deaf to the harshness, even pomposity, of her consort. The best political spouses seldom are. Herod could have done with a Lady Sadoc.

'Is there nothing we can do?' she asked.

That evening, when Simeon was doing some light digging in the pots on his verandah, a thought germinated in his head. The next day, equipped with a trowel, small sack and some of the most deliciously garlicky olives sold by Onesimus, he strode out of the Valley Gate, skirting the Hinnom and passing the Snake Pool on his right. A brisk walk brought him to the edge of a wild olive grove. Later he diverted towards the Dung Gate and the area where the temple aggregates were piled. Outside a depot hut he found Phut.

'Shalom, chatterbox.' Phut raised a silent hand in salute. Simeon produced the garlicky olives. 'Go on. They're for you.' Phut clopped over and took a sniff. 'I thought they might take the edge off your appetite.' The wordless giant took the olives tenderly into his large hands. From his grunts it was evident that the olives were acceptable.

'If there are two things I know about you, good Phut, it is these,' began Simeon. 'First, you are a God-fearing soul who does what is right. Second, you like trees almost as much as you like olives.' Phut ceased his chewing for a moment and looked slowly at Simeon. When he ate, his jaw had a slight sideways motion, like a ruminant. 'That is why I have come to have a chat with you. Well, not so much with, more at.'

After the olives had been reduced to a neat pile of stones Simeon headed back to Deuteronomy Square. Preparations were soon put in train for a ceremony that evening. All Ezekiel was told was that he should wear a clean tunic, brush his hair and try to scrape at least some of the dirt from his fingernails.

'Why?'

'Surprise,' said Reuben.

A small crowd gathered, Simeon stepped forward holding one of the little sacks he had taken on his morning expedition, and Reuben tapped the side of a plate to gain attention. 'Ladies and gentlemen,' said Simeon, 'we are gathered here this evening to give our friend Ezekiel a present.'

'A present?' said Ezekiel.

'Some time ago we suffered a grievous loss. Lady Sadoc is with us to help repair that loss. Ma'am, you are most welcome.' Hear-hears and applause. 'The loss of the almond tree was felt dearly by Ezekiel, and indeed by the sparrows and robins who used to live in it. We cannot resurrect the almond tree but we can do something similar. Ezekiel, I am going to give you your present. It is in this sack and you will look at it and think: "What a swizz." But then I will explain.' He gave Ezekiel the sack and Ezekiel looked inside, pulled out a small, wonky piece of vegetation, and indeed expressed puzzlement. 'It is,' continued Simeon, 'a wild olive seedling. Near where the poor almond tree stood we have prepared a hole in the ground. It has been dug and filled with sand and grit, for which we must thank our friend Phut. It has even had some fertiliser added, for which we must thank our friend Javelin. And now it is to be planted by Lady Sadoc.'

Sadoc's wife received the seedling with reverence and made sure that it was heeled in and staked. Tabitha played her harp. Jonah was prevailed upon to say a small prayer and Lady Sadoc completed the formalities by unveiling a small plaque which read: 'Ezekiel's Olive Tree – planted by the Lady Sadoc, in memoriam amygdal.' Lady Sadoc kissed Ezekiel on either cheek, everyone clapped and the crowd shouted: 'Speech, speech!'

Ezekiel shrivelled. 'Speech, speech!' cried the crowd.

'All I'd like to say,' said Ezekiel, accepting the inevitable, 'is that I am very touched by this wonderful . . .' As he started crying everyone cheered.

In the following months Ezekiel watered the seedling and on icy mornings wrapped it in wool. When upmarket ladies came to buy almonds they were given a full account of how many inches the olive seedling had grown. Everyone speculated on its future fecundity. Kedar was displeased. He felt 'the authorities' should have been consulted. He would, at the very least, have liked to have been invited to the tree-planting ceremony. In the normal run of things he would have marched over to the olive seedling, wrenched it out of the ground and dumped it on Ezekiel's counter. But Lady Sadoc's name was on the plaque. Lady Sadoc had planted it. The plaque bore some Latin writing which Kedar was not entirely able to understand. The olive seedling survived.

And so Ezekiel, who had lost one tree, won another and gained a dream. As the olive became a sapling, and then a juvenile tree, the almond seller rediscovered his smile. The grief of loss yielded to the pride of watching something grow. The tree's first blossom was almost like a bar mitzvah. The first fruit appeared. Ezekiel was a father! Soon there were abundant olives that Reuben placed on customers' tables. Everyone would tell Ezekiel he must be proud, which he was, and at the first oil-pressing there was a special toast – 'to absent friends' – at which gestures were made to the empty space where the felled almond had stood. The good Lord taketh away with one hand and, sometimes helped by a Lady, he giveth with the other. If you go to Jerusalem today you will find an ancient olive, its branches now gnarled and twisty. Deuteronomy Square itself has gone the way of all flesh. The layout of the streets has been altered at the behest of important men with retinues of architects. Yet they have not yet touched that revered olive tree, reputed to be older than the Wailing Wall. Some things, happily, are bigger than 'progress'.

News from Jericho

ONCE a month or so Musa set up his anvil in Deuteronomy Square and dispensed news from distant parts. And the kingdom of Onesimus, greengrocer, would become riven by tensions.

Musa was a farrier and a follower of chariot-racing. Some find chariot-racing a bore. Onesimus did. He thought it irresponsible and modern and Roman. Yet that was why others liked it. There was talk of a track being built at Caesarea. Hippodromes were quite the thing. Where there was chariot-racing there needed to be farriers to tend to the horses and repair smashed chariots. Musa was often found jobbing round the backs of the stadia.

'Tell us about the hippodrome at Jericho,' said Benjamin.

'What a place. Seats three thousand. Twenty chariots race at breakneck speed. Wheels drum on wettened sand, horses pant, whips crack, the crowd goes mad. It's the women who scream the most. Your mother would love the hippodrome. It brings out the beast in them.'

'I will be a charioteer one day, Musa.'

'Why not, laddie?'

'Jonah the Pharisee was saying the other day that chariots are a Roman corruption.'

'You don't want to listen to everything those Pharisees say.'

Onesimus was not by nature a despot. His wife, Deborah, once told him he was as sweet as a nectarine. A certain dependability in life was what he hoped for each day when waking before dawn and going down to stir the porridge. At that hour there were no interruptions. Deborah was not pecking him. Benjamin was zonked to the world. If left, their son could lie abed till noon, dreaming of the hippodrome. Benjamin had a one-track, two-wheel mind.

Onesimus did not mind the boy having impossible dreams. What he objected to was a long-haired farrier sparking that dry tinder. They were in the fruit and veg' business, for goodness' sake. Life meant early starts, sacks of carrots, cockroaches in the shed and evenings at an abacus. He forbade Benjamin from talking to Musa and he told Deborah that any man with a medallion and tattoos was unsuitable company for a married woman. Both of them ignored him but Onesimus did not notice. In his mind he was in charge and that was all that mattered.

There were other farriers, with proper smithys, but Musa drove into the square and repaired your animal there and then. He was cheap, too, and there was the added satisfaction that when you paid him he rang a merry bell that let out a hollow clonk and made people laugh. Musa had no building to maintain. Nor, possibly, did he always remember to pay his taxes. He never stayed long in one place. By the time his rivals had prodded the publicans to investigate him for tax avoidance Musa had long left for the next town.

'You have a good husband,' he told Deborah as he scraped mud out of a carthorse's hooves. 'He provides for you.'

'Onesimus is dependable,' agreed Deborah dully. Musa removed his jerkin and tied his hair into a ponytail as he prepared to extract a red-hot shoe from the coal. The glow made Musa's muscles glint. From ten feet away Deborah felt the heat.

Musa had worked at Masada when Herod built the fortress overlooking the Dead Sea. He took his anvil to Alexandrium where prisoners were brought to the desert to work. Some dropped from fatigue, others were locked in the very dungeons they had dug from the hillside. At Sebastia he'd seen slaves strain at ropes to raise vast blocks of dressed stone. Some were crushed when a column toppled. 'What goes up can come down,' said Musa, 'stones or men.' Some prisoners at Alexandrium were educated gents who got on the wrong side of power. 'Keep moving, friends. Stay limber.'

Initially his scepticism scandalised Simeon. Herod was doing all he could to strengthen Judaea. Such naked swagger made Simeon bristle. This farrier did not just bring bad news, he *was* bad news. But every platoon needed a rebel. From his army days Simeon could remember at least that. Doubt kept the officers honest.

No one quite knew where Musa came from. 'I am a citizen of nowhere. So, apparently, was my father.' He could order his supper in Syriac, Greek, Latin, Hebrew, Qatabanian, Phrygian, even Gaulish. As a boy he sailed to Gaul and he told Reuben about the Gallic cooking.

One of his routines was to mimic a Gallic man chatting up his girlfriend – a mass of writhing eyebrows. Noor and Deborah couldn't get enough of it. His multilingualism had its uses. 'If I use Phoenician when denouncing that klutz Kedar he will not understand me. I can say: "Brother Kedar, your testicles are the size of pine nuts and your mother had a tamarin's moustache," and he will think I have been polite. Petty, but it amuses me.' In Dedan, Musa camped alongside Scythian turquoise merchants and heard them plot in their Tumshuqese. They thought he was a thief and proposed to knife him. He escaped at dead of sly night.

But animals trusted him. The jumpiest stallion would let him scrape its hooves and affix a shoe, always with that hissing kiss of steam and the smell of singed horn. And then the tap-tap-tap of nails. He had once been ordered to help at a crucifixion. Centurion Lucilius told him: 'Report to Golgotha tomorrow at noon and there'll be thirty denarii for you. We need someone quick with a hammer.' Musa left town that night. Another moonlight flit.

Javelin was limping and Benjamin worried he had pushed her too hard. Musa was the man to put things right. Javelin had known Musa all her life. She did not try to bite him or wander off mid-shoeing. A steady supply of black grapes from the pocket of his jerkin helped. The cause of the limp – a stone in one hoof – was soon removed. It would be sore for a few days but she should be back to 'full speed' in a week.

'She's never going to be the quickest,' reflected Benjamin.
'Mules can run up slopes that would defeat a horse.'
'That's no use in racing.'
'In a chariot race, no. Horses for courses. I could never

be a temple priest or a greengrocer. Others would hate living on the road. Javelin will never win the gold cup but she will be a champion in other ways.' When Simeon heard what Musa had said he liked the farrier better.

Musa brought news from Jericho. Young Aristobulus the high priest had drowned in a pool at the palace. 'It had been hot. There had been a lot of foolery. Maybe everyone had too much to drink, or boys were being boys and got carried away ducking one another in the water. This went on after dark. Aristobulus may have bumped his head. His body was pulled from the water next morning. Herod and his cavalcade departed without waiting for the funeral. He could at least have made a pretence of grief. The people were not impressed. He's cock of the walk at present but it won't last.'

Few in Jerusalem spoke like that. 'When you have property or family, you don't, do you?' said Reuben afterwards.

'Well, I have neither property nor family, but I don't,' said Simeon.

'Not yet,' said Reuben.

A Pot Was a Pot

REUBEN and Simeon had been friends since army days. 'You were a terrible soldier,' said Simeon as Reuben slopped early-morning tea into a cup and toasted some stale bread. The fire was sputtering. Reuben shivered. This misty start brought back an army morning in Galilee. Their kit was wet, the horses had escaped and bandits were rumoured to be massing beyond the ridge. Reuben had shuffled and shivered that day, too. Both of them were corporals, Simeon by merit, Reuben because he was the company cook.

'Harsh but true,' said Reuben, prodding the fire. 'Fighting was not my thing. My job was to feed the troops, brew tea and refuse bribes from suppliers. The quarter-master liked those for himself. Most soldiers are useless.'

He had a point. History enthuses about tactics and muscular valour without relating the reality for most recruits. Sore feet, blunt swords, arbitrary discipline imposed by maniacs: that was soldiering. The money wasn't bad, though, when you added the bounty collected from enemies who contrived to be even more inept. Simeon was one of the better fighters. Yes, he was impertinent. There was something about his posture that betrayed the word 'Why?' Dig a trench, polish your belt, do fifty press-ups, salute the colours. Simeon was enthusiastic but his cast of face often betrayed a 'Why?' even if he did not utter the word. His platoon was the laxest and happiest in the company. Sergeant Major Yadin nicknamed him Socrates because he was so clearly sceptical. Yet Simeon was good in a fight. Efficient in the kill. He could sing, too. The men liked to hear his voice.

Farmers and fishermen were excused conscription. Rabbis and the children of prominent landowners usually dodged it, too. Almost everyone else was nabbed, unless they were crippled. Reuben did think about claiming to have early-onset leprosy but realised it would mar his professional reputation. 'Oi, Chef, is this part of your thumb floating in my stew?' Reuben joined up. A pot was a pot, wherever you were stirring it. He was excused most parades – there were onions to chop – and because Sergeant Major Yadin never made him do press-ups, Reuben made sure the sergeant major never went short at supper.

General Ephron's division was garrisoned outside Nazareth. Civilians wandered in and out of the camp: saddlers, tailors, butchers. And dancers. Anna was a dancer. She moved well and was bold and the soldiers loved her impressions of General Ephron. She got the sadistic old tusker to a tee. On the night she first saw Simeon in the lower ranks' mess she looked him directly in the eye and said: 'Not bad.' Someone said Simeon was known as

Socrates. Anna threw back her dark curls and scoffed. 'The Greek Socrates was no use to women.' Another soldier disclosed that the corporal had married his childhood sweetheart. 'Interesting,' said Anna. 'I like a married man.' She would watch him, rapt, as he sang sentimental love songs. Some may have found it odd that a corporal who could apparently think so little about plunging his spear into a bandit's flank could lose himself in song. Anna was not one of them. Simeon was a braw lad, alive to the moment, full of appetites.

He was young. It was a different time. On a long posting the dock lines had loosened. Widowed Anna herself had no ties. After one of her dances she sauntered to Simeon's table, told his neighbour to scram, and sat roughly at his side. 'Buy me a drink, Socrates. Provided it's not hemlock.' An everyday garrison affair? It became more than that. Anna was older than Simeon or Hannah. She made Simeon feel worldly. She would talk about spiritual possibilities and claim to be in touch with 'the other side'. From anyone else it would have sounded kooky but she was so matter-of-fact, so convinced, that it seemed normal. She knew a little scripture and did not scoff when he admitted he would have liked to sing in a synagogue or even the temple at Jerusalem. 'Sing to me instead, my beautiful cantor.' And while he sang of loss and love and trembling mountains and dewed valleys she would close her eyes and pray or meditate – one was much the same to Anna. After they slept together she told him: 'Mercy and truth are met together – righteousness and truth have kissed together.' She told him his army life, if God spared him, would one day yield to something braver, which was peace and mercy. Simeon had been reared never to say the word God. Anna thought this a daft rule. It wasn't improper over-familiarity. It wasn't even God's first name. God was a force that passed all understanding. God was no more called God than men and women called one another 'being'. We should approach God with a straight eye and raised chin. Why cower? 'The only people who've benefited from controlling our thoughts about God are those leeches the Pharisees and Sadducees,' said Anna.

One of her skills was sleeping draughts. She used valerian, frankincense and lettuce milk. Combined with boiled water and a little mint it helped stressed army boys to sleep. The army. The bloody army. Most of the skirmishes involving General Ephron's division were farcical mismatches. Usually they found the enemy asleep, befuddled by wine or too much lamb. Peaceful capture of enemy fighters did nothing for the general's political prospects. He wanted them slaughtered. Before Simeon was made a corporal his unit was seconded to a Roman force in Syria and they were attacked by cataphracts. The Roman officers noticed Simeon's work in the close fighting, thrusting at the armoured horses with his pugio. The Judaean with the scar on his forehead was a soldier worth having.

On a night attack outside Kinneret the unit was creeping into an enemy camp when a young trooper tripped over a guy rope and thought it was a booby trap. They all took cover save Simeon who severed the remaining guy ropes, collapsed the enemy tent and speared its occupants. The screams brought other enemy soldiers to the scene. Simeon accounted for ten of them that night. Even Sergeant Major Yadin was impressed. In due course so was the local governor, Herod.

'It nearly killed Yadin to praise you in front of the governor,' laughed Reuben. He imitated the sergeant major's deep voice. '"This, Excellency, is the man who led the operation on brigands near Kinneret. May I present Corporal Socrates?"'

Yadin stood a rigid distance from the governor. General Ephron was at that parade, too. The general was craziness embodied. Herod was younger, more courtly, a scent of rosemary evident off his lustrous flesh. He had a civilised voice. He was attractive.

'When did you get that mark on your forehead, Corporal?'

'Years ago, Excellency.'

'More heroics in battle?'

'A snake bite. I was a young man.'

Herod grunted and started to move to the next man before he paused. He returned to Simeon. 'A snake bite, did you say?'

'Yes, Excellency.'

'Where?' asked the young governor sharply.

'Petra.' Simeon wished he was elsewhere. Having once been bitten by a snake, you do not want to venture too near another. The governor leaned in close, until Simeon could smell aniseed on his breath. The scar throbbed.

'Is your name Simon?'

'Not quite. Simeon, Excellency.'

'Simeon, that was it! Thank you, Simeon.' Then more loudly: 'Thank you for your gallant service, Corporal. Galilee is grateful.' He clapped Simeon's shoulder before moving on, saying: 'Now, Sergeant Major, who have we here?' The memory still made Simeon proud.

But other memories were more painful. It was a month later, back at barracks in Nazareth, that the message about Hannah was sent. There had been complications in the birth. The messenger hurried by horseback and made it within a day. Simeon should come immediately, said the message. But he was not in the barracks when the message arrived. He was with Anna and she had given him something to help them both sleep. He received the message only when he returned early the next day.

He was allowed to go at once and travelled as fast as his legs would permit. But by the time he arrived the following afternoon Hannah's funeral had been held. 'We could wait no longer,' said her mother. 'Oh, Simeon, she loved you.'

'And I loved her,' he said, and he sobbed like a boy, which in some ways he still was.

He held the infant they had pulled from her womb and tried singing that song to the child. It was the song he had written himself, celebration of a much-anticipated arrival, a hymn to salvation. He had practised it in front of Anna, a thought that now shrivelled him. He tried singing but the words just bounced back off the ailing infant's uncomprehending brow.

Stephen lived three days. A wet nurse tried to suckle him and the other women of the village ensured there was sufficient air in the lowly room where the infant was being cradled and soothed. The softest blankets were provided, the choicest herbs hung, and permission was given for the mourning rituals to be suspended while the household fought to save the baby's life. To get Simeon out of the way, as well as to give him something to do, Hannah's family told him to climb Mount Gerizim to offer prayers to Abraham and the forefathers. *The Eloowwem of Abraahm we bless you, soften your anger with us and grant us mercy and goodwill.* The uphill path soon left behind the crops and shrubs of the village and the landscape became stony. Dabb lizards darted, a cacophony of crickets crowded in on his mind and he stooped to pull a mandrake from the barren earth. Dry-mouthed, he sucked on its root for relief from his thirst as he trudged onwards and upwards along the steep mountain way. Was that a headless Blemmye jumping behind that dolomite tor, two enormous eyes throbbing between its shoulders? Marmini loitered behind him, he felt sure, taunting him with charred tongues and foul ditties, though every time he turned to confront the bastards they disappeared, slipping into drifts of toadflax with no more than a vanishing ankle. He hurled the mandrake into the distance and as it described an arc in the air it took flight, fluttering like a bat, a savage torment of black, hairy wings.

Stephen died before he could be circumcised. Simeon opened his own guts to God. For days he roamed the ridge of Gerizim, that broad shoulder of lifeless soil. He howled and sobbed, clawed the air, flayed his back with the thorns of a dead jujube branch. He rent his raglike robes and scrabbled the ground until his fingertips bled as he pleaded for a second chance. Next time he would not fail. Next time he would pass the test. Please! These begging laments would have grieved the hardest heart; yet Mount Ebal, Gerizim's counterpart, stood unmoved across the valley. All Simeon could taste was dust and ash, wormwood and gall.

The child was buried as he had briefly lived, an innocent. The Samaritans bore their losses with dignity. 'She was beckoned back early and now she has been joined by her angel,' they said. 'We should be so lucky.' Simeon went to the joint grave with flowers – blue lupins and two white lilies. As he approached he moved a beetle which would have been crushed. There had been enough death. In the mountain silence he wept, great blobs of grief on the dust, until he thought he could smell summer rain. He tried to pray but his thoughts stayed inside him, refusing to take flight. Singing was no good, either. The Final Song of Moses turned to pebbles in his throat. The music had died in him. He felt he would never sing again.

When he crouched to lay the flowers, the two mountains marched in and wind blew as if some vast swan was beating its wings on the bank of a wide, black river. Daylight vanished and was replaced by a dazzling whiteness. A voice, if it was a voice, asked: 'Well, what are you going to do now?'

'Who are you?'

'Never mind who I am, who are you? What are you made of? How are you going to make this good? You wanted a second chance, didn't you?' Simeon shielded his face from the light and dust and he cowered. 'Oh, please,' said the voice, 'don't crumple on me. Grief is one thing, whimpering surrender is another. You were such an army tough-guy, quite the goat.'

'I shouldn't have done that,' said Simeon. 'I know it was wrong.'

'Now he says.'

'I'm sorry.'

'Maybe. But what next? Weeping endureth for a night but what comes in the morning?'

'Joy.'

'You wish! Penance. Penance comes first.'

115

'How?' asked Simeon. 'Do I dress in burlap and smear myself with ashes?'

'Little point in that. Burlap is for show-offs. No, you're going to make your way to Jerusalem and wait. Make for the temple, wait and watch. You will stay there until the time. Think of it as sentry duty. One day a great force will arrive – a prince of peace – and you will have a small but useful part to play. God's dominion is over all the generations. You are no more than a beetle in the dirt. Go to Jerusalem, earn your passage. You will know when you are free.'

Another wind gusted so strongly that Simeon fell hard on the ground. The whiteness evaporated as fast as it had formed. Some shape flew up and away until around Simeon there remained only the last eddies of dust and departing air and a long, screaming silence.

And then: 'Simeon! Are you okay? Simeon!' Reuben was running towards him up the mountain. He arrived panting. 'Sorry I startled you but I suddenly saw you.'

'Reuben, what are you doing here?'

'When a mate's in trouble, you've got to help. The village said you were here. I wanted to say, you know, sorry. I wish I'd met her. And the kid. It's really tough.'

They did not embrace. A jumbled Simeon just nodded and Reuben pulled him to his feet. Simeon patted down his torn clothes, shook a thorn twig out of his hair and tightened the latchet on one of his sandals. They rearranged the flowers which had been scattered by the wind. Among them Simeon found a large white feather. Reuben said it looked like goshawk or great egret. Simeon was less sure. He tucked it into a pocket inside his tunic. Slowly they walked down to the village, two soldiers, subdued, dented, and one of them a little wiser.

On returning to the garrison Simeon sent word to Anna to tell her what had happened. But Anna had gone. Sergeant Major Yadin had heard about the affair and taken a dim view. He had never liked Anna. She had been a distraction and was too intelligent for young soldiers. The sergeant major had her banned from the camp and told her she would be denounced as a harlot if she ever came back. Simeon only learned this much later. At the time he presumed Anna had left to give him space to grieve. She had returned a tunic he had left at her apartment. Wrapped inside it was a figurine of Astarte, goddess of love. Two months later Simeon left the army and moved to Jerusalem. His stepbrother had agreed to buy his share of their father's incense business and that gave him enough money to live on for a while.

Simeon had been in Jerusalem a month when he received a message from the palace. The king sent his condolences. Miss Hannah had been a much-loved part of his childhood. Unless Corporal Simeon had other plans, a vacancy existed for a guide to be employed in Temple Square to assist visitors. It carried no stipend but he would have the king's blessing if he felt able to apply for the position. Simeon took the job because it was at the temple and because he felt that if any new prince was going to arise, it would be no disadvantage to be in with the royal family. One of his first customers was Philippos the Greek, who stopped to chat one morning and offered Simeon extra money for the Aramaic lessons he did not need. 'Tell me, Simeon, how does one say in Aramaic: "His Greatness sends his best wishes"?'

A year later Reuben followed him to Jerusalem and opened the tea stall. Simeon made Reuben curious. There was something unusual about him but what the heck. The army hadn't been much fun without him. A pot was a pot, wherever you were stirring it, and it might as well be near his friend Simeon.

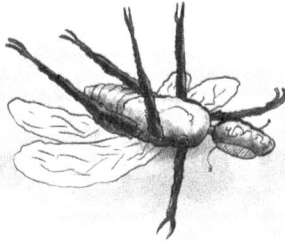

Lord of the Flies

KEDAR was not the only person who attracted flies. Simeon was also driven mad by them. *Bzz-bzz-bzz* they went all day, squadrons having dogfights over his bed, crowding into the window corners, mating. Deuteronomy Square was clouded by houseflies, horseflies, fruit flies, awl flies, bluebottles, blowflies, midges, gnats. Damn flies were all aiming their snouts at him. Jonah, without a second thought, squashed one on his arm while praying. Noor flicked one off her chopping board as if it were a crumb. When Tabitha felt a fly on her brow, she wafted her hand as if adjusting a strand of her lovely hair. Simeon found such nonchalance impossible. Each fly on his leg or neck became an infuriation. At night they were replaced by mosquitoes. Simeon tried scented candles. These made him sneeze. He tried smearing his wrists and ankles in lemon juice but that make him sticky, and the mozzies still bit him. He jammed a pillow over his head. It stopped the *wheeeeee* but eventually he had to come up for air and

119

mozzies pounced like diners who'd been waiting for the restaurant's all-you-can-eat buffet to open.

In one of the Job's Alley ironmonger shops he spotted a fly swat. Maybe this would see off the little pests.

'You want me to wrap it?'

'No need,' he told the shopkeeper. 'I intend to go to war immediately.' He swished the swat around his head like a conductor's baton.

'Some people are martyrs to flies. Others barely notice them. Same with doubts. And sins.' The ironmonger peered at Simeon. 'You sure it's only flies that are worrying you, brother?'

Simeon hurried from the shop, irked by the man's curiosity. Niggles were forgotten when he put the new weapon to use. It was superb. Flies stood little chance under the super-fast swat. Corpses soon littered the floor and Simeon decided a small drink would be in order to celebrate his victories. Further slaughter followed. Wine had improved his timing with the swat. Another glass would further aid his marksmanship. His room was soon empty of targets – the enemy had been routed – so he sat on the terrace where the day's heat was easing. Six more flies and a couple of wasps met their Maker. Simeon emitted a mock-evil cackle and inspected his swat with approval. It had been a good buy, worth that impertinence from the ironmonger. Doubts? Sins? He was merely rectifying a long-overdue imbalance in power. The flies had had things too easy for too long. Long live His Greatness Simeon!

Grapes were starting to show, cucumbers were inching across the terrace and the aubergines were plumping. All was well with the kingdom. Noor called him down to supper – lentils and okra – and Simeon feasted royally, infecting Noor with his cheer. 'Okra is good for the brain,' he declared, 'for its core is shaped like the seal of the mighty Solomon. We will be wise tomorrow, sweet Noor, just you see!'

'If I didn't know you better, Simeon, I'd say you've had a glass of wine.'

'Or three, Noor. But a wise ruler knows when to stop. Let me help with the dishes.' He made to lift the cooking pot but wobbled on his bench and Noor told him she would sooner do it herself and have everything in one piece, thank you. Simeon tottered upstairs.

All was quiet in his room. He left the curtain open because the last of the light was beautiful. His Jerusalem was at peace, subsumed by that well-fed smokiness she attains at dusk. Not a fly stirred. Simeon patted his full tummy and grinned. Yessss! Doziness crept up on him.

Bzz.

He had just started dreaming.

Bzz-bzz.

One of Simeon's eyes clicked open.

Bzz-bzzzzzzzzzzzzzzzzzzzzzzzzzzzzzzzzzzzzzzzzzzzzzzzzzzz zzzzz!

He was out of bed in a flash, naked, swat brandished in warrior hands. There was just enough light left for him to see the interloper. A single fly. There, on the wall. A survivor, or scout? He swatted. Damnation. *Bzz-bzz.* There, on the windowsill. Another miss. A flicker of movement brought yet another flashing swish and the swat came down on the small bedside shelf. There was a noise as the swat made contact, a smash yet also a tinkle. The buzzing stopped. Simeon was pleased about that. But it had not been without cost.

On the floor, in three pieces – one for each love of his life – lay the little statue of Astarte. Its arms had snapped off. Simeon put down the fly swat, lit a candle and collected the figurine in one palm. The breaks were clean. Could they be repaired? Maybe. All for an errant fly. A tear formed and dropped down one of Simeon's cheeks. It was soon followed by a counterpart from the other eye. Then came a legion more tears.

'Feeling sorry for yourself?'

Simeon jumped. 'I was alone.'

'That's what they all think.'

'I broke it. The Astarte.'

'So you did. Stupid of you.'

'She gave it to me.'

'Years ago.'

'Who are you?' asked Simeon. 'Where are you?' He felt a rush of air to his right. It darted to his other side, then to the back of his neck, then shimmered at the verandah doorway, making the curtains sway.

'This self-pity won't do.' There was a smell of something not quite like summer rain.

'I miss Hannah,' said Simeon. 'Our child did not live. And now I have broken Anna's token. God has no interest in me.'

'Defeatist nonsense. Get a grip.'

'What for?'

'For the coming of the rest of time. You know what's right.'

'I don't!'

'You will at some point. You will when it matters. Temple tomorrow morning, full shift, every working day, no muckin' about. Do it and you do God's work. And now let's have no more of this pathetic blubbing.'

The candle was extinguished by a draught. Simeon rushed outside to see where the visitor had gone but there was nothing save a sky of stars and the last of the city's supper pots being washed and a fading hubbub. The smell of summer rain was still discernible. Or was it?

Simeon slept fathoms deep. Next morning he felt rinsed. Where the broken Astarte had lain, now she was again whole. Had he dreamed it all? Or was there, as he ran his fingertips over the figurine, the tiniest of scars? When he put his feet on the floor he felt a layer of clay dust, milled as fine as turmeric.

At the Races

JAVELIN would be a champion in her own right one day, Musa the farrier had said.

Finally the hippodrome at Caesarea opened. Benjamin relished Musa's descriptions of the arena and the chariots whizzing round its track. 'I'd love to see it,' said Benjamin.

'Go.'

'I can never get the time off.'

'I can't live your life for you, lad,' said Musa.

Judaea had a shortage of chilli peppers. The harvest had been small and customers were paying over the odds. When Onesimus heard a shipment of chillis was expected at Dor he told Benjamin to head there and buy a cartload. The return journey might take five days but think of the profits. Benjamin broke his usual habits and hit the great west road at dawn. The wide Roman road was a credit to Herod's reign. At Lydda they rested and Benjamin gave Javelin some nosebag before turning north on to the old road. After Antipatris and a night's rest it would be a left turn towards the sea. The hills were fresh and life was good.

The next morning, drinking down the cool of dewy dawn, they were rounding a bend when they met trouble. A covered Phoenician wagon stood at an angle in the road with two hooded men on its driving seat, whipping an uncooperative horse. In the ditch alongside lay an elderly man, possibly dead, and two women weeping and wailing. Benjamin accelerated to the incident, jumped down and told Javelin to wait. The mule stamped to attention. Benjamin hurried to the ditch. The women explained that the men were stealing their wagon and that the old fellow in the ditch was their husband and father who had been struck on the head when he confronted the thieves. The wound was bleeding and he was groaning, which was at least better than being dead.

'Our cart!' said the older woman.

'I'll chase it,' said Benjamin.

Hippodrome-goers will tell you that a mule normally stands little chance against a horse. They have shorter legs. You might as well race a fishing smack against a trireme. But up a hill, particularly when the horse is being bullied by an unfamiliar driver, the mule may be at less of a disadvantage. The pursuit occurred on rising ground. Benjamin's cart was empty and he had a light touch on the reins. For months the little mule had listened to Benjamin's fantasies about chariot-racing and her own had taken flight. Here, now, was a real race.

At the first corner both vehicles skidded. At the second, one of the thieves fell off the cart and landed in a thorn bush. On the next straight Javelin pulled almost level. They went into the third corner alongside each other and as they came out of it Javelin had the strength to keep her line, though it was a close-run thing. There was a grinding of locked wheels. Javelin grimaced at her bit and leaned her shoulder into the opposition, to the extent that a clerk-of-the-course might have ruled foul play. A moment of peril saw Benjamin's cart teeter on two wheels but Javelin gave another yank to her left and corrected her wagon. The stolen vehicle was pushed off the road into a thicket of rock rose, thistle and terebinth trees. It stopped with a jolt and the remaining thief leapt to the ground and ran. Javelin gave a triumphant whinny and was answered by the horse from the hijacked cart who soon calmed down thanks to a carrot from Benjamin. It had been a tremendous tussle, one to relive for months to come.

The old man from the ditch recovered and he and the women – his wife and their daughter – were effusively grateful. Benjamin managed to get their cart out of the thicket and back on the road. With a little tightening of wheel-nuts he was soon escorting them the remaining distance to Dor. The old chap, Mr Jacob, had a house there. 'Can we put you up for a night or two?' Benjamin accepted. He liked Mr Jacob and his family, and the chilli ship was behind schedule. He could leave his cart at Mr Jacob's house, let Javelin rest in a shaded stable, and walk the few miles south to Caesarea to catch an afternoon at the races.

Mr Jacob insisted that he and his family would accompany Benjamin and they would travel by carriage in grand style. Although many thought Musa exaggerated his stories, he had under-reported the marvels of Caesarea. Above the stadium entrance, pennants snapped in the sea breeze and hundreds of spectators flocked to the races.

They had seats with a fine view of the first bend. Hawkers sold nuts and cups of wine. Benjamin was placed next to Jacob's friendly if slightly plain daughter.

The first race saw a tight finish between three chariots. The second race had to be re-started after carnage at the first corner when two chariots collided. There were six races in all and between each one the racegoers placed bets with bookmakers. Mr Jacob made a profit on the day because he backed three winners. His delight at the third win quite compensated for his disappointment that young Benjamin did not seem romantically interested in his daughter. They left the hippodrome on a high of excitement and wine and on the way out Mr Jacob bought Benjamin a present: a pair of charioteer reins for Javelin. Just wait until he showed those to everyone in Deuteronomy Square! The next morning Benjamin, heading back to Jerusalem with a cargo of chillis, was still on such a high that he nearly forgot he had seen Jonah the Pharisee in the crowd as everyone surged out of the stadium.

The Accidental Matchmaker

ON the eve of Faunalia, Simeon hobbled down to the pool of Bethesda. The Pharisees did not approve of Roman festivals but Faunalia was surely a bit of harmless fun. Youngsters gave each other anonymous love tokens and concocted terrible poems about daisies and true hearts. For one day a year, Lysander had competition.

The pool of Bethesda was beautifully still at first light. Unrippled and black, it had an almost oily quality. Lepers slept under the portico and a water boatman skimmed across the surface. Two swallows swooped but they seemed more interested in taking a drink than in catching the water boatman, who either had nerves of steel or did not notice the swallows. Maybe, like Simeon these days, they were hard of hearing.

Simeon had slept badly, worrying about Noor. Sometimes he sneaked a sideways glance and found her mouth turned down at the edges. Was she sad? Ill? Noor had no kin in Jerusalem. Her father kept a vineyard in

Emmaus and now had a second brood. The closest thing she had to family in the city was her distant cousin Shoom. Otherwise Noor's world revolved round cleaning her flat, making sure Simeon was in one piece and baking for Reuben's tea stall. How could Simeon cheer her up? A new dress? An afternoon outing? Pay her more rent? Well, not that last one, obviously. But there must be some way of raising morale.

The swallows took it in turns to duck and dip and bank at speed. One would perch on the portico and the other took that as an invitation to perform its aerobatics, darting down again to the water's surface, taking a tiny sip, then lifting sharply to avoid hitting the end wall, and all while making little clicks to its friend. Simeon felt like applauding but that would have been intrusive, for this was the swallows' special time. Maybe they were courting.

'That's it!' thought Simeon with a thunderclap. That was what Noor needed. A boyfriend. That evening he had a talk to God. He sank to his knees and stared hard at the feather. 'Look, Noor makes a wonderful couscous and attends temple every week but she's lonely. How can this be fair?' The feather remained motionless. Simeon eased some pins and needles in his right foot and continued: 'Noor leads a life of virtue. She is just the sort of person you should bless, not burden with sadness. Stick and carrot is fine but stick, stick, stick is unacceptable. She needs love in her life. I really think you should fix this. Think about it. Promise me you will at least do that.' A less watchful eye would have missed it but Simeon could have sworn the feather swayed.

If Noor had a weakness it was for almonds. She could spend ages at Ezekiel's almond stall ogling the goodies.

Ezekiel sold almonds in their skins, almonds in vinegar, almond paste, almonds with honey. There were pickled almonds, almond cakes, almond pastes, almond butters and macaroons. The way Noor liked her almonds best was roasted, lightly fried and salted. No one did them better than Ezekiel. And who else was single? Who else needed a romantic tickle? Ezekiel!

'I know a beautiful lady who loves those,' said Simeon when bachelor boy was roasting his next batch of almonds.

'Who's that?' asked Ezekiel.

'That would be telling,' said Simeon.

'I won't pry.' Ezekiel resumed his chores. This was possibly going to be harder than Simeon had anticipated.

'What I am saying,' Simeon continued, 'is that I know a beautiful woman who loves Mr Ezekiel's roasted, lightly fried, salted almonds and who would be grateful for a present this Faunalia festival.'

'I can do you a gift pack if you want, mates' rates,' said Ezekiel, still not twigging. 'I must confess I thought you were past that sort of thing, Simeon. I'm impressed.'

'It is not what *I* want!' exclaimed the hapless matchmaker. 'I am thinking what *she* might want. This beautiful woman. Who might be looking for love and who might be able to draw an obtuse nut seller out of his shell.'

'Hmmn?'

'For goodness' sake, Ezekiel. I'm trying to play Cupid and you're not making it easy. Tell me, are you lonely?'

'I've got my almonds.'

'Do you want a girlfriend?'

'I've never been much good at that sort of thing.'

'Here's your chance.'

'Really? What do I do?'

Simeon had it all worked out. Every evening, as the frangipani was starting to unleash its scent, Noor brushed her hair, slipped into a fresh frock and sashayed to the tea stall. There she would chew the fat with Reuben and help him shut up shop. She was obviously prettifying herself in the hope that some handsome customer would be there. A dashing gallant. A square-jawed adventurer. But it never happened. She always returned alone.

Here, Simeon realised, was Ezekiel's chance. The little almond Romeo should lay a honey trap, more accurately an almond trap. 'It'll never work,' said Ezekiel.

'How do you know?' asked Simeon. 'Every evening your mystery lady, Miss N, walks down this alley. It's worth a try.'

A piece of balsa wood was carved into a love-heart. On it, in charcoal, Ezekiel wrote the letter N. It was attached to string and suspended over the alley's entrance at eye height. At the other end of the string was a small bell and a bag of Ezekiel's roasted, lightly fried, salted almonds, secured in pink cloth. This carried another message which said: 'To my one fair love N, from an admirer who is nuts about her.'

'Where will you wait?' asked Simeon.

'In the fig tree.'

'Perfect. Right, the frangipani is starting to smell. When you hear footsteps in the alley and the bell is pulled, leap out and declare yourself.'

'You're sure this is a good idea?'

'It's a no-brainer!' Simeon had heard the young use this expression. He did not fully understand what it meant but it sounded positive. He limped off to the square to tell Reuben his clever ruse.

Ezekiel had changed into a new shirt and his best sandals. The fig tree's leaves were as big as frying pans and he could not see entirely clearly what was going on in the street but the bell would tell him when to emerge. Passers-by came and went. He heard a cart and thought he detected a low voice like a pigeon's coo. Ezekiel was nervous. It was ridiculous. Whoever this N lady was, why should she accept him, the nerdiest almond vendor in Judaea? But Simeon had promised him that she was looking for love.

Tinkle!

Disentangling himself from the fig tree took longer than he had hoped. By the time he was able to present himself, the trapped prey had read the message attached to the nuts.

'Ezekiel!'

'Shoom!' What was she doing here? Poor Ezekiel was thrown into a frightful fluster. Shoom was Shoom. Shoom did not begin with the letter N.

'Did you write this?'

'Er, yes.'

'I had no idea. How did you know?'

'Know what?'

'My name.'

'Shoom?'

'Nava. The N. My real name is Nava, though hardly anyone knows it.'

'Simeon told me.'

'Simeon? But I just came to see him and he isn't there. I came to give him his gout treatment. Cousin Noor must have told him my name.'

'That'll be it,' said Ezekiel, thinking what a beautiful voice Shoom had.

'Are these truly for me, Ezekiel?'

'Happy Faunalia.'

'Ezekiel, I don't think I've been so surprised for years. Not since . . .' She was going to say: 'Not since I found my husband dead from a seizure on the floor a month after we married', but thought better of it.

'Good-oh,' said Ezekiel.

'Shall we share these nuts?'

'But they're for you.'

'It would make me happy if you joined me,' said Shoom, and her lips formed a smile, rather a pretty one at that.

At the tea stall things had not gone as Simeon expected. Reuben, hearing of the plan to match Ezekiel with Noor, laughed acidly. Simeon was about to tell him there was no need to be unpleasant when Ezekiel and Shoom appeared at the corner of the square and walked, moony-faced, to the bench by the bougainvillea where they nibbled on roasted, lightly fried, salted almonds. It was a scene repeated quite a few evenings afterwards. Ezekiel and Nava, whom everyone still called Shoom, collected one another at the end of a working day. Sometimes they walked to the pool of Bethesda to hold hands and watch the swallows. Nava means 'pretty'. Ezekiel thought her just that. The name Ezekiel speaks of the strength of God, and in her beau's quiet dependability, not to mention his rare skill at roasting, slightly frying and salting almonds, Shoom thought he had a measure of that. Two lonely hearts were made one and somewhere a little festival faun kicked its rear hooves in delight. When the lovers married it was Simeon's privilege to act as a still slightly puzzled best man. The square had a wonderful party that night. As Noor and Reuben shut up shop afterwards they reflected that love, like bread dough, sometimes needed a prod.

Law Report

SIMEON was trying to teach his apprentice Caleb Roman numerals. Barely had he drawn a line in the dirt than the wind blew it away. This amused Caleb but did not help him learn. While they were at their so-called studies a stranger wandered up, cloak billowing in the breeze.

'Are you Simeon? I am told you know everyone.'

'That's not quite true but how can I help?' said Simeon. 'Who are you after?'

'Anyone who can hire me. A site foreman, I suppose. I'm hoping for a few months' work on the temple.'

'Hiring is officially Kedar's department but Hiram pretty much runs the site. He's the stonemason.' The visitor, in his mid-twenties, had a dependable air, broad shoulders, a hint of northern accent. He carried a tool kit and Simeon could see saws and a straight-edged measuring rod. 'You're a woodworker?' The man nodded. 'Caleb will take you to Hiram. Have you found somewhere to stay?'

'The construction camp.'

'Not much clean water there. Make sure you look after those, too.' Simeon pointed to the tools. 'Things go walkabout in that grotty camp. Caleb, take our friend to the masons' yard and see if you can find Hiram.' The carpenter rooted in his tunic for a coin but Simeon told him to save his money for his family.

'No family yet – but one day, God willing.'

'God is sure to will it,' Simeon found himself saying.

Pilfering was on the rise. Thieves were given stiff sentences – crucifixion in extreme cases – but the severity made little difference. Once you could leave a bag of tools out for a week. Now they'd pinch your shadow. It was a couple of months later that Caleb reported that there had been a set-to at the construction camp. 'You remember that Galilean carpenter? He has accused a local lad of nicking his gear. The bloke's going to be charged.' A mob soon came shouting up the hill. In the middle was a quartet of officers escorting the rope-bound suspect. They were heading for the Sanhedrin building. Caleb persuaded Simeon they should follow.

In court the suspect was named as Abar Abbas and was pushed into a pen where his arms were freed and he waved at his supporters. These shouted encouragement, some chanting: 'A-Bar! A-Bar!' The magistrate called for order and hit his gavel on the table.

'The court is in session,' cried the magistrate.

'My lord,' began the carpenter, 'I accuse the youth in front of you of theft.' The plaintiff had recently discovered his chisel was missing. Another worker in the camp dormitory complained about losing a copper bracelet. A third had lost a leather pouch of coins. The carpenter concluded that the camp had a thief. So at the fruit and veg' shop he bought a bucket of green walnuts.

'Still in their outer skins?' asked the magistrate.

'Yes.'

It was declared that Onesimus should be brought to the court to corroborate this evidence. 'Fetch Onesimus!' shouted an officer of the court. 'Fetch Onesimus!' shouted a marshal of the outer precinct. 'Fetch Onesimus!' whooped wits in the public gallery. The magistrate whacked his gavel on a piece of slate. It cracked down the middle, just like a walnut shell. The public gallery jeered. Some there had been drinking. Simeon recognised some members of the Zealots. They were muttering that the carpenter was a foreigner. You could never trust a northerner.

The plaintiff explained that he removed the walnuts from their green skins and pressed the husks to extract their liquid. He applied this to his tools. 'Good for the blades?' asked the magistrate.

'My lord, it was the handles I treated. Over the next days I left my tool bag unattended at the camp and at evening reapplied the walnut juice to the handles. Nothing went missing until this morning, when I saw my table saw had gone. It is one of my prized possessions, having had a distinctive double V. A carpenter without his saw is not much use, as you may appreciate. At the site this morning I looked at my workmates' hands. When I saw the suspect, I knew who had taken my tools.'

'How?'

'The juice from green walnut husks has a distinctive quality.'

'It does?'

'It stains the hands.'

Abar Abbas looked down at his fingers. The magistrate gestured and the prisoner reluctantly lifted his hands, showing the backs of them to the court.

'Other way round, man,' said the magistrate. 'Show us your palms.'

Abar Abbas slowly did so and the crowd saw that the young man's fingertips were darkened. 'He was cleaning fireplaces for me this morning,' shouted one of his supporters. 'Anyone from round here knows that's his second job. What a farce this court is.'

'Most of them aren't from round here,' shouted another. 'With so many foreigners about, it's no wonder things are being nicked.'

The magistrate observed that if it was merely dirt from a fireplace, it would wash off. 'Fetch some water.' By now Onesimus had appeared.

'Do you sell green walnuts?' asked the magistrate.

'Not at the moment,' said Onesimus. 'I had some but they were bought by the plaintiff. Do you want me to order you some? I'll do you a good price.'

'Are you sure the plaintiff was at your shop?' snapped the magistrate.

'I never forget a customer.'

An attendant arrived with water. Abar Abbas was told to wash his hands. He rubbed hard at his fingers. It made no difference to the stains.

'I was peeling walnuts at my cousin's yesterday,' the youth claimed.

'Who did your cousin buy them from?' asked the magistrate.

'Onesimus.'

'Mr Onesimus?'

'The plaintiff bought the lot almost the moment I put them out for sale. I was the first greengrocer in Jerusalem to have any. Always am.'

'We found these!' shouted an army officer who had entered the court with new evidence. It was brought to the front. A sack of tools was upended and it included a table saw marked by a double V motif. Also in the pile of items was a copper bracelet and a small leather pouch, though it contained no coins. 'They were among the defendant's belongings.'

'That's my saw,' declared the carpenter.

'Bring it to me,' ordered the magistrate. The saw was handed to him gingerly by an attendant. He sniffed its handle. 'Smells a bit.'

'Lemony with a hint of pine wood?' asked the carpenter.

'That'll be extract of walnut husk,' said the court attendant.

'Did you handle this saw earlier?' the magistrate asked the soldier.

'Yes, your worship. I examined it when we found it.'

'Show me your hands.' The soldier did. His fingertips were starting to discolour.

Abar Abbas was found guilty and turmoil ensued. Caleb was nearly knocked over as Zealots surged towards the front of the court. Someone threw a stone. 'Silence!' said the magistrate. He was ignored. Chanting of the thief's name recommenced. 'SILENCE!'

The magistrate rose. 'Look, no one wants to see a lad's life ruined. How old are you, boy?' Abar Abbas said he was fourteen, though he looked older. 'Which of us in all honesty,' continued the magistrate, 'could claim never to have misbehaved at fourteen, or sixteen? When a court reaches a verdict, that verdict must stand. At sentencing, however, allowances can be made.

'It is a tradition of Jerusalem courts, sometimes overlooked, that the victim of a crime can request clemency for the guilty defendant.'

All eyes turned to the carpenter. 'Well?' shouted a voice. 'What's it going to be, mate?' The magistrate signalled for the plaintiff to approach his seat. They had a conversation. The carpenter gave a fed-up throw of his head, picked up his retrieved saw and returned to his place.

'In light of the recovery of the stolen goods, with the permission of the plaintiff,' said the magistrate, 'the court sentences Abar Abbas to ten lashes and a fine of three weeks' salary. But he will not go to prison.' The thief gestured thanks to the magistrate. 'And before leaving this court the guilty man shall kiss the hem of the plaintiff's coat.' Abar Abbas's friends laughed as the youth went to do as bidden. The carpenter tersely indicated that it was not necessary. He gathered his robes and left the court.

Simeon and Caleb heard later that he had gone home to Nazareth. His name was Youssef.

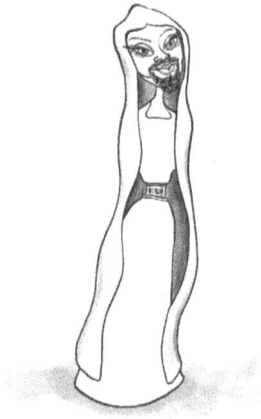

Social Glue

TABITHA lived next door. From his room Simeon could hear her practise on harp, lyre and viol. He wished she'd play more viol. It carried better across the courtyard.

One weary evening he was struggling at the entrance to the alley with his stick and two bags of vegetables when a young Roman officer said: 'Let me help you with those, sir.'

'Thank you.' It was rare for a Roman to be so polite. 'They are a little heavy.'

'More awkward than heavy, really.' The soldier was in the soft tunic, leather sandals and red cloak that officers wore off-duty. He had a handsome head of black hair. 'Where are we going? Down this alley?'

'Through this door on the left and then if you could put them on the kitchen table, that would be most helpful.'

'Easily done,' said the Roman. 'My name is Capillus. I'm fairly new to Jerusalem.'

'Simeon. I have been here as long as a tortoise. Thank you, Capillus. We are glad to have you here.'

'That's something not often said to a Roman.'

'No, well, that's the way of the world.'

'I'm looking for the house of Tabitha the musician.'

'Tabitha and her parents live just across the alley.'

'I've come to see her about lessons.'

'You teach Latin?'

'No, no. Music lessons. I sing. Or did back home. I've fallen out of practice. Someone gave me Tabitha's name. Do you sing?'

'I did once. A long time ago. This is her door.'

Simeon unpacked the shopping and pottered upstairs. He soon dozed, he was not sure how long, and woke to a decent baritone doing arpeggios. A viol played an introduction and the baritone launched into a song about a lovesick bumblebee. It was one Simeon dimly recalled. His grey head danced on its ball-bearings and his lips moved to the lines he remembered.

Around that time it was announced the king was expecting a VIP from 'back home'. This was how some Sadducees referred to Rome. If planning a trip to Italy they would say: 'We're thinking of making a trip home next summer,' even if they were Judaeans born and bred. Several generals and senators had come to Jerusalem recently. A welcome ceremony was to be held at the palace and the old temple choir, under the baton of the celebrated Levi, would provide musical magnificence. This was encouraging, for there had been doubts about the future of the choir, accountants complaining that it cost too much and plenty of senior courtiers taking the same view. It is the fate of choirs ever to provoke such envy and to endure such attacks.

The palace chamberlain assured Levi of the VIP's importance. It was 'essential' that the concert go well. 'We'll give it a bash,' said the choirmaster. If Maestro Levi had a fault it was that he could be *calmando* when officialdom expected *vivace*. The palace chamberlain took the view that if the choir was a flop, Levi would deserve everything that came his way. Preparations began. The all-male temple choir polished some psalms and canticles and worked up a few secular Roman songs – one was about rustic lovers crushing grapes by foot – to make the VIP feel at home. With less than a week to go the tenors were struggling for the high notes and the basses sounded muddy. Kedar looked in on one rehearsal. The high priest discerned that things were going badly. Levi protested that all would be well but Kedar was unconvinced. Kedar, like many ecclesiastical managers, had no understanding of choirs. A more musically minded soul could have assured him that rehearsals always went badly, did they not? Yet Levi's normally calm brow was furrowed. Maybe something truly was awry.

The following morning a furtive figure, in bustle and size not entirely unlike Choirmaster Levi, appeared at Onesimus's stall and asked in a disguised voice: 'Got any lemons?'

'Pips or peels, we sell it. How many do you want? One? Two?'

'Two hundred.'

'Two hundred?'

'Pips or peels, you sell 'em, right?'

'I may need to ask around, Mr Levi.'

'Don't ask too much. And how did you recognise me? I need this kept quiet.'

Levi's choir had gone down with the lurgy. If the authorities heard of it, they would use it to their own anti-musical ends. Levi's next call was to Bildad the bee-keeper, from whom he bought three bell-jars of honey. 'That's cleaned me out,' said Bildad.

'Well, you'll just have to plant some more, or whatever it is one does with honey.'

The remedy, as prescribed by the temple physician, who as a doctor was bound to discretion, was hot lemon and honey. Great pots of it were brewed and administered. No matter how much of the concoction the choir members drank, it seemed to make little difference. Levi's sangfroid evaporated. 'The basses are even more useless than normal and the tenors are pinking like pheasants.'

Bildad, by way of conversation, told Levi: 'I sing to my bees.' But the maestro was too consumed by worries to listen, or so it seemed.

With each day that passed, the palace checked that everything was in order, Kedar fretted and the high priest himself, taking Levi to one side to express his growing anxiety, said he was dumbstruck. 'If only my tenors were,' said Levi. It was becoming obvious that some of the singers were not likely to recover in time. In desperation the choirmaster summoned Bildad.

'You said you can sing,' said Levi.

'I didn't think you noticed.'

'Are you any good?'

'The bees don't complain.'

'Try this.' Levi plucked five notes on a lyre. Bildad repeated them in a fruity tenor. 'Not bad,' said Levi. 'Got any mates?'

'Don't tell him I told you,' said Bildad, 'but Lysander was once a choral scholar. He gave up because he thought no one was listening. Lysander lacks self-esteem.'

'Many in my choir have the opposite problem,' said Levi.

'There is one other person I could try,' said Bildad. Like some of the older people of Deuteronomy Square, he knew Simeon had once sung. He went to Simeon and explained that Levi was in a bind.

'It's too soon, Bildad,' said Simeon.

'This is an emergency. It's all hands to the pump.'

'I am sorry. But it still hurts.' All these years on, it did.

Bildad did not push the matter. Bee-keepers are good like that. A world run by bee-keepers would be a soothing place. Yet he did extract a couple of extra names from Simeon, and Levi was grateful. 'I'll certainly arrange those fake beards,' the choirmaster told Bildad.

The VIP from Rome arrived and the welcome ceremony was imminent. Levi's choir and selected guests shuffled nervously into the royal courtyard on a day of broiling heat. The king and his queen entered to a fanfare from the state trumpeters and the national anthems were played before the dignitaries were shown to curule chairs on a dais. The VIP was a plump thumb-twiddler from Rome's foreign affairs committee. As the choir launched into its psalms and canticles he did not seem terribly interested and stifled a yawn. The choir sang reasonably well, despite the basses having been placed in direct sunshine. Bildad propped up the tenors and Lysander was a revelation as the solo countertenor. In the basses the Roman army officer Capillus did sterling work, his performance only slightly impaired by the false beard he was obliged to wear to fit in with the Judaean men. From ten yards you would not have known but up close it was obviously black wool stuck on to a base of birch bark tar.

It seemed possible Maestro Levi might get away with it. But then came an unexpected problem. '*Psst*, your beard is coming off,' Tesserarius Capillus was told by a fellow bass. The sun had dried the birch bark tar and it had lost its stickiness. Part of Capillus's disguise was dangling off his chin. He looked like a half-sheared sheep.

'O all ye beasts and cattle, praise ye the Lord,' sang Capillus *con gusto*, 'praise him and MAGNIFY him for ever!' You had to give that 'magnify' a good push. In the effort another clump of fleece left its moorings. Choirmaster Levi did not notice, being so deeply immersed in his art that his eyes were closed. Capillus sought to repair his difficulties by pushing the wool back into place. He half-succeeded before Levi reopened his eyes. Capillus thought he had got away with it, and as far as Levi went, he had. But one does not become a member of Rome's foreign affairs committee without having a capacity for observation and Capillus's difficulties were spotted by the VIP. Whereas earlier the visitor had been bored, now he started enjoying himself. He clapped heartily as the Benedicite ended. The shorter piece about the vineyard rustics followed. While perfectly tuneful, it possibly did not merit the loud approval given by the VIP who had watched with delight as Capillus, first with one hand then two, fought with increasing desperation to pat the beard back on to his face. At one point he had to crouch down to retrieve a handful of wool that had dropped, all while continuing to deliver the bass line. The VIP was delighted and when it ended he stood and shouted: 'Bravo! Bravo!'

145

Not wishing to make him feel left out, the king and queen did likewise.

'Tremendous stuff!' enthused the Roman as the dignitaries were withdrawing to the royal apartments. 'Much better than the Circus Maximus. I'll have to tell Octavian.'

A grateful chamberlain waddled over to pump Levi's hand and offer congratulations. Capillus was merely glad to rip away the last of the dreadful black wool. Our second fake-beard wearer waited until getting back to Deuteronomy Square. Ezekiel stood guard while some choir robes and, yes, false whiskers were handed back out to him from the makeshift changing room at the back of his almond stall. 'What a relief,' said a familiar voice.

A few women can sing tenor and Shoom, the husky-voiced garlic seller, was one of them. Ezekiel removed a last strand of wool before giving her cheek a soft peck. 'Well sung, Nava,' he whispered. The two of them hopped from foot to foot in shy affection, like young rustics pressing grapes with their toes.

The Battle of Mersu

DEBORAH arrived at the tea stall with two sacks of dates. She dropped them with a thud at the table under the bougainvillea and disappeared shouting: 'Don't let anyone touch those – they're for the mersu.' Soon she reappeared with two more sacks, this time pistachio nuts. Another thud. 'A woman's work is never done.'

'Want a hand?' asked Simeon. He was playing solitaire and did not really want to leave his table. Off trudged Deborah. 'Don't know about you,' Simeon told Reuben, 'but I can smell burned martyr.'

'Makes a change from charred lamb. I wish she'd chosen another table. Jonah and his lads are expected. They always sit there.'

Jerusalem was overcast and scratchy. Cart drivers squabbled at junctions. Provincials moaned about prices. The humidity even got to Zillah, who threw a priceless vase at Tambal. He caught it and then tripped over his sandals, smashing the thing. She was furious.

It was nearly Volturnalia, the Roman festival celebrating a god of water. This tended to be celebrated with large amounts of wine. Water barely came into it. Mersu balls were another Volturnalia custom. Noor and friends used Reuben's kitchen equipment to prepare the sticky cakes. They would be sold for charity. The money went to the temple building fund. Didn't everything?

Mersu could be dry but Noor's recipe was irresistibly gooey. Sure enough, here came Bildad with honey. Noor and her girlfriends had already started grinding the pistachios and laying them out on floured trays, singing as they worked. Jonah's lads arrived. They hovered, twisting their curls. Women made them shy at the best of times. There was muttering and whisker-tugging before Jonah asked Reuben how long the women intended to occupy 'our table'.

'They've only just begun. Will another table not do?'

'We like that one.'

'So do they, by the look of it.' Laughter was rising from the bougainvillea where Noor was holding a pestle and drew attention to its shape. She started singing a round about a hen chasing a cockerel through a farmyard. The more her friends clapped, the more Noor threw her hips into the song, her nose and hair dusted by flour. Simeon had not guessed what a spirited mover Noor could be. Reuben was rapt.

'But it's our table,' persisted Jonah.

'It's actually my table,' said Reuben. 'You lot may be creatures of habit but this tea stall has a first-come-first-served policy.'

Jonah stamped his foot. 'Please! Judas is coming. We have important matters to discuss.' Judas the Zealot was a bigshot with a jutting beard. For months he had been luring Jonah's Pharisees to his cause, and vice versa. Negotiations were at a sensitive stage.

'And mersu is not important? Tell that to the square.'

The mersu makers were starting to be noticed. Children ran up, begging licks of honey. Passers-by fanned their faces under Ezekiel's almond tree. The humidity was worsening. Benjamin clattered past with a load of guavas and shouted: 'Faster! Faster!' at the pistachio grinders. Even Javelin looked hot. Tambal marched up and imposed what he said was a 'mersu tax'. He was rewarded with a dollop of half-ready mersu amid rude comments about Judaea's tax rates. The louder the noise, the grumpier Jonah and his confederates became. Someone started playing a penny whistle. Another struck a rhythm on spoons. Noor and Deborah started an ad-hoc dance of the seven veils. Both women pushed up their hair to keep cool. Reuben found himself hypnotised by the lines of Noor's neck.

Amid all this, Jonah failed to notice the arrival of Judas and four stooges. The hairy Zealots scowled that their entry had gone unacknowledged. Judas's beard dropped at an angle, a bull preparing to charge. From his blackening brow and delving bristles, Judas was in no mood for a party. Are Zealots ever? Two women disporting themselves under a bougainvillea! It confirmed Judas's view that Volturnalia was decadent. Come independence, Volturnalia would be banned. He didn't much care for that big Nubian goofing around with his mouth full of dough, either. There were a few too many black faces in Jerusalem so far as Judas the Zealot was concerned. Independence would sort that out, too.

Judas's aide-de-camp tapped Jonah on the back to alert him to his boss's arrival. Jonah swung round with a careless elbow and accidentally hit the man, just as the first rumble of thunder was heard. Jonah was starting to apologise when Noor threw her scarf into the crowd and in the melee another of Judas's men went tumbling. Shouts of 'Steady on!' were followed by: 'There's no need for that.' Bystanders yelled that everyone should calm down. That only further quickened tempers. Two chaps tried to separate the jostlers but one of the would-be doves stepped on Judas's foot. 'You clumsy oaf,' said Judas.

'Don't look at me in that tone of voice!' responded the peacenik.

Fisticuffs erupted. Simeon watched from his draughts table. A Pharisee might hold that the outcome of the conflict was written in the stars. A Greek would place greater premium on tactics and training. It soon became evident Simeon's game of solitaire might not be completed. Tea was being spilled, cups went flying, the women sang louder and the mersu production line accelerated. Now came a sharper retort of thunder and a wind arose. In the melee Jonah lost his skullcap and responded by pushing Judas in the chest. This had a knock-on effect and a rolling maul surged towards Simeon's table and upended his draughts board just as he was about to complete the game. He still had the final piece in his hand but the table collapsed. That did it. Simeon's inner debate about Pharisee and Greek was discarded. Out came his inner Ahab. When a man is robbed of his solitaire game – the first for months in which he was set to go out – a line is crossed. With a bark of 'Right!', Simeon pushed through the battlefield to where Judas the Zealot was wrestling with some previously placid tourist from Antioch. Simeon tapped Judas on the back. When the Zealot turned round, Simeon with one hand grabbed his black beard and said: 'This thing does have a use, after all.' With the other hand, more technically fist, he delivered a resounding blow to Judas's hooter. It carried such force that Judas and his beard, minus some strands which remained in Simeon's hand, flew several feet backwards until he hit the bougainvillea table, spilling piles of dates and pistachios. A not quite empty jar of honey landed on his head. At which point the rain started in pelting sheets. The conflict ended as fast as it had started, just as Centurion Lucilius turned up with a squad of soldiers and, at their rear, Kedar.

'Nobody is to leave until I give permission!' cried the centurion. With the thunder overhead and the commotion of the downpour he was largely inaudible. Most people raced for shelter – most, that is, except Judas the Zealot, who was sitting under the bougainvillea table with his head in a honeypot, from whence there came an echoey: 'Why has it gone dark?'

The thunderstorm lasted only five minutes but it left a scene of devastation: benches and tables awry, pots smashed, the mersu mixture wrecked by rainwater. Centurion Lucilius swished his vine staff in the air, frustrated not to have been able to crack it over a Judaean head, and returned to the Antonia to write a report. Kedar also left, shaking his head. A dazed Judas the Zealot was released from his honeypot and taken away for questioning. The authorities had been after him for some time.

As the sun came out and the gutters stopped gurgling, Tabitha appeared at the bottom of Deuteronomy Street, dry in a summer frock. The birds serenaded her as she drifted across the square with a young man on her arm, blissfully unaware of all the trouble. As the beauty and her consort passed one of Lucilius's guards, the soldier snapped to attention and said: 'G'afternoon, sah!'

'At ease, Calvus,' said Tesserarius Capillus.

Turning a Blind Eye

THOUGH work on the temple complex continued, the holy of holies needed to be blessed. It was going to be quite an occasion and the king, eager that the high priest should not steal all the attention, said he would pay for a big band. The palace booked the city's finest musicians to provide a medley of sacred and secular tunes. There were to be shofars, cymbals, drums, trumpets, tambourines, lyres, sistrums, pipes, zithers, bells and a large harp. The harpist, naturally, was to be Tabitha. Deuteronomy Square was proud.

Two spanners were thrown into the works. First, the Sanhedrin met to consider public disorder charges flowing from the mersu riot. Several protagonists, including Simeon, Jonah, Deborah and Judas the Zealot, faced charges. The director of public prosecutions, a stuffed shirt with a nasal voice and no sense of humour, was seeking stiff fines. The Zealot faced a prison sentence.

The trial, overseen by Sadoc, opened with an account of the brawl. What did the defendants have to say for themselves? The answer was 'not much'. Simeon, apologising for being slow to stand in court owing to his gout, said his memory was foggy these days. Jonah claimed that the Pharisees had assembled that day merely to encourage the good ladies' charity-mersu drive. Noor gave a comely shrug and said it had been a 'hot 'n' bothered sort of day' and the thunderstorm made it hard to hear the lovely centurion's commands. Judas said blackly that he did not recognise the illegal occupancy of the Roman militia. 'Order!' cried Sadoc.

The prosecution relied on the testimony of Lucilius. It was weakened by the fact that the centurion and his riot squad had arrived only as the brawl was ending. No one else was found to give evidence. The prosecution had hoped to call Kedar but at the last minute he sent an apology, being stricken by wisdom-tooth trouble. Everyone else from Deuteronomy Square that afternoon had either been looking in the other direction or had been too busy clapping along to the pistachio grinders to notice the altercation.

'Lying hooligans!' barked Centurion Lucilius. Sadoc was inclined to agree but his room for judicial manoeuvre was limited. Judas was sentenced to a month in prison for his impertinence to the court but there was insufficient proof of individual culpability. A blanket verdict of community affray would have to suffice for the rest.

And the sentence? 'This court rules that residents of the Deuteronomy district will not be admitted to the blessing of the holy of holies. We don't want a repeat of this ill-discipline.'

Sadoc's sentence caused serious dismay. The mood at the tea stall was forlorn. Then Ephraim brought word of the second spanner in the works: Tabitha had been replaced as harpist.

'She wasn't even in the square when the fight happened,' complained Reuben.

'The alleged fight,' said Simeon.

'This is wickedly unfair,' said Ezekiel.

'The Sadducees have pushed it too far this time,' said Jonah.

'It's not connected to the fight,' said Ephraim.

'The alleged fight,' said Simeon.

'It's because she's blind,' said Ephraim. 'The priests won't have a blind musician playing at such a holy event. They call her blindness ungodly.'

Disbelief was followed by disgust, followed by uproar. Tabitha might be blind but she was the best harpist in Jerusalem and she was their friend. Noor arrived to report that Tabitha was at home, weeping. An immediate public meeting was declared. Speaker after speaker stood on Reuben's bar-top to denounce the Sadducees and priests. Jonah, who normally put much store by religious cleanliness, averred that the priests should spend less time with Greeks and Romans and more time with working Judaeans. This won firm applause. The crowd voted to march to the Sanhedrin and a throng was soon outside the Hall of Hewn Stones with tunic sleeves rolled. The people of Deuteronomy Square vowed to boycott the blessing in protest at the mistreatment of Tabitha. Sadoc appeared on the balcony and was greeted by a blizzard of chucked radishes and tomatoes, provided by Onesimus at a very reasonable price.

'You can't boycott the ceremony,' said Sadoc. 'You've been disinvited from it already.'

Various members of the crowd shouted that had they been invited to the ceremony they would not have gone. Sadoc told them that was unpatriotic. It was their duty to attend great civic occasions. 'We've been banned!' cried the crowd.

'Well, now you're unbanned,' snapped Sadoc.

'You can't unban us without a retrial,' shouted a crowd member in what was proving to be a quick game of tennis. Sadoc was enough of a lawyer to see they had a point. The crowd started celebrating a great victory. The Sanhedrin had been bested! But had it? For Tabitha was still weeping at home. Her dream of playing at the blessing – an event they themselves had so looked forward to – remained in tatters. After a certain amount of chin-stroking Simeon and Jonah were admitted inside the Sanhedrin for a parley with Sadoc. This lasted so long that they had to send out for refreshments: ale and filled pittas. Reuben explained that these things could never be rushed. Zillah sent Tambal with a tray of halva to sustain the protestors. Zillah said she would have joined them but she was having her waxing treatment. That did not stop her cheering: 'Power to the populus!' from the beauty-parlour couch.

A deal was reached. The ban on Deuteronomy district residents attending the blessing could not legally be altered but the authorities could forget to enforce it, provided the people of Deuteronomy Square behaved. That was naturally provisional on Tabitha being reinstated as the event's harpist. Sadoc's people found that the high priest would be so dazzled by the beauty of the new temple that

Tabitha would not be the only unsighted person in the city. A blind eye would be turned to her blindness.

On Judas the Zealot, mind you, the authorities would not budge. He would remain in prison. Simeon was unfussed and Jonah also found he could live with that.

A Buzz at the Temple

NO matter how much he licked them, Bildad's fingers were always sticky. Such is life for a bee-keeper. Bildad's white jacket was stained and tacky and his hair was often matted by blobs of honey. He was haloed by bees drawn to these splodges. Or did they follow him out of love?

Bildad did not mind. Bees talked less than humans. Bildad's stickiness earned him the suspicion of Reuben, whose one obsession was keeping his draughts pieces clean. Bildad was forbidden from playing at the tea stall. No offence was taken and he retired to a corner table to sip mint tea, chew on a knish and wave at the occasional child. They were more tolerable than adults.

Bildad's hives stood at the bottom of a lemon orchard in the Tyropoeon valley, where the bees could be left to their own devices. Bildad regarded them not as his possessions. To him it was the other way round. He was their servant. Bildad could come and go almost undetected. Lightness of foot helped in his line of work, for bees dislike clumsiness.

Sometimes Reuben would find Bildad at the counter. 'Begob, Brother Bildad, you did give me a fright. I never heard you.' And Bildad would beam; but not this day. Instead of his usual mint tea he asked for a goblet of Gaulanitis wine. Now another. Wildness darted in his eyes.

'Everything okay?' asked Simeon.

'No,' said Bildad, and took a tug of wine. After a few more gulps, Bildad blurted it out. 'Hornets.'

Hornet scouts had arrived at dawn. Bildad knew at once it was trouble. Soon the scouts returned with warrior comrades and started to kill sentry bees. Hornets have big jaws and no sense of mercy. Bees curled in death, the ground soon thick with bodies. Bildad ran for his aprons and net-hat and squashed a few attackers. A few hornets can wreck one hive in a day. Even Rome was not that deadly.

'My beauties are fighting hard,' said Bildad. 'They surrounded one hornet and balled on it, stinging and suffocating. After that the bastards retreated to a tree to re-form. They're still there. I know they'll be back. So do the bees.'

The next two days were terrible. The hornets returned. One hive was exterminated. Then another. On the third day Bildad appeared at the tea stall without his white bee-keeping outfit. He buried his head in his arms.

'What news from Actium?' asked Reuben.

'Disaster,' said Bildad. 'The bees have absconded.'

'The whole lot?'

'Gone,' said Bildad. 'Not one set of wings is left. The silence is terrible.'

'Where have they gone?'

'Up the mountain, off to a wood, to Egypt, who can say?'

Days passed. Yom Kippur was approaching and Reuben felt wretched. For years he had banned Bildad from playing draughts for having sticky hands. Now his hands were as clean as anyone else's. Simeon sat with Bildad and listened to his laments. Words flew out of him. He described his bees like a bereft lover, twisting a rag in his fingers. Benjamin invited Bildad to pet Javelin. He managed a few strokes but then had to turn away, blinking back tears. Jonah promised to say prayers for those in grief, and gently reminded Bildad that bees always climb upwards, so were bound to be heading to heaven. Bildad's sorrow was infectious. Consumption of honey fell, not because it was impossible to buy – there were other bee-keepers – but because it made people think of Bildad's lost sheep. Well, not lost sheep. Lost bees. You know what I mean.

Then, news. Habib the street-sweeper was resting over a brew at the tea stall. No one else was around except Simeon. Reuben had gone to help Noor prepare challah loaves for Yom Kippur.

'You know what?' said Habib.

'I know not what,' said Simeon. 'What know you?'

'Those bees.'

'Bildad's bees? There's nothing to be done.'

'There might be. I reckon I've heard them.'

'You've found them?' said Simeon.

'It may not be easy grabbing them.'

Habib disclosed the tale ploddingly. Yom Kippur was the one day in the year that the high priest entered the holy of holies. No one else ever stepped foot there. That, at least, was the ideal. But a holy of holies has to be cleaned. In a year a room gathers dust. When the high priest enters you don't want him smothered by cobwebs. The dust might set off his allergy. Someone had to clean the place. But no one was meant to enter it. Problem. 'Unless,' as Habib put it, 'you find a Gentile such as me, who doesn't really count as a soul.'

'You've been inside the holy of holies?'

'Can you keep a secret?' asked Habib.

'I promise,' said Simeon.

Habib studied his tea. 'It was a sideline I had in the days of the last temple. A week ago the high priest's office told me to resume the arrangement with the new building. I have the temple-gate password so I can get past the sentries at dusk and start giving the holy of holies a going-over. I have a special duster for the ceiling. Made it myself with a giant banyan branch. Not that I used it yesterday. The moment I entered, I heard them.'

'Who?'

'The bees. Making a racket. I'm surprised the priests haven't heard it from outside but I suppose they're always being deafened by trumpets and cantors and animals having their throats cut. In that room, you can't miss the noise. Not that I could see them. It was dark, and I'm not overly fond of bees. I didn't want to disturb them in case they attacked me. But Bildad's bees are safe.'

'Praise the Lord.'

'Never mind your Lord,' said Habib. 'The question is, how are we going to get them out?'

'We?' asked Simeon. Habib looked up from his tea leaves and gave an emphatic nod.

'Can't do it on my own, can I? I don't speak bee.'

* * *

'Found?' asked an incredulous Bildad.

'Found, indeed . . .' said Simeon. He could not finish the sentence because Bildad embraced him. It was some time before Simeon could add: '. . . but not yet recovered.'

'Take me to them. Now, please.'

'There's a small problem,' said Simeon. 'Can you keep a secret?'

'I promise,' said Bildad. It was true, for he could. Unlike some.

The strategic priority was to locate Ephraim. Simeon spotted the gossip on a bench in the square. Whatever work he did – something in the civil service – was light enough to allow him to work from home.

Simeon limped over and sat on the bench with a sigh.

'Simeon, dear heart, you sound tired.'

'Just getting old.'

'Aren't we all?' said Ephraim. 'Aches and pains.'

'My own fault I didn't sleep well,' continued Simeon. 'I shouldn't have closed the window. Normally I prefer some air at night.'

'An Athenian doctor friend says fresh air is good for the brain.'

'I didn't want to risk it last night, though. Not until this troubling business is out of the way. Ooof.' And with that Simeon blew his nose at ponderous length, leaned back on the bench with legs extended, and closed his eyes.

The fly was cast. 'This troubling business . . .' Ephraim did not move. For ten minutes he remained on the bench while Simeon's chest rose and fell with a suggestion of sleep. Actually, it was more than a suggestion, for Simeon did indeed drop off for a while. Until some carter dropped a plank of wood.

'Feel better for that?' asked Ephraim.

'Humph,' said Simeon.

'You were well away.'

'Catching up.'

'Why couldn't you sleep last night?'

'It's all this talk of the presence,' said Simeon, returning to his task.

'The presence?'

'I'm not sure I believe it but some people are convinced. Not rational types like you but the more impressionable sort.'

'Try me,' said Ephraim softly.

'You really haven't heard? Well, apparently there's talk of a presence up at the temple. A visitation. I did think I heard something last night.'

'A visitation?'

'A throbbing sound, like the fluttering of wings. Distant. In the margins.'

'At the temple?'

'Thereabouts. The temple guards are talking about it, and you know how world-weary they are. One sharply told me not to talk about it. It was almost as if he was afraid.'

'Interesting,' said Ephraim.

'No doubt a load of hocus-pocus,' said Simeon lightly, 'but it might explain why some of them have been a bit jumpy.'

Onesimus's wife, Deborah, came past carrying a new besom and announced she was off to give her home a good sweep, what with all the dust. 'Never seen dust like it!' she hooted. 'Anyone would think the angels have been having a knees-up in the rafters. If angels have knees, that is. Cheerio!'

Ephraim waited until Deborah was out of earshot. 'Nice enough woman but those varicose veins will give her trouble.' He returned to their previous conversation. 'Wings fluttering, you said.'

'Wings, yes. That's what it sounded like to me.'

'Angels have wings, even if they don't have knees.'

'It seemed a few blocks away, a lowish, regular noise. Might just have been the wind. God moves in a mysterious way. I'd best be off, Ephraim. Work calls. Mum's the word.'

'Shalom, Simeon. Mum is indeed the word, as always.'

Within eight hours word had spread from the morning market to the souvenir shops, from lower-town hovels to upper-town turrets. It was known outside the Sanhedrin and in Zillah's fountained cloisters. At the Antonia fortress it was reported to the duty officer as local intelligence, probably nonsense but worth entering in the ledger all the same. Reuben was stacking benches at the tea stall and cocked an ear, half-wondering if he could detect any hint of wings. Og and Phut, at their modest lodgings, were chewing on supper – a mound of couscous flavoured by raisins and chives – when Og said 'Shushhh!' and strained his hearing. Phut, who had never been shushed in his life, ceased his bovine chewing, grains of couscous dropping silently from his empty upper gums. At the washing pool Cephas the temple stockman tied a double knot in the cow-gate fastening to ensure his animals would not break free if spooked by any presence. Philippos, sitting in his cool apartment with its mountain view beyond the city ramparts, made a diary entry about mumbo jumbo sweeping through the Jews. And in the temple guardroom the sentries assembling for their shift sat in thoughtful silence. Any idea they had previously been jumpy was, I blush to say, sheer invention by Simeon, just as Deborah's intervention was a plant. But the temple guards now knew the rumour of the celestial presence and it nibbled at them.

Habib wheeled his barrow to the temple at dusk. He chose a shadowed entrance on the eastern side. The password worked and Habib proceeded through the narrow doorway with his barrow and long banyan pole. The guard had to step aside to let him through. Habib clumsily dropped some of his clobber and amid the distraction the sentry did not notice the soft-soled second figure flit past him.

At that twilight hour Jerusalem succumbs to a smoky stupor, supper fires throwing a companionable pall over the city. Habib ambled across the open ground between the cloisters and the sacrifice court, his barrow making its customary squeak. It would have been a keen-sighted sentry who spotted anything amiss. Bildad was crouching under the long, bushy banyan branch, almost entirely hidden from overhead view. They reached the steps to the sacrifice court and Habib stopped. He would leave his barrow here. 'Put on your overalls in that niche,' he whispered. Bildad withdrew a ball of clothing from under a skep in the barrow. He nipped into the recess to don his white bee-keeping outfit.

Sentries conducted regular circuits inside the site. Habib gestured when it was safe for Bildad to emerge. They were about to head inside the sanctuary when Bildad remembered the straw skep in the barrow. As he was lifting it, the skep dislodged a broom which started to slide down the side of the wheelbarrow, making a grating sound. Habib caught it before it clattered on to the steps. Inside his bee-keeping jacket, Bildad felt sweat drop from his brow. The slightest noise would echo round the high-walled court. To both sides stood the great hooks and pulleys of the sacrifice tables. Ahead loomed the holy of holies. Its door opened with surprising ease. It was probably only nerves that made Habib forget to close it.

'Bzzzzzzzzzzzzzzzzz.' Inside, the hum was at once audible. Bildad fell to his knees. Overcome to be in the holy of holies? Praying for deliverance? Habib prepared his banyan branch. With a couple of adjustments it was long enough to reach the ceiling, though he dreaded to think how the bees would respond when he tried to dislodge them. He raised his gaze to where he expected them to be. That was odd. Not there. Maybe another corner. But no. Not there either. He rubbed his eyes. The bees were not to be seen yet still they were audible. Did swarms not always lodge high in trees or on buildings? The air was almost vibrating with their noise. Then he noticed Bildad gesturing. A digging signal. Habib padded over. 'They're in the Well!'

So it was that the Gentile Habib and the Jew Bildad entered the very bowels of godliness, that crevice of Creation known as the Well of Souls. A meagre passage led them under the temple's floor and they found themselves in a small cave in which the bees had settled. Upstairs, meanwhile, the open door of the holy of holies was spotted by an attentive sentry. He poked a head round the doorway to check for signs of any intruders. Instead he just heard a tremendous buzzing – and it was coming from the infamous Well of Souls. The sentry, fearing that molten spirits were about to erupt from below, turned and fled. It was said he was never quite the same man afterwards.

Bildad laid a sheet while Habib, using a telescoped version of his banyan branch, knocked it against the swarm. Down plopped the bees like a bunch of mistletoe.

'Now what?' hissed Habib.

'Now we wait,' replied Bildad.

'Wait?'

'It shouldn't be more than a few hours.' Bildad moved the sheet near the skep which he arranged so that the bees could climb inside. As Jonah had said, the noble bee has an instinct to rise to the top. Bees are admirable toilers, communitarian yet aspirational, cooperational yet hierarchical, always looking to climb. They are entomology's reproof to communism.

'Hours? It'll be the middle of the night before we get out of here.'

'I have to let the bees settle in the skep.'

'But my barrow is out there. I'm normally gone inside the hour.'

'I know the way out. Just tell me the password.'

'It's potty.'

'Potty is the password?'

'No! Leaving you in the temple is potty.'

A compromise was agreed. Habib left Bildad in the Well of Souls and moved his barrow back across the courtyard, parking it in the shadowy colonnades. Bildad waited for his bees to climb into the skep. During those hours he talked to his little friends and they to him. He helped some climb inside the basket and they thanked him by shaking their wings and signalling to other strays. Inside the skep they regrouped around their monarch and past upheavals were forgiven. Bildad soothed them and he himself was soothed by the restoration of order. It was going to be all right.

When the last stray had been collected, Bildad covered the bottom of the skep with netting and reverently took his leave of the Well of Souls. He was still in his waist-length bee-keeper's garb with its strangely shaped hat, broad shoulders and big gauntlets. A yellow moon was now high in the sky and the white bee-keeping outfit acquired a luminous quality. He held up the skep in front of him.

Another sentry, peering in disbelief, was inclined to brandish his spear until he noticed in the strange light that the white form appeared to have no legs. It held an upper limb at a strange angle, as if pointing east. The sentry was a God-fearing man. His orders were only to prevent human trespassers, not the supernatural. Who was he to intervene, especially amid such a crescendo of angels' wings? He became the temple's second runner of the night, dropping his spear and legging it for safety. Bildad was concentrating so hard on keeping the skep steady that he barely noticed a thing. Habib picked up the handles to his barrow and hastened after the bee-keeper as much as he was able amid his laughter.

To this day neither man has uttered a word about having stepped inside the Well of Souls. Members of the temple sentry community, for their part, when the moon is yellow and the owls hoot, speak quietly of 'the night of the honey moon', but only among themselves.

An Unhinged Demand

FROM the palace came word that the king was unwell. A headache had made him sensitive to loud noises. Palace sentries were ordered to change guard without their traditional shouts and foot-stamping. The state trumpeters were sent on leave until His Greatness was feeling perkier.

Kedar was summoned to the palace. Boaz was about to announce his arrival outside the chamberlain's hall and had already filled his lungs when a footman tapped the herald's shoulder with a reminder that shouting was currently not preferred. Boaz and Kedar ambled into the hall where the chamberlain was deep in administrative duties. 'Pssst!' went Boaz. 'Pssssssst!' The chamberlain heard the second attempt.

'His Greatness demands that the temple gate's hinges be muted,' whispered the chamberlain.

'What?' said Kedar.

The chamberlain wearily rose to his feet, tiptoed to the other side of the desk and softly repeated the sentence in Kedar's left ear.

'No, I heard you first time,' said Kedar. 'But how can we possibly meet this command? The gate has to be opened and shut every day.'

'Some people say the hinges' squeaking can be heard in Antioch.'

'They're certainly not quiet.'

'His Greatness considers the noise to be torture.'

'He'd know more about that than me.'

'Are you being disloyal?'

'What can I do about the noise made by the temple gate? It's a fact of life.'

'You are the captain of the guard?'

'I am.'

'Well, that's a fact of life too, chum. Do something about it or His Greatness may have a sense of humour failure and then it won't only be the hinges that squeak.'

It was a disconsolate Kedar that traipsed back to the temple. He was in no mood for gaiety when Ephraim fell into step alongside him on Deuteronomy Street.

'Interview at the palace go badly?' asked the gossip.

'How do you know I've been at the palace?'

'Walls have ears.'

'Bugger off,' said Kedar.

As Kedar crossed Temple Square he saw Simeon talking to a group of visitors seated in a semicircle on the ground while Caleb offered them peanuts and dates. This was part of a new 'tastes-of-Jerusalem' promotion the boy had devised to 'improve the visitor experience' and make a small profit from sponsors. Provincials liked having Jerusalem food outlets recommended to them. It irked Kedar that Simeon was so independent but there was little he could do about that. He could, however, do something about traders who pushed their luck inside the temple precincts. His path to the high priest's office took him through Huldah Gates, up the stairs and along the colonnade. The first person he saw was Shoom, who regularly trailed down the royal stoa selling garlic to the scribes, moneychangers and professional speculators who, under licence from Kedar, had infested this area.

'Shoom, shoom,' sang Shoom. She did not so much walk as glide through the cool-shaded colonnades, the braided garlic round her neck resembling the hair of a fairytale princess. The draught caught the sun-bleached dress she had once worn at her husband's funeral. Shoom was no beauty. Her eyes were a little too close together. Yet she exuded a peacefulness which was what Kedar lacked right now. That, and his personal distaste for garlic, made him scratchy.

'You there! Garlic woman.'

'Shoom?'

'No, I don't want any garlic. But I do want to know who gave you permission to sell your wares here.'

A man selling lottery balls waved amiably at Shoom. She sold him a bulb and started to continue on her way.

'I'm not finished with you,' shouted Kedar. 'I asked you who gave you permission to sell your stinking garlic in my temple.' Soft Shoom replied that nobody had issued her with permission because she was a free widow of Jerusalem and the temple belonged as much to her as to any other Jew.

'You're wrong there, lady,' said Kedar. 'I run this temple on behalf of the high priest and unless you have accreditation you can sling your hook. You can come here for worship but not commerce. Formal measures are in place to regulate such matters. Out!'

And that, it seemed, was that. Kedar bristled off to the high priest's offices to discuss what could be done about the king's mad order. Officially the palace had no sway over the temple but it was not as simple as that. The high priest owed his position to His Greatness and when His Greatness was moody it made sense not to provoke him.

Important personages were summoned for a testing of the hinges. The gate was so heavy that forty men were needed to push and pull it shut. The moment they started to do this there was the usual horrendous creaking. 'Stop!' cried the high priest, all in a dither. Fleeces were placed on the hinges to act as mufflers. They were unsuccessful. Hot water was poured on the offending area. It only made the hinges seize up completely for ten minutes. Someone suggested axle grease. No joy.

'Personally, I think the noise is magnificent,' said Micah, one of the older priests.

'They've made that noise since we first got them,' said the high priest.

'The fitters said the noise would reduce after a decade,' offered Lemuel the architect.

'A couple of decades!' said Kedar.

'There's nothing wrong with the stonework,' said Hiram the mason. 'It could be the metal pins or those olive-wood knuckles but you'll have a job changing anything.'

'Too heavy to lift,' agreed Micah glumly.

'No room to insert wool,' added Lemuel.

'In nuce and omnibus perpensis therefore, gentlemen, what is our executive summary?' asked the high priest. He may have been an unprepossessing little man, wet as a snipe moor and cursed with a wheedling voice, but his committee skills were spotless. The executive summary was that no one had a clue. The meeting was adjourned pending consultations.

'They're in a stew,' said Ephraim to Simeon at lunchtime. 'Kedar's talking about going on holiday until the king's better. The high priest has told him that would be an act of desertion. Levi threw an artistic tiff when he was told the gate-closing ceremony will now be a cappella with no brass or percussion. The Romans are washing their hands of the whole business. By the way, do you know you smell of garlic?'

'Sorry. It's my gout treatment. Shoom's oil. Works wonders.'

'Shoom sells oil? I wonder if it might cure my psoriasis.'

'It has certainly done me some good. Reuben says garlic oil has miraculous qualities and works into the tiniest, tightest fissures, "bringing viscous relief from the most persistent friction".'

'Well, that's nice,' said Ephraim.

Their faces settled into that pleasant inaction faces assume when their owners have run out of anything to say. Five seconds later both men slapped their foreheads and said: 'Hang on a minute!'

Kedar, on hearing Ephraim and Simeon's bright idea, was dismissive. 'I won't have that woman in the temple precincts.'

'What if it works?' said the high priest.

'It's worth a try,' said Micah.

'I won't have that garlic woman interfering,' said Kedar. 'She gives me the creeps.'

'She's a widow,' said Simeon.

'Are you surprised?' said Kedar. 'If I was married to her I'd have jumped off a cliff. Misery on two legs. Garlic hung round her neck like a prayer shawl, bloodhound eyes and that terrible voice of doom. Shoom, shoom, doom, doom. Drives me insane.'

After a longish pause, Ephraim said simply: 'Anyway.'

The high priest then caused astonishment by announcing he was going to make a decision. 'I would like Mr Simeon to approach the Widow Shoom and ask that she might assist us.'

Shoom's garlic oil worked a treat. One phial for each hinge was sufficient to stop the squeaking. Shoom declined payment. There was, however, one small request she had. 'I imagine you would like to be allowed to continue offering your wares in the temple colonnade,' said the high priest.

'That I am not much fussed about,' said Shoom. 'I can see it probably is wrong to sell things in a holy place.'

'Oh.'

'What I would like you to do is this,' said Shoom, and she flicked open her knife – to a moment of alarm from the high priest – and cut free one of the garlics from her neck. Now she cut into the bulb and released its cloves. She placed one in each person's hand. 'Plant these,' said Shoom. 'If done with sufficient care, each clove will in turn produce a whole new bulb. Sunshine, a little water, eternal garlic. Regeneration in perpetuity.'

'Thanking you,' said Kedar with much twitching of his nose.

'Commendably sustainable,' said Lemuel the architect, examining the clove with a certain amount of doubt.

The high priest said: 'I've never been much of a gardener, really.' He pocketed the clove and got on with the rest of his day and it was another three months before he found it still in that pocket, dried out and useless.

Mrs Mizrahi

CALEB'S mother was a woman of determination, her stumpy gait distinct from afar. Simeon saw her enter Temple Square. 'Look sharp, lad, your mother.' The boy ceased some cursory mining of ear wax and jumped to his feet. Simeon remembered doing much the same when he was on army exercises and Sergeant Major Yadin loomed over the horizon. It invariably presaged a telling-off. Join the army, live the dream.

'Loafing about as normal!' bawled Mrs Mizrahi. Her right arm swung, lending martial impetus. Visitors at the temple entrance turned to inspect this source of guttural admonishment. Widow's weeds and a large bag, possibly containing enough small boulders to stone a Mede, accentuated a forthright nature. Two eyes, as of garnet, shone from sockets that were hedged by black brows. Her greying hair was drawn into an imperfect bun. The voice had stentorian reach. Caleb said she once brought a marching platoon to a dishevelled stop with one of her sneezes. Some of the squaddies mistook it for a 'halt' from their NCO while others presumed they were under attack from a siege engine. Mrs Mizrahi had long, and successfully, conveyed the impression that she took no prisoners. And yet she considered herself bottom of the pile and was not without kindness.

'Is that lump of mine being *any* use, Mr Simeon?' she demanded.

'We were just talking about you, and with the greatest affection,' said Simeon.

'I'm surprised you can wring a word out of him. All I ever get is grunts.'

'Hello, Mum,' sighed Caleb.

'You forgot your sling,' Mrs Mizrahi told the boy. 'You'll be needing it later for cadets. I had to come uptown to get some blades sharpened so thought I'd bring it.' She threw the sling at Caleb. 'He'll be forgetting his feet next.' Finding herself within range of her son, she gave him a whack round the head and then pressed a food package in his hands.

'Thanks, Mum,' said Caleb in the voice teenagers have used since Noah's flood.

'Such a kind mother,' said Simeon.

'But is he actually being any use? Is he learning anything? If he's not learning, he might as well be sent to the coast.'

'I am here, you know,' said Caleb. 'You don't have to talk about me like some idiot.'

'Seems a fair description of you,' remarked Mrs Mizrahi.

Caleb was accustomed to hearing this threat of naval conscription. The Romans always needed rowers for their ships. 'We have had a productive morning,' ventured Simeon. 'A scholar from Istakhr was seeking accommodation and Caleb carried his luggage. The Levantine trade delegation had to deposit bags while being given a tour of the temple. Your son is a natural coat-check clerk. An elderly woman from Sychar was feeling faint. Caleb found her a chair and she rewarded him with a tip. He is indispensable.'

'If you say so,' said Mrs Mizrahi, hooking a lip over one of roughly three teeth protruding from her gums. Her scepticism was not unwarranted. When the Levantine traders had turned up, Caleb was kicking a sheep's bladder against the wall and Simeon had had to yell at him to attend to his duties. But Simeon was not one to squeal. 'Good to see you looking so well,' he told the widow. Mrs Mizrahi hawked up a ball of green phlegm which shot past one of the dental palisades and flew ten yards before double-bouncing off the ground like a pebble skimming the waves.

'Sychar?' she said. 'That would be a Samaritan woman.'

'Yes,' said Simeon.

'A Samaritan!'

'A Samaritan.' Caleb rummaged in his pocket and produced the coin he had been given by the woman from Sychar. Mrs Mizrahi brooded on this information for a few seconds before she grunted: 'Well, I suppose Samaritan woman are likely to feel their age as much as the rest of us. So long as he's being helpful, Mr Simeon. So long as he's learning. He won't earn much with you but my late husband said a boy should first learn not earn. He's an apprentice to wisdom.'

'I am not wise, Mrs Mizrahi.'

'A little of it goes a long way these days. Shalom, Mr Simeon. Caleb, count your lucky stars you're not rowing for Rome.' With which she left to find the blade grinder, and a few passers-by moved smartly out of the orbit of her swinging bag.

'Count your lucky stars!' repeated Simeon in comradely mimicry. And then: 'Caleb, your mother is a genius. Counting stars is precisely what we're going to do. What time do you finish cadets?'

'Sundown.'

'When you finish, come to my place for an hour. You're going to learn your way round the night sky. You're going to count stars.'

Miscarriage of Justice

EVERY summer the Roman garrison threw a party to celebrate the first grape harvest and to improve community relations. A buffet of Roman delicacies was prepared, music was played and greenery was hung from the Antonia's ramparts to make the fort appear less threatening – although actually it just made it look camouflaged. The soldiers were told not to wear swords and to pinch bambinos' cheeks and to be friendly. When some of them tried to smile there was a cracking as of dry leather. The Pharisees naturally wanted no part of any of this and stood outside chanting: 'Romans out!'

Zillah sailed past them, waving to Jonah. He discreetly waggled a pinky in return. 'I'm surprised they have nothing better to do,' she said to no one in particular. 'Is there not some sacrificial blade that has to be cleansed or some pretty lamb simply dying to have its throat slit?' Most of the tea stall followed Zillah's lead. If the Romans wanted to hold a party it seemed churlish not to go. Were Jews not encouraged to accept hospitality if it was generously offered? Free food and drink was manna, almost.

Zillah was this year's matron of honour. She bridled a little at the term 'matron' but was pleased by the attention and happy to present a laurel to the farmer who produced the best grapes. She liked farmers. They knew how to handle a ewe. Grapes were exhibited on trestle tables in the courtyard. Simeon found Benjamin and his parents there. Onesimus was one of the judges. Benjamin's cart was to be used as the stage for the awards ceremony. A carnival atmosphere prevailed. Even Kedar and his wife were mingling. Kedar greeted Zillah with a certain stiffness but Simeon smoothed things over by complimenting Mrs Kedar on her hairdo of plaits and blooms. Mrs Kedar received so few compliments in life that she warmed to Simeon and chatted about her day and how they had enjoyed trying Roman food. 'Much better than the grapes,' said Mrs Kedar.

'Are you not a grape person?' enquired Simeon.

'I am. But my husband has trouble with them. They make him, you know . . .'

'Sneeze?'

'No, you know.'

'Angry?'

'No, not that. Well, I don't think so. No angrier than he normally is. No, Mr Simeon. They make him . . . pop-pop.'

'Oh, right, pop-pop. Yes. I can see that could be a problem. To a man of his importance.'

'You two are getting on well,' said Kedar. 'What's the joke?'

'Nothing, dear,' said Mrs Kedar.

Javelin found the event less interesting. Standing in a Roman fortress, attached to a cart, while the humans talked was not Javelin's idea of fun. Mind you, was that a table of grapes over there? Javelin was tethered to a ring in the wall but when she pulled on her rope she found that the masonry was loose. The ring fell to the ground. Javelin wandered towards the grapes, which had now been judged. Javelin, like all mules, was keen on grapes. She quietly got stuck in.

An hour or so passed and the moment for the presentation arrived. Zillah climbed on the cart. Beside her was Lucilius the centurion, rugged, unable to obey the instruction to smile, generally all man. While Lucilius suppressed his habitual urge to strike something hard with his vine staff, Zillah proposed a toast to the emperor, to the king, to the harvest and the height of summer. May it be fruitful. Now for the awarding of first prize for the grapes.

'And the winner is . . .'

Prrrrrrrrp!

It had come from somewhere near the cart. Zillah looked with surprise at Lucilius who took a moment to realise what she suspected. He gave a 'not I' shake of the head.

Prrrrrrrp!

'The winner, with the most delicious collection of lovely, juicy grapes . . .'

Prrrrrrrp!

'Ow!' said Kedar to his wife. 'What you do that for?'

Prrrrrrrp!

Zillah was struggling to complete her ceremonial duties and Lucilius, for the first time in living memory, was not only smiling but felt a strange, shaking sensation in his chest. For a moment he feared he was having a seizure. In fact it was laughter. Zillah finally managed to name the winner, who struggled through the crowd to collect his prizes. 'Oh you are *awful!*' Zillah told Lucilius, who by now was practically weeping with merriment.

Everyone agreed that it had been the best fete for years. Relations between the citizenry and the garrison were boosted and Lucilius wrote a warm report to his praeconsul in Antioch. Mrs Kedar told her baffled and defensive husband she had 'never been so embarrassed in my life'. It was only that night that Benjamin admitted to Onesimus that grapes always gave Javelin frightful wind.

Justice Javelin-style

ONESIMUS told Benjamin to deliver some dates to Zillah. He decided to combine the job with a trip to the rubbish tip and his cart was loaded with vegetable and fruit peelings. It was a little ripe on the breeze but people tolerated far worse in those days. 'Don't dawdle,' Onesimus told his son. 'Zillah wanted these pronto. Lovely and juicy they are. The food of love.'

Javelin happily trotted through the streets. Zillah's house was in a smart street shaded by palm trees. This was the life: a sand-brushed roadway, plenty of room for turning, houses with scented courtyards and a tranquillity quite different from Deuteronomy Street. Javelin started moving like a dressage horse, daintily lifting her hooves and nodding her head. Benjamin had never known the little minx assume such airs. They came to a crisp, correct halt outside Zillah's gates where another vehicle – a low-slung chariot – was already parked. One of Zillah's grooms was unharnessing the chariot's horse to correct a problem with its halter. As Benjamin dismounted, Javelin gave a proud nicker and shook her Caesarea reins. While Benjamin heaved the box of dates off the back of the cart and headed for the tradesmen's entrance, the chariot horse shot Javelin a short, superior look. He was a handsome so-and-so: a tall, muscular chestnut with a plaited, pale mane.

'I'm not going to feel socially inadequate,' thought Javelin, so she gave another cheerful nicker. Jerusalem was as much her town as anyone's. The chariot was a magnificent piece of work, white-painted and carved to give an impression of speed. It sat on the ground low and sleek, its side panels decorated with carvings of the wind and breaking waves. Its platform had a bronze bar for the driver to grip, plus a small sculpture of Neptunus Equester, god of racing. The wheels were supersized with gold-painted spokes and hubs tipped by sharp prongs. At high speed they could do some damage. Javelin was staring at the wheels, gulping a little, when she noticed that the chariot horse had strayed a few paces from the groom. The horse wandered up to Javelin and waved his head airily, baring some impressive teeth.

'Tsssh, Sagitta, tsssh,' muttered the groom, soon reabsorbed by the halter. Sagitta. So that was the stranger's name. Javelin looked up at him – the height difference between the two was pronounced – and snorted. Sagitta ignored this rudeness and inspected Javelin's cart with its steaming load. It was a minute or two before Javelin realised what he was up to. A tug on the cart made her look round. 'Oi!' Sagitta was helping himself to some of the fruit peel on the back of the cart. Jupiter stamped. The gesture only encouraged Sagitta to chew faster.

The red mist descended and Javelin let out the most enormous '*Eeeee-ORRRRRR!*' which made the groom shout at Sagitta to behave. Roman horses pay little heed to Jerusalem ostlers. Sagitta continued to gorge himself. Snacking on someone else's payload! Javelin noticed that Sagitta's long, salon-teased tail was within distance. Come to think, it did look a little like the silk at the top of a corn on the cob. She took a good bite.

'*Yeowwww!*' went Sagitta.

'*Eeeee-ORRRRRR!*' laughed Javelin.

The noise brought Benjamin running from the mews behind Zillah's house. He was accompanied by a blond young Roman, Cornelius. Once they established what had happened the two lads exchanged apologies. Benjamin patted Sagitta and Cornelius gave Javelin a palmful of sunflower seeds. Cornelius was Zillah's nephew.

'Your chariot's a beauty,' remarked Benjamin.

'Thanks,' said Cornelius. 'I have only raced her once and it frightened the life out of me, but Sagitta knew what he was doing.'

'Raced at the stadium?'

'Not here in Jerusalem,' said Cornelius. 'It was a novices' race at Jericho. Amazing track. We managed to avoid coming last.'

Benjamin's eyes burned: speed, danger, competition.

Zillah appeared. 'Have your horses stopped fighting?'

'His horse. My mule,' corrected Benjamin.

'Javelin may officially be a mule,' said Zillah, 'but we all know that in her heart she is an Arab thoroughbred. And look at those charioteer reins. Very smart.' Zillah patted Javelin's snout and Javelin, had she been able, would have blushed.

'Come and have a drive some time,' said Cornelius.

'Could I?' asked Benjamin.

'I bet you're a natural.'

The goodbyes exchanged by Javelin and Sagitta were cooler.

L'dor V'dor

JONAH'S Pharisees were at their prayers, blocking much of Deuteronomy Square, when Adom the undertaker tried pushing through them. 'Show some respect!' shouted a young Pharisee. Others told Adom to be patient. The undertaker explained that he was hurrying to attend a corpse in the Sanhedrin. Prayers were important but a corpse could not wait.

'Actually,' said the first devotee, 'that's not quite right. A dead body is hardly going to run away, is it? And you surely mean the corpse is at, or outside, not in, the Sanhedrin.'

'Please,' replied Adom, 'why must you people argue everything? Someone has died inside the Sanhedrin. Always I must repeat myself!'

'Don't lose your rag.'

'I am NOT losing my rag!' raged Adom. 'Now allow an undertaker to earn his living.'

'Who's died?' asked another Pharisee.

Adom smote his forehead. 'Okay, this needs to be quick. I must tell you that one of our most revered ancients, Old Jonah of Jerusalem, snuffed it in the chamber today.'

'Not Old Jonah!'

'And during a speech,' continued Adom, warming to the pleasure of breaking bad news. Undertakers are not alone in relishing misfortune but for them there is the added frisson of possible work. If they can get to the scene first.

'Whose speech?' asked the onlookers.

'His own. Now I must press on or I'll be beaten to it by my so-called rivals. Undertaking is a fight to the death.' The Pharisees parted like the Red Sea and Adom hoisted his tunic to betray a set of shapely ankles as he sprinted to the Sanhedrin.

Old Jonah of Jerusalem had been a member of the Sanhedrin since eternity, or so it seemed. His career had begun in the days when giant crocodiles and sea snakes swam in the River Jordan. Children were assured that Old Jonah once danced with a girl who had danced with a man who had danced with a great-great-granddaughter of Solomon. His dandruff was the very scurf of history. His father hoed the Garden of Gethsemane when it was a cabbage patch. Old Jonah became as shrivelled as a sultana and his voice had the bleat of a kid goat. A great life had ended.

The Pharisees headed for the Hall of Hewn Stones to lead lamentations. Their own, younger Jonah was quick to grasp that his namesake's death would create a vacancy in the Sanhedrin. Leading public obsequies would do no harm, no matter how vulgar some of the Sadducees thought him. At the Hall of Hewn Stones mourners heard how Old Jonah had met his end. The Sanhedrin that airless day had not been busy. The house fell to considering the case of a Samaritan leper found guilty of eating an owl. Had he transgressed Leviticus's instruction against the consumption of certain birds? Or, given his leprosy, was his flesh already tainted? Old Jonah rose slowly and said he was 'going to be brief'. Everyone knew this was code for: 'I'm going to talk my knees off.' As Old Jonah began dilating on the matter – making the slow progress, say, of a tramp chewing on owl wing – members' eyes grew heavy. Doorkeepers swayed. The chief clerk drooped at his table. Old Jonah's speaking manner had always been slow, marked by pauses while he cleared his rattly throat. Who notices the exact tock when a clock ceases ticking? Who sees a shower's final raindrop? So it was with Old Jonah's speech. One minute he was upright, leaning on his crook, head angled and eyes closed in their customary expression of deep thought; the next minute he was still upright, supported by his crook but now thoroughly dead. A couple of Sanhedrin members presumed he must be waiting for the next sentence of inspiration. Only after a few minutes of silence did the chief clerk tiptoe up and gently touch his shoulder, making his body crash to the floor. Old Jonah of Jerusalem was a goner.

'Basically, suicide – bored himself to death,' concluded Zillah, en route to the hairdresser. A teenage girl was with her. 'He came to one of my summer parties,' continued Zillah. 'Frightful windbag. I'm amazed he didn't take anyone with him. Simeon, this is Eve. One of my nieces. She's come to Jerusalem for finishing school. If she'd met Old Jonah, he'd have finished her off. Eve, this is Mr Simeon, one of the few almost sane men in the city. No one quite knows what he thinks.' Simeon inclined his head and the young girl gave an embarrassed wave. 'Right,' rasped Zillah, 'I must dash. Conubia wants me to try an afro but I'm not sure.' While Zillah strode off, Simeon noticed Benjamin's cart stopping at the Hall of Hewn Stones' side gates. It was today being pulled by two mules: Javelin and a younger beast.

'Hearse duties,' Benjamin told Simeon. 'Any chance you could hold the reins? I must let Adom know I'm here.'

'Who's the new mule?'

'Isn't she a cutie? I'm calling her Little Javelin. It'll save remembering a new name. She's still learning the ropes.' Benjamin dashed inside.

'Good morning, Javelins,' said Simeon. Little Javelin tried to bite Simeon. 'You're a frisky one. Well, we all were once. L'dor v'dor.'

Renewal. Regeneration. Nothing ever quite changed, or stayed precisely the same.

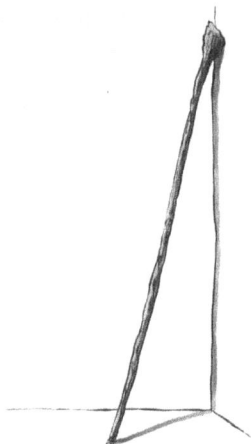

An Innocent Tramp

GLUMNESS prevailed. Bread prices had shot up and a late frost wrecked the peach blossom. The Romans for once had no war to keep them busy so were making a nuisance of themselves, building roads and causing traffic jams. For days it rained. Streets filled with puddles, country roads became wadis and nothing could dry. After a shivery night Simeon stared at a bowl of unsweetened porridge Noor had plonked in front of him.

'No honey?'

'Bad for the waistline. I must say I'm rather enjoying this diet.'

'I'm not. I'm cold.'

'Take some exercise.'

'You're being a sergeant major.'

'I'm only doing what you told me. Starve to live. Remember?'

She was right. Simeon had indeed complained about becoming fat and had announced noisily, after a drop too much drink, that he was embarking on a regime. 'Be strict with me,' he told Noor in a moment he now attributed to early senility. Only lunatics encouraged their housekeepers to be martinets. It was like surrendering to Pompey. You could expect no mercy.

Noor swept from the room, angles imperious. Simeon had miscalculated her capacity for torture. The porridge was solid enough for Og and Phut to use as mortar. He flicked a gobbet of it at the ceiling. It stuck there. Reuben was unimpressed by this dieting, for he now had no one with whom to share his morning buns. Buns are less fun when eaten alone. Jonah heard about the fasting and congratulated Simeon. What was the cause of his penitence? 'I'm too fat,' said Simeon. Jonah, himself not small, laughed weakly and said yes, but seriously, what was the transgression that had caused Simeon to seek the path to righteousness? Simeon: 'No, I'm just trying to shed my gut because I'm beginning to look like a baker's wife.' The Pharisees started to give Simeon a wide berth, holding their hats as they scurried past him in the square. Fasting for slimness was poor form.

Caleb told Simeon he was 'weird'. Although Caleb had no intention of dieting – Mrs Mizrahi would not permit it – Simeon's asceticism made the young man feel guilty about his packed lunches, which were substantial. This could not be said of his master's provisions. Each day Noor handed Simeon a dry pitta bread, sunflower seeds and a stick of celery. Simeon loathed celery. It tasted of sour disapproval. Encountering Menachem the Essene, he handed him his entire packed lunch for that day. Menachem, initially excited, looked at its contents and handed it back with a look that was part sympathy, part betrayal. 'Maybe next time,' said the Essene.

Visitors who consulted Simeon outside the temple had been told to expect a twinkly fellow but instead found a crabbed misery. 'Well, you aren't much fun today,' chirruped Jethro. The little tramp came splashing up to Simeon on another day of incessant rain. He had fashioned a hat for himself from palm leaves. Its brim served as a gutter. Under it, Jethro beamed.

'Your shoes will get wet,' grunted Simeon.

'It may have escaped your notice that I possess no shoes,' replied Jethro.

'Anyone sensible is staying at home.'

'I have no home either.'

'Well, I don't see why you're so bloody cheerful.'

'I'm no different from normal, brother. It's you and half Jerusalem that's changed. I've never known the city in such a grump.' With which he produced, from behind his back, a kitchen sieve. It was the sort of utensil in which housekeepers rinsed rice. 'My all-weather begging bowl,' explained Jethro. 'Generous patrons, in such weather, may hesitate to drop coins into a cup filling with water. With this device they know their donations will be safe. It is proving most successful. Look.' On his leprous stumps he waddled to a family of visitors. Rain was lashing them from all sides. Jethro, in his mad hat, hopped about with the sieve and exuded crazy cheerfulness. The visitors were so grateful to have some amusement amid the downpour, they dropped a coin into his sieve.

'No begging!' bawled a voice. It was Kedar from his portico. 'Someone arrest that tramp!' None of his goons felt like coming out into the rain so Kedar himself strode over and ordered Jethro to go and find some work. The authorities had recently announced a crackdown on begging. 'There is no shortage of employers looking for staff,' Kedar told Jethro. 'Get a job, sponger.'

The rain stopped, as it generally does, and summer reasserted herself. Commerce recommenced. Menachem the Essene was allowed to drift round the square holding out his begging bowl; but not Jethro. One noonday Simeon heard a sharp shout and the swishing of a whip. 'Owwwww!'

'Get out of here, you filthy tramp!'

'Owwwww! All right, I'm going. Holy Moses, what's wrong with you? I'm going.' Jethro was thrown down the temple steps with a bump, bump, bump until he came to a rest near Simeon's pitch. One of the guards threw his crutch down after him. It had been snapped in two. As an afterthought, the guard also threw the bone from a lamb cutlet.

'Jethro the Jebusite, greetings. Been waving your stump under the wrong noses?'

'Oh, hello, Simeon,' said Jethro, tenderly feeling his head. 'As a matter of fact, I was minding my own business in the cloisters, sleeping off breakfast, but Kedar had me chucked out for thieving. He said I was unclean.'

'Harsh but true. You are a bit whiffy. Let me help you up.'

'He accused me of stealing that lamb bone but it fell off the cart,' said Jethro as he tried to re-bandage what remained of his right leg. 'I didn't nick it. I was merely tidying up. They don't complain when sparrows pilfer nutshells.'

Simeon examined the crutch. It was ruined. 'Beyond salvation,' he concluded.

'That's what they say about me.'

'You must never believe it, Brother Jethro.' By way of cheer, Simeon offered Jethro a quarter of the orange he was cutting. It was good and juicy, bought from Onesimus's stall that morning as a supplement to Simeon's diet. Jethro made proper use of his piece, sucking hard and rubbing his gums with the peel once he had extracted everything he could from the fruit. Simeon gave him a second quarter. Jethro accepted it with reverence, cupping it in his shaky hands and mumbling.

'What did you say?' asked Simeon.

'We forgot to say grace,' said the little tramp. 'Shehmaa our Eloowwem.'

'Amen,' said Simeon. And then: 'I didn't know you were a Samaritan.'

'How else do you think they get away with treating me so badly?' asked Jethro. 'Happiness all your days for one hundred years, comrade.'

'Happiness,' echoed Simeon, and the word, or the idea, almost made him sob. That happened sometimes. More often as he became older. Sadness could pounce out on you from the most unexpected alleyway.

While chewing on the orange they watched the trickle of visitors. It was always the same. People entered the temple tentatively, voices lowered. The scale of the site awed them. From deep inside the temple came a sound of silence yet here in the heat of the square there was a hubbub of chatter and animals. Stepping into a quieter space had an effect. Simeon remembered a cave near Eudaemon. He and his father were on a ship with a consignment of copal and there was a scare about pirates. The captain took shelter in a cave. As they approached it, all the noise of the open sea receded and the temperature and light dropped. A slow slap of water on prow replaced the froth of white horses. Having earlier had to shout over the sea, now their whispers were echoing, the dank cave's silence almost confronting them. The pirates never found them.

'I may not be everyone's model citizen,' said Jethro, 'but I have feelings. These skinny wrists have a pulse. My tear ducts leak. And like anyone else I become peckish after a night on the tiles.'

'Night on the tiles?'

'Last night. I may have overdone it. A family of tourists was leaving the temple after a visit. They were so happy they gave me a handful of coins. I spoke a blessing and told them God would smile on their generosity to a poor old man. One of the Levites heard me and said I should not be selling benedictions. I invested some of the money in Mount Carmel wine and woke up this morning feeling a touch frail.'

'Where did you wake?'

'The temple. In my cups I must have found a hidey-hole near the moneychangers. I probably could have gone undetected but for my snoring.'

'You mentioned being peckish.'

'You know how it gets, Simeon. A few scoops of vino. Then you realise you could do with some solids. The temple was closed for the night and next to the priests' court they load a wagon with the bones from the altars. Some still had meat on them and it was only going to go to waste. I took a couple of chops to my hidey-hole. Slept the sleep of kings, full of meat and wine. Then woke to a shouty priest calling me a dosser.'

Simeon made a few sympathetic noises before saying: 'Look, you'd better use my staff for a while until you can find a new crutch. My gout's not bad at the moment. I'll have the stick back at some point. It's an old friend.'

The next day was the Sabbath and Jethro was begging at the corner of Deuteronomy Street and Temple Square. Details of what happened next remain sketchy but it is said Kedar was promenading with Mrs Kedar and told the leper he should not be working on the Sabbath. 'This is the day of rest.' Jethro asked Kedar if begging was now to be considered a form of work. Had he not, days earlier, told him to find work instead of begging? Yet now he seemed to be saying that begging *was* work. Kedar said he would not be spoken to like that in front of his wife. As soon as the Sabbath was finished Jethro was arrested and charged with theft. His body was later reported to have been thrown into the paupers' graveyard. Natural causes, said the coroner. Regrettable but routine.

In due course an official arrived at Simeon's pitch in Temple Square and returned 'the property stolen by that tramp'. It was the walking stick. 'I lent it to him,' said Simeon, and a great surge of anger flared within him. 'He didn't steal it from me! He was innocent, damn you. Damn you all! He was just trying to live.'

Kedar's man merely gave a shrug that as good as said: 'Not my problem.'

A Familiar Gait

LIFE went on. Life does. Construction continued on the outer parts of the temple complex, arches and adornments sprouting like an English garden in May. Hiram the stonemason moved into a large new house in upper town and sent his children to be schooled in Athens. Lemuel the architect, somehow less rich than the mason, complained that the whole temple had basically been ruined because his proposals for a domed visitor centre were rejected on cost grounds. Its circular cella with oculus could have put Jerusalem on a par with Rome and Lemuel was 'frankly disappointed' that Herod had baulked at the costs. Centurion Lucilius broke several more vine staffs and was said to be in line for a posting to Illyricum. Calvus was made the garrison's community-outreach officer. His friendship with a widow from Beitar had resulted in her becoming great with child; they made a delightful couple. Zillah's nephew Cornelius won several races at the new Caesarea hippodrome and became a pin-up of charioteering. And in Deuteronomy Square the cardamon puffs and fig dainties continued to evaporate from Reuben's counter. Jonah plotted his ascent to political glory. Noor baked and blew flour dust from her nose. Mrs Pappo continued to cast an eye at Onesimus's grapes, half-hoping he would give her another kiss. And there were rumours that Herod intended to conduct a nationwide census, recording every household in Judaea, down to every last lamb and piglet. 'Nosy parkers,' said Reuben.

Jethro's death went little remarked on, because such things were best not discussed. Simeon brooded. The cruelty of it stewed deep inside him. At the baths he told Philippos the tale factually, including the detail that Jethro had been a Samaritan. Philippos could interpret his mood and do with it as he saw fit. Is that not the purpose of a good intelligence officer?

There were two other matters. The first he would tell Philippos. The other he would not.

Menachem the Essene reappeared in town. He regularly disappeared for months to a commune by the Dead Sea but made visits to Jerusalem to visit an elderly sister in the upper town and, it was joked, to do some banking. With his begging bowl and gaunt shoulders Menachem was hardly a spreader of joy. Most people ignored him. Those who said hello could find themselves detained by long sentences about wastefulness and spiritual drift and the pointless vanity of the new temple. Menachem was both a caution and an annoyance, at worst a briar, at best a reminder of our prideful transience. But now that Kedar's men had seen off Jethro they decided Temple Square should be spared the Essene and his unpatriotic moaning. What had been tolerated for years would be tolerated no more. The removal was not violent. Two large guards approached Menachem in the square and spoke some explanatory, official words. The Essene lifted his long beak and started to reply. While he was speaking the two men simply lifted him off the ground, one under each cavernous armpit. They carried him, still talking, to a nearby cart and deposited him in the back. Menachem was still holding his begging bowl. Once in the cart he ceased bothering to talk. He just sat there as the cart was driven away. Simeon shouted: 'Are you okay, Menachem?' The Essene gave a limp wave. That was it.

The other matter occurred at the water-libation festival, when the temple precincts filled with pilgrims and water was carried from the Pool of Siloam, through Huldah Gates, up to the courts where the men were kept separate from the women. That partitioning always led to good-natured eyeing-up and wooing. Many a romance had its origins in the water-libation celebrations. Simeon was past all that, of course, but he and Reuben still went through the motions of laddishness. 'Who's that one over there, in the veil?'

'She must be the new washroom attendant for the women's court,' said Reuben. 'I heard she was from a community in the Qumran area. Essene, I guess.'

'Like poor Menachem.'

'Poor Menachem? Few in Jerusalem eat better – and no taxes to worry about. Shall we go and have a drink?'

Simeon saw the veiled woman again a couple of weeks later, across the temple courts. The partitions of the water-libation festival had long been dismantled but other, invisible barriers remained. Attendants of the women's court, particularly of the women's washroom, largely kept to themselves. Simeon saw her empty a bucket into a drain. There was nothing unusual about that but for a second he thought he saw something familiar about her cast of head and the way she turned and walked. Simeon told himself he must be going dotty. Really, age was becoming a trial. When would God let him go?

Jonah's Prospects

COULD the younger Jonah inherit Old Jonah of Jerusalem's seat among the seventy-one of the Sanhedrin?

Zillah asked Simeon to come to her villa for early-evening drinks. The invitation was delivered at breakfast-time by Tambal who said he would wait at the door until Simeon gave a reply. 'Don't be silly, Tambal. Come inside for a spoonful of honey and some chopped apple.'

'I'm a slave.'

'You're not my slave. Anyway, we're all in servitude one way or another, to work or routine or to destiny. My own cruel mistress is grief.' The bench creaked as Tambal lowered his bulk and inspected the honeypot with the daintiest of enormous fingers. He gave a connoisseur's grunt of approval.

Jasmine trailed its evening scent across Zillah's verandah. From her lily pond there was a view of the Antonia fortress. Evening was touching the top of the Judaean Hills to the south. The fading sunlight caught the bleached hairs on

Zillah's arms. She wore a flowing white robe and her skin glowed. Her loveliness was a glory to God's creation.

'Tambal says your honey tastes of rosemary and is among the best he has tasted.'

'Was.'

'He ate the lot?'

'It was a pleasure to watch an expert at work.'

'Tambal, you're a disgrace!' shouted Zillah, laughing. 'You finished Simeon's honey!'

'It was the greatest compliment I could give,' explained Tambal. 'Wine?'

Zillah tucked her bronzed toes under her thighs. She held a goblet of wine close, almost stroking her neck with it, and they soon fell to gossip about Jonah's bid for the Sanhedrin.

'How radical is he, Simeon?' The wine was light, white and had been kept cold in the lily pond.

'He's certainly religious.'

'Religion doesn't have to be political. Probably shouldn't be, actually. Is he married?'

'Not yet.'

'But he likes girls?'

'He does. They just aren't so keen on him.'

'What does he think of Herod?' She sensed hesitation. 'This is a private conversation.'

'His Greatness provokes strong feelings in his subjects, not least with all this talk of a census and more taxes.'

'Would he betray the king?'

'Not to the Romans. He's not keen on them, either. But Jerusalem is a city like any other. No one can be trusted entirely. Except you.' Zillah rewarded him with a laugh.

Simeon added: 'The Sanhedrin is hardly over-endowed with innocents.'

'The Sanhedrin is full of lizards and it needs to be. It places them in the spotlight and stops them scuttling behind walls. In the Sanhedrin they must show what they're made of.'

'People like politicians to be outspoken,' said Simeon. 'In the army we knew that the more ruthless our officers were, the more effective they would be in battle.'

'Let's hope we never again have to fight the Romans.'

'It would be a massacre. That doesn't stop the Zealots fantasising about it.'

'It's their insistence that I find so exhausting. Tambal, please take the air out of Simeon's goblet.' Tambal padded over with enormous feet. The sound of wine being poured captured the intimacy of the moment. 'They are interested in Jonah not despite his anti-Herod views but because of them.'

'Jonah is not subtle,' said Simeon. 'Or without flaw. You will have heard that he makes a lot of noise against Roman decadence, not least chariot-racing and hippodromes.'

'I had heard that, yes.'

'Yet he is himself not without decadence. Young Benjamin saw him at the races in Caesarea.'

'No!' gurgled Zillah. She loved this gossipy plum. 'Oh, that's perfect.'

'In a way I like him better for that. It shows a human side.'

'The occasional hothead, even when hypocritical, helps establish political contours for the Romans. Having him in the Sanhedrin would make some other members look more reasonable.'

'Could they bear him socially?'

'Even the progressives are starting to see that the Sanhedrin have leaned too far to Rome. Unless they pull back a little the nationalists may rise and the balance of Herod's settlement will be squandered. I hope I'm long gone by then. Ah, Eve, here you are.' Zillah's niece floated on to the verandah. She and her aunt exchanged kisses light as meringues.

'Good evening, Mr Simeon,' said Eve. This time it was Simeon's turn to blush, for the young woman was transformed. Her long auburn hair floated in her wake. In a few years, Eve would be the new Zillah. Simeon bowed.

'Tambal might find you some wine, darling,' said Zillah. 'Simeon, we must cease gnawing political bones. It is boring for young ears.'

'I must be going,' said Simeon.

'I haven't even broached the question of my concert.' Zillah was organising a fundraiser for the temple.

'Will you be singing, Mr Simeon?' asked Eve. 'I am told you have a beautiful voice.'

'Who told you that?'

'I forget.'

'My singing days are long gone.'

'That's a shame, Mr Simeon. Singing is so good for us.'

'He doesn't want to talk about it,' said Zillah. 'We should not have raised it.'

Tambal escorted Simeon to the door, lighting candles as they went. 'We have a few coming for dinner,' he explained. 'She would have asked you to stay but I think she likes to keep you her secret.'

'I am hardly the right class, Tambal.'

'There's that, too.'

It was cooler in the street. Simeon stopped to tighten his cloak. He was still there when he saw Philippos the Greek arrive at Zillah's door. He was followed a few moments later by two litters that bore Sadoc and his wife. The sound of marching boots cautioned him to remain in the shadows. They came to a halt and a stern voice commanded its junior companion to 'come back in an hour and a half and rescue me'. That thigh-slapping epicurean Lucilius the centurion was the last of Zillah's dinner guests. Simeon headed home with relief.

Simeon's Secret

HEROD was said to reckon everyone had a secret. Reuben was offended. 'How dare he think we all nurse something dark in our hearts?'

'It may not be quite that,' said Simeon. 'It may be a wider observation about human nature.'

Reuben continued to chew on the matter, just as Shlomo would often chew at his paws. 'I bet Kedar has secrets. And any member of the Sanhedrin.'

'That's politics for you,' said Simeon.

'Onesimus is a dark horse, too.'

'A successful business executive must keep some cards close to his apron,' agreed Simeon.

'Benjamin? A secret girlfriend, maybe.'

'Javelin would divorce him.'

'If anyone discovered my malabi recipe I'd have to kill him,' admitted Reuben.

'Naturally.'

'But Habib the street-sweeper? Bildad? Our silent friend Phut? What secrets could they have? And is it likely Menahem has secrets? An Essene renounces ownership, and what is a secret if not a possession? I'm not sure the king is right on this one.'

'I'll let him know,' said Simeon, earning a playful kick under the table.

There was a silence while they watched Shlomo locate and deal with a flea in his flank. Satisfied that he had dislodged it, Shlomo settled on his front and yawned enormously. Dogs slept for hours yet they yawned. Ants worked ceaselessly but when did you last see one yawn?

'How about you?' asked Reuben.

'What about me?'

'Do you have a secret?'

'Maybe.'

'That means you do.'

'Maybe.'

'What is it?'

'If I told you, it would not be a secret.'

'Any chance of a mint tea around here?' interrupted a voice from the counter.

'You have a customer,' said Simeon.

Once Reuben knew Simeon had a secret, it itched him worse than a flea. This wasn't entirely logical because as we already know, Reuben himself had a secret, which was how he concocted the beautifully sticky, pink-tinged malabi rice pudding. Everyone knew malabi contained rice and coconut and strawberry juice and a measure of flour for thickening but in what proportions and in what order and at what temperature? How was Reuben's so good? That was for Reuben to know and no one else. If Reuben could have a secret, why not Simeon? Reuben did not see it like that. He dwelt on these things throughout the days. Sometimes Simeon would catch him watching from the counter. Simeon asked what he was staring at and Reuben replied: 'I'm trying to work out your secret.' Another time, over a digestif on Simeon's roof terrace, Reuben asked: 'Is it a woman thing?' Simeon laughed and threw a cashew shell at him. 'A man thing?' continued Reuben. 'Nah, it can't be a sex thing. You're too old for that. It's probably money. Maybe you've come into an inheritance and intend to leave me everything when you die. Is it that?'

'I just changed my mind. You've blown a fortune.'

'Yeah, yeah,' said Reuben.

Zillah's temple fundraiser now had a name, Concentus, and the programme was coming together nicely. She had persuaded the palace to let the royal trumpeters give a fanfare at the start of both halves. That would ensure things opened with a parp. Centurion Lucilius had been prevailed upon to allow the garrison band to pump out a few tunes. Tambal would demonstrate Nubian drumming. A highlight would be Tabitha playing her harp while Philippos the Greek intoned love poems by Ovid. Zillah thought an hour in total should suffice, including an interval when cups of ayran could be sold. There was talk of singing from Jonah's lads, if the Pharisees would step foot in the theatre. Tabitha's involvement might persuade Jonah to forego his usual qualms about that den of iniquity. Ibrahim the artist had proposed a modern dance lullaby, although it was pointed out that might send the audience to sleep. Lysander offered to read some of his poems. Zillah told him he was 'a darling to make such a generous offer but this is really a musical evening, so sadly we don't think it will be possible to have a spoken item'. Lysander said he hadn't supposed anyone would be terribly interested, anyway, so not to worry. This naturally made Zillah feel wretched, though she soon got over it.

Publicity would be handled by Ephraim.

When tickets went on sale there was a flurry of business. A sales image was produced of Tabitha playing her harp, her cheekbones thrust forward while a wind caught her flowing locks. One of the king's daughters or wives – His Greatness had several of both – bought most of the third row of seats. The high priest sent regrets but made it plain he had no theological objection to a public performance which helped the temple fund. Jonah declared the event kosher and, yes, his lads would sing. There was a request for seats from the Antonia garrison, whose senior officers would attend in togas rather than uniforms as a diplomatic gesture, to indicate the universal fellowship of the arts. Zillah floated around the city like a bigshot impresario. All of which created pressure on the performers.

'Mr Simeon,' said Tabitha one evening, 'would you do me a favour? Philippos can't make it for a rehearsal this evening. Could you read the Ovid poems while I practise?'

Simeon was thrown. 'Ovid?'

'We have them written down.'

'I am flattered you should ask but music is not my forte.'

'I just thought . . .'

'Would you allow me to find someone more suitable?'

'I thought it would be convenient because we're neighbours,' said Tabitha.

'Indeed we are, and I count my blessings, but I should hate to let you down. Leave it with me. I will find a solution.'

Reuben stepped into the breach. Simeon claimed he had a headache.

Tickets were going like raspberry basbousas but Simeon still had not bought one. Jonah reported that two Sanhedrin members were in a bidding war for some prize seats near the royal box. There was talk that the king himself might attend. Zillah announced that a travelling troupe of Egyptian tumblers and pipers had agreed to perform for free, along with an up-and-coming Roman minstrel who had been on recent engagements at Tyre. She had also booked an Illyrian fiddler and a Levantine clown. It was going to be quite the occasion. 'Where are you sitting?' asked Philippos next time they were at the baths. At that very moment there was a gush of caldarium steam and Simeon's answer was lost.

On the evening itself Jerusalem dressed in its finery. Kedar stepped gingerly down Deuteronomy Street in new boots which were plainly giving him blisters. One step behind him walked Mrs Kedar in a bright green gown that shimmered like mackerel skin and clung to her portly hips. Everyone told her she looked a million shekels, while hoping the dress would not rip when she sat. Sadducees attended en masse. Reuben wore a pink rose in his jacket. Even Habib scrubbed up for the occasion, the first time he had been seen in anything but his street-sweeper tunic.

'You coming?' asked Reuben, wiping the last tables before heading for the theatre. Simeon said he would follow after a quick trip to the loo. 'Don't be long,' said Reuben. 'You won't want to miss the king's arrival.' In the event, Herod did not attend. It was said he was suffering from a cold – or from worry about assassins.

Reuben, from his aisle seat, craned his neck in search of Simeon and finally spotted him near one of the exits at the back. The nincompoop must have left it too late to buy a better ticket.

The tumblers tumbled, the Illyrian fiddler fiddled, Jonah's boys sang and Zillah was a natural as mistress of ceremonies. Even Ibrahim's modern dance routine was well-received, not that anyone, least of all the artiste himself, had a clue what it was about. The highlight of the evening was Tabitha's harp music. The audience fell into enthralled silence as she strummed and stroked the strings and Philippos proclaimed Ovid's love poems. Wind, created in the wings by slaves flapping fleeces, picked up Tabitha's curls and made it seem she was the figurehead of a cruising trireme. This led into a stirring medley of Judaean popular songs diplomatically interwoven with snatches from a Roman imperial march. For an encore she played a Eurydicean lament. Emotion streamed down the cheeks of grown men, women hugged their sisters, children watched from their dads' shoulders and Jerusalem, it seemed, was lost in love. Reuben cheered like everyone else. Everyone, that is, but Simeon. For Reuben noticed that his friend's seat was empty. And with that the shekel dropped, and a grin spread on his chops.

'Did you enjoy Concentus?' he asked Simeon later.

'What a success.'

'The music?'

'The music!'

'You liked it all?'

'It is hard to say which I liked best.'

'But which you liked least?'

'That would be unfair.'

Rising from the table, Reuben shot a finger at Simeon and said: 'I know your secret but I won't tell anyone, certainly not her. You hate harp music!'

Three Blundering Eejits

SILHOUETTED in this pre-dawn light Simeon's eyebrows jutted like a mountain crag. A good sentry seldom sleeps and even less so in old age. Simeon's dark eyes were nowadays failing him but his jaw stood square to the coming days. He had been on the roof terrace all night, since Caleb described the stars to him and mentioned a moving light that appeared in the east a week or so ago. 'Where is it now?' asked Simeon. 'How bright? Could you be mistaken?' After Caleb went home – his mother still expected her son to be prompt for his supper and it did not pay to cross her – the old man stayed out here and waited. Something was up. Something was stirring. A warm wind created whirls which blew towards his face. Simeon licked at the dust.

Presently indigo hills and the outline of rooftops emerged. That much he could still see. By this hour, even on a Sabbath, Jerusalem should be stirring. Today there was no noise. Not a cockerel crowed. Javelin and her crown princess were usually honking for food by now; today, nothing. 'Are you up there?' Noor called gently from the stairs. She arrived on the roof terrace with tea and some bread, hobbling a little. Like the rest of them, beautiful Noor was becoming no younger. 'How long have you been up here?'

'A few hours.'

'Why?' asked Noor.

'I was watching.'

'At dawn on the Sabbath?'

'Why not at dawn on a Sabbath? Things could happen any time. God wouldn't observe our stupid rules.'

'And did they?'

'Did they what?'

'Happen.'

'I don't know,' he laughed. 'Maybe.' Noor handed him the tea and bread. Before wandering back inside she touched his shoulder and let her hand stay there a while.

Later that morning he moved downstairs and sat on a bench by the street. It was a place to watch things, even on a subdued Sabbath. The occasional bent widow creaked past and Shlomo wandered over to lie down on all fours in the watery sun. Ants went about their normal commute, impervious to Leviticus and its Sabbath injunctions. Long after sweet death's oblivion, ants will be busy at our eyelids.

Ephraim stopped for a gossip. 'You'll have heard about the sheikhs.'

'Sit down and tell me,' said Simeon.

'Well,' exclaimed Ephraim with melodrama. 'They arrived in the night. Took the best rooms at the inn opposite the high priest's house. Their luggage train is enormous. Ten camels, roped through the nose.'

'From the east?'

'Yes. And *not* light packers. Silk, scents, lacquer ware, jade, jewels, furs, tents, great chests of stuff.'

'Who are they?'

'That's what's odd. They're not merchants. Not trying to sell. They seem to be divines or magupats of some sort, unarmed and learned and constantly smiley. You don't expect such riches from holy men. They've sent a messenger to the palace requesting to see His Greatness. On the Sabbath, I ask you. Bang goes the royal lie-in.'

'That explains things.'

'Explains what?' said Ephraim sharply.

'Why I had a disturbed night, that's all. It must have been the noise of their arrival.'

'I thought you were looking tired,' said the gossip. 'Well, I must be getting on. Things to do, stories to hear. Ginseng tea might do you some good. Mrs Kedar swears by it.'

Though Jonah and his Pharisees disapproved, the Roman baths operated seven days a week. Simeon could see no logic in the ban on washing on the Sabbath. God could hardly disapprove of cleanliness. Steam whooshed and billowed and the bathhouse carried its normal smell of woodsmoke from the furnaces and oils from the unctorium. 'Over here, old friend,' said Philippos from an invisible perch when Simeon's stick came tapping.

The Greek talked more quietly than normal. Once or twice Simeon had to ask him to repeat himself and he worried he might be going deaf. 'Ephraim's full of some story about holy men arriving in the middle of the night,' said Simeon.

'If that's what they are.'

'What do you mean?'

'I don't know how innocent they are. No one can be so unworldly. They're claiming to have followed a star here. The astronomer royal, Miqrah, doesn't work Friday evenings so the king is not sure if he believes the story.'

'My apprentice saw something like that in the sky.'

'Your apprentice might do well to zip his lip.'

The visitors were Parthians of some sort and by seeking an audience with the king they had, wittingly or not, made a diplomatic statement. Jerusalem was accustomed to priestly pilgrims but few presented their credentials to the king. Herod normally played hard to get but the magnifici sent him a tray of gilded walnut baklava and, for the ladies of the royal household, a pewter bowl filled with aniseed body cream. Herod had a weakness for both walnut baklava and the scent of wifely flank massaged in aniseed, so the visitors were admitted. At first all went well. The trio took it in turns to pay florid tributes to Herod and his court, these being relayed by a smooth interpreter. They purred about the splendour of his reign. They complimented him on the opulence of his palace and the rising glory of the temple, which they compared favourably to that of Ecbatana. It was impossible to tell which of them, if any, was the leader, for they took it in turns to speak and when they did so it was in soft, lisping voices accompanied by plump hand gestures. Everyone was wreathed in smiles – until the visitors asked to be allowed to pay their respects to Herod's successor.

'My what?' said the king.

'The new king of the Jews whose appointment is emblazoned in the stars,' replied the visitors amiably. They added that they marvelled at the wisdom of a ruler who was clement and far-sighted enough to pass the torch of monarchy without the usual bloodshed and unhappiness. What a remarkably generous man King Herod was, haghighat daareh! This occasioned great nodding of heads and namaste palms.

'Oh dear,' said Simeon.

'At first Herod laughed. Then he thought their interpreter must have made a mistake. Then things went a little quiet.'

'Were you there?'

'I was watching from the minstrels' gallery. The king dropped his teeth to the knuckles of his right hand and gave them a bit of a chew. Courtiers froze. The queen, on tiptoes, reversed from the room before the gifts could be snatched back. The visitors stood on the carpet in front of the king, fanning themselves slowly, beaming innocently. I don't think they realised anything was wrong. When the king did speak his voice had a low, guttural quality. He diligently begged the visitors to say more about the star they had followed and why they had come so far on such a speculative mission. They waxed lyrical about a vision telling them that the prophecies of the Nevi'im were bearing fruit and how, most fervently, being scholars of religion, they wished to be there to pay homage to the Christ. The king wafted his hand at this, scripture not being his forte, and he invited them to retire to a side-room for refreshments. The moment they were out of earshot his language deteriorated. Boaz was despatched to fetch the high priest and to bring the blasted Miqrah with him. The high priest and his acolytes arrived pink in the face, lugging various ancient scrolls, and when Herod heard their diagnosis of Bethlehem being the birthplace of a great king, he threw his goblet at them. By now the astronomer royal had been pushed through the doors, looking greatly indignant. The king said: "There you are – for years I pay you and the one time you're needed, you've taken the night off." The astronomer royal confirmed that there were indeed reports of an unusual moving star.'

His Greatness: 'Where is it now?'

'Well, it's hidden by the sun at the moment,' said the astronomer royal.

'No, you halfwit. Where was it last night?'

'Roughly over Bethlehem.'

'Bethlehem!'

'Yes,' said the astronomer. 'What's wrong with that?'

'You're fired,' screamed the king.

The astronomer did not take his dismissal well. He was pulled from the royal salon with a browned-off expression, shouting: 'That's not fair,' and: 'I demand an appeal.' Apparently all the king said was that if the astronomer had been any cop he would have anticipated his fate in the stars.

Philippos eased his neck amid the bathhouse's billowing steam. Simeon leaned on his stick and laughed about the astronomer royal, who had never been much good in the first place. It was another couple of minutes before Philippos continued.

'Soldiers are being summoned, Simeon. This census has already annoyed the people. Things could become sticky. It would be helpful to know what is being said in the square.'

'Is he going to arrest the three sheikhs?' asked Simeon.

'Not yet. He is going to have them followed. If they have any sense they will make themselves scarce and head home by another way.'

'It doesn't sound as if they do have much sense,' said Simeon.

The next few days in Jerusalem saw a frenzy of activity and, for the good souls of Deuteronomy Square, considerable botheration. Guards on the palace gates were doubled and traffic in that area was banned. Herod's sons were confined to their quarters and a dusk-to-dawn curfew was imposed in the upper city, causing difficulty for Zillah's soirees. Ephraim heard that the garrison commander was 'watching developments closely' and numerous turmae cantered out of the Antonia each day to assert Rome's presence with a noisy clattering of hooves. There was even a rumour that Herod had died. When had the king last been seen in public? Could it be true his guts were leaking out of his groin? Screams had been heard from his private apartments, it was alleged. Why was it so long since the king had visited the temple? In earlier days he loved riding through town in a litter. Why not now? Jonah became excited. 'It's the endgame, Simeon!' The young Pharisees around him grinned and rocked and ate enormously. Philippos, meeting Simeon in the bathhouse, announced that he was being called away to Tyre on business and might soon be gone for several weeks. He urged Simeon to keep his head down but Simeon wafted away his worry. Que será, será.

The three sheikhs left town hurriedly a couple of moonless nights after their royal audience. The king, when he discovered their disappearance, threw a terrible tantrum. He tried to discover where the moony-faced trio had gone. Ostlers and watchmen were interrogated roughly but nothing came of it save for a rumour – reported by a goatherd and clearly ridiculous – that the sheikhs had gone to a farm and hailed some peasant girl's child as the next king. The goatherd was charged with wasting police time.

'A contact of mine on the city walls did see a line of camels taking the Bethlehem road,' Ephraim told Simeon. 'But that's between you and me, of course. We don't want to get those three wise men into trouble.'

'Three blundering eejits, more like,' snorted Simeon, and he brushed a small itch off his forehead.

News from Bethlehem

THIS Musa was not the carefree Musa the square knew. He worked quietly and kept his voice down, accepting customers' money with little more than a grunt. The old Musa used to ring a bell every time he was paid.

Benjamin dropped Javelin for her usual service and there was none of the usual spoiling. Today it was straight to business with no treats. Javelin's hooves were scraped in silence. When Benjamin handed over some coins the farrier muttered: 'A touch of seedy toe. Otherwise not too bad. I've seen a lot worse these last few days.'

'All this rain must have been causing problems.'

'I'm not talking about hooves,' said Musa. 'Hooves can be healed.'

'What's wrong, Musa?'

'You don't want to know.'

The story came out of him unevenly. He began by muttering that Herod was a cruel bastard and we'd always known that. But what was the point of the Romans if they didn't stop the king acting like a barbarian? Then: 'I'm talking too much,' and he started to pack away his mobile smithy.

Benjamin fetched tea. Once Musa had finished tightening his saddlebags he sat down, drank the tea and gave a heavy sigh. 'I was working in Bethlehem. It was awful.'

'We did hear a rumour. Something about babies.'

'It was true.' Musa blinked.

'Why did Herod do this?'

'You don't want to discuss it too loudly, lad.'

'Why not? It's terrible. Babies!'

'Herod was spooked by those sheikhs, those idiots flashing their money in Jerusalem a week or so ago. He had them tailed and once they'd gone, he sent his thugs into action. I wish I hadn't been there. The women were all crying. Men tried stopping the massacre but they were pushed aside and some were speared. The babies themselves never made a noise. Not the ones I saw. That only made it worse.'

The first morning at Bethlehem had been normal. Musa had set up his brazier near the market where he always worked and his little bell had busily clonked for a couple of hours as various customers paid. Around midday a cavalcade of Herod's men swept in from Jerusalem, left their horses by the aqueduct and started going from house to house, asking about any newborn infants. After that, Musa's trade evaporated, and with it much else.

Proud parents and grandparents are always delighted to bring their babies to the door. That was almost the worst of it: the innocence of their initial happiness, for there was no suggestion of a threat when they were asked to produce

224

the children. Many presumed it was part of the damn census. The slaughter wasn't done by Judaean soldiers. It was Thracian and Galatian mercenaries. It happened so fast that there can't have been time for many to escape, although a lot of people fled Bethlehem afterwards, in shock.

'Herod has spent years building up this country, trying to make us proud with his buildings and this temple. Then he goes and does this. It's madness. Killing babies because he fears one of them is going to topple him! Threatened by a babe in a cot.' Musa rubbed his stubbled face. 'I'm getting out of Jerusalem. The city doesn't feel right. The Romans must know he's finished.'

'The Romans created him,' said Benjamin.

'He wouldn't be the first puppet to have his strings cut.'

Deuteronomy Square that evening was a subdued version of its normal self. Only a few of Jonah's lads joined him at the long table and they kept to themselves, muttering. Ezekiel closed his almond stall early owing to a lack of custom. Few shoppers were on the streets. Simeon, troubled that his own king had done such things, did not join the draughts table. He took a jug of Pramnian wine to a table near the bougainvillea where Phut was working his way through a mound of ka'ak al-quds. Phut could be relied on not to speak. Silence was all that Simeon sought. Oblivion in a flagon of puzzlement. 'Come on, little Herod, let's go and get you dressed.' He confessed to his thoughts in the Roman baths the next morning. Philippos merely said that there had been a muted atmosphere in the palace. 'Things are a little *piano*,' was how he put it. 'It's hard to be sure how matters will develop.' Before they left that day,

Philippos added: 'My Tyre trip has been cancelled. They now want me to take some leave for a few months.'

'Athens?'

'Rome, actually. Mainly pleasure but a little business. I will see you on my return, I hope. Look after yourself, old soul. I have so enjoyed our chats.'

'I Sing'

AND when the days of her purification according to the laws of Moses were accomplished, Mary brought her baby to the temple to present him to the Lord. She had been looking forward to the trip, never having visited the big city. Her husband told her it was a dreadful place but Mary's head swam with dreams of Jerusalem's walls and the food and the crowds. She had heard much about that wonder of the world, its temple. In her young mind Jerusalem was a citadel in the clouds.

Simeon had bookings for three presentation ceremonies, all to be supervised by old Rabbi Micah. Already two had failed to turn up; now the third was late.

'It's all very odd,' Simeon told the boy. 'You'd better go and tell Micah we've drawn another blank.'

'No need, he's just come out of Huldah Gates and is heading towards us,' replied Caleb. 'Did we get deposits from the no-shows? He'll be after us for the balance.' Families had to pay a presentation fee to the temple and they often gave the money in advance to Simeon so he could handle arrangements. Few country people liked to carry many coins around the wicked city.

'What ho, Micah.'

'Shalom, Simeon. Where are your families?'

'They are not exactly my families.'

'You know what I mean. Where are these people? They made a booking and now they fail to honour it. The scribe will soon start wheedling about his fee. Two cancellations already.'

'And now the third lot are late, if they turn up at all. Running scared maybe.'

Simeon clocked an unusual number of Roman guards in the square. The authorities had the jitters, all because three blundering busybodies had appeared from the East, asking dumb questions. And because the king, his king, had gone mad. 'They might yet turn up.'

'Alternatively I could knock off early,' said Micah. 'The money still has to be paid. You know that.'

'I only pass on what I am given. I'm not liable for no-shows just because Herod is throwing his weight around.'

'You should watch your tongue, Simeon,' said Micah. 'I don't mean that as a threat. You and I have known each other long enough. But you never know who is listening.'

The third couple on Simeon's list was Mary and her husband. The streets were clogged by spot-checks. Local troops were stopping carts and searching loads. Simeon was about to give up on the couple when Caleb said: 'Those two with a child might be them.' The mother, in a purple shawl, clutched a swaddled infant. The father had deep-set eyes and powerful shoulders. He looked, Simeon thought, familiar.

'It's Mr Simeon, isn't it?' said the father.

'I recognise you, I think,' replied Simeon.

'You helped me once when I was looking for work.'

'The Nazarene carpenter!'

'Well remembered. Yousef. This is my wife, Mary. There were soldiers everywhere. We had to leave our donkey tied to a trough in the lower city.'

'The place is on edge.'

'Have we missed our appointment?'

'Fear not, little flock. Caleb will run and tell Micah we're in business after all. You're the first couple to turn up. The rest cancelled.'

'They cancelled?' said Mary. There was an innocence about her.

'They lacked your good manners,' said Simeon. If Mary had not heard about Herod's proclamation it might be better to keep it that way. Caleb caught Rabbi Micah in time but the scribe was keen to pack up for the day. Micah said his verger could take down the official details and submit them the next day. Caleb said Simeon would be grateful. He hated to disappoint couples.

'You seem to be on your own. Couples normally bring relations and godparents to bear witness.'

'They are back in Nazareth,' said Mary. 'We travelled straight from Bethlehem. We were there for the census.'

'Bethlehem?' said Simeon. He rubbed the scar on his forehead.

'I rode the donkey with our little one. Yousef walked beside me.'

'My dear, you misunderstand me. Can I check? Do you mean your son was born in Bethlehem?'

'Yes, Bethlehem. For the census. The baby came on earlier than expected.'

'Is something wrong?' asked Yousef.

The old man stopped them halfway up the stairs leading to the Gate Beautiful. Worshippers and traders were pushing past them. The new temple, even on slow days, had become a marketplace. But maybe it helped to discuss this in a melee.

'Look,' said Simeon, 'the authorities are arresting any new parents from Bethlehem. I wouldn't risk it.'

'Risk what?' said Mary.

Caleb interrupted. 'That's Micah's verger at the top of the stairs. He's gesturing at us to hurry.' A party of passing Pharisees was making a din. A candle-seller hawked his wares. Two urchins were goofing about, one trying to punch the other. A beggar-woman yelled for alms. Noise everywhere. Mary clutched her child.

'When they ask where you had your son, say you're from Nazareth,' said Simeon.

'He was born in Bethlehem,' said Yousef.

'Just say: "We're from Nazareth," and the rest will be understood. Keep Bethlehem out of it.'

'We need to hurry,' said Caleb. The verger came up and crossly explained that the priest could not wait for ever. Simeon knew the man only by sight. He would not necessarily be trustworthy.

'Just fudge it!' he hissed to Yousef.

Micah greeted them with: 'Here they are!' and accepted the turtle doves Yousef had brought. Caleb produced the wax token to prove the birds were bought from an approved dealer. On behalf of the young couple he also dropped the presentation fee through the slot into the large wooden chest for temple dues. The sum was in the approved temple coinage. Mary and Joseph were told to stand beside each other before the altar while the flapping turtle doves were handed to orderlies and had their necks wrung.

'Where are the family members?' asked Micah.

'There aren't any,' said Simeon. Again he rubbed his forehead. It was hellish itchy.

'No one to bear witness? No one to hold the baby?'

'Nope.'

'You and Caleb will have to do it,' said the priest. And the baby was given to Simeon.

'Rabbi Micah,' began Caleb, 'we give you Joseph, a carpenter from Nazareth, and his wife Mary, also from Nazareth.' Micah repeated the names to the verger who scratched the details on a wax tablet before Micah recited the opening liturgy. Mary gazed happily at her handsome husband and for a moment everything seemed okay.

Simeon had not held a baby for more than half a century. 'The infant, please,' said Micah. At first Simeon did not hear. In his arms little Yeshuah was contentedly gurgling, chewing his tiny fist. Simeon could smell the child's milkiness. He was so light. 'The infant, please,' repeated Micah. 'Simeon, step forward, please.'

'Rabbi,' said Caleb, 'we give you Yeshuah of Nazareth.' He steered Simeon forward so that he was standing in front of the priest.

'Date of birth?' asked Micah.

The verger took it all down on the tablet.

'Nazareth, you say?' said Micah.

'Yes,' said Simeon and Caleb.

'That was where the child was born.' The way Micah said this, it could have been a statement. There was no reason to respond.

'No,' said Mary. 'We were in Bethlehem when he was born.'

'They're from Nazareth,' said Simeon. Turning to the verger, he added, in an almost jocular manner: 'Such a bonny baby.' Yeshuah was stirring. He stopped sucking his fist and reached out with his hand. Simeon inspected the child. The eyes were blue, the rich, layered blue of apatite.

'Place of birth, then,' said the verger, 'it is not Nazareth? It is Bethlehem?' He paused to check what Mary wished. Mary nodded. Yousef and Simeon felt unable to contradict her. The stylus worked its letters in the wax.

The rest of the ceremony played out according to the customs, even if Micah seemed distracted. The liturgy was spoken, prayers were chanted. Maybe it was all taking a little longer than normal. Micah and his verger bowed to each other, bowed to the altar, bowed to the participants, then bowed a second time to the altar. The parents bowed to Micah and to the altar and to one another. Simeon, still holding the infant, bowed three times before he raised Yeshuah to Micah so that he could anoint the baby's brow with sacred oil. Simeon's mind raced. Why could Mary not have told a white lie? Bethlehem! The child Yeshuah again reached out his hand and his tiny fingers curled round the lower reaches of Simeon's beard. The blue eyes were ablaze, not with temper but with something more forceful than that and, though this was an odd thing to say, ageless. Simeon felt the gaze of those eyes intensely. They drilled into him. They triggered and, somehow, cauterised a deep memory. Simeon realised that his brow had entirely ceased its itching.

There remained a joint prayer still to be said. Micah was about to begin it when the verger spoke into Micah's ear. Micah shook his head and told the unhappy verger to stay put. Caleb spotted what the problem was. Leaning over to Simeon he whispered: 'The scribe is about to leave. The verger wants Micah to hurry.'

Little of the ceremony remained. All that would happen now would be that Simeon would be expected to return the baby to its mother, Micah would impart a final blessing, everyone would do some final bowing and then the congregants and their family members, not that they had any here, would hug and celebrate while the wax tablet was borne to the registration desk. Simeon started handing Yeshuah to Mary but he felt a sharp tug on his beard. 'Ow! That hurt.'

'He doesn't want to leave you,' laughed Mary.

The verger pounced on the moment of informality to ask Micah: 'Rabbi, shall I proceed?' He was anxious to run the wax tablet over to the scribe, whom Simeon could now see in the distance. The man had risen from his table and was collecting his scrolls.

Baby Yeshuah continued to direct that kingly gaze at Simeon. He reached his second hand to Simeon's beard and flexed another set of tiny fingers. 'One moment, please, Rabbi Micah,' said Simeon. 'I would like, with your permission, and as a sign of gratitude to you and the temple for conducting this beautiful and important ceremony, to sing a short prayer.'

'You sing?' said Micah.

'I sing,' said Simeon. 'I sing.'

Sentry Duty Almost Done

SIMEON lifted his head in defiance and, if truth be told, to stem a tear, as he said: 'I sing this.' Yeshuah was in his arms so he started softly and let the volume rise gradually. The voice had not been raised in song for years yet from its first note its pitch was practically perfect.

'Lord, now lettest thou thy servant depart in peace, according to thy word.'

Caleb turned with surprise. He noted the emphasis with which Simeon sang the word 'now'.

'For mine eyes have seen thy salvation, which thou hast prepared before the face of all people.'

Over at the registration desk the scribe closed his box of quills, tucked his bench under the table, adjusted his hat and headed down the cloisters. The verger noticed what was happening. He ached to chase after the scribe but was duty-bound to remain by the altar for as long as the formalities continued. Rabbi Micah had not yet given the blessing and words of dismissal. Leaving before that would be improper. Micah remained impassive in his priestly position, hands clasped. He had enough aura of command to root the whimpering verger to his spot.

Simeon's singing did not go unheard. From her place in the women's court washroom Anna caught it on the breeze. The long years had left it no less distinctive. Anna had never expected to hear him sing again. And that tune: the words had changed a little but she had heard the melody before, one night a lifetime earlier, from a young soldier who had composed it for his son. She left the washroom and started walking to the source of the song.

'*To be a light to lighten the Gentiles*,' sang Simeon, himself stepping slowly towards Mary and Yousef. His voice grew in confidence. With every word it gathered defiance. Caleb had had no idea his master possessed such a voice. Visitors in the courts could now hear it and they were turning in curiosity. A soaring, powerful tenor. A voice worthy of any cantor. A voice worthy to address God.

'*To be a light to lighten the Gentiles*,' sang Simeon, repeating the phrase and building towards his musical peak. '*And to be the GLORY of thy people Israel. Amen.*' The word 'glory' was stretched to several notes, as was the Amen. The song flew from his ribcage, as if from a song thrush. Onlookers became entranced by this ancient with the infant. The baby's eyes blazed like shafts of sunlight through clouds. Simeon's joy, his relief, radiated out of him and Anna knew that she could no longer keep away from him. Having covered the distance from the washroom she removed her veil and wordlessly reached a hand to Yeshuah before clasping her heart and bowing. Micah bestowed a long, loud blessing, in which he thanked God for the gift of Simeon's prayer and for Simeon's voice and for this young couple from Nazareth. Mary accepted Yeshuah back from Simeon. She told him it had been a beautiful song and she would never forget it. Yousef silently shook the old man's hand. Anna dropped to her knees and kissed the hem of Yousef's tunic. She imparted blessings of her own to Mary. Little Yeshuah continued to gaze at Simeon. The babe would not stop staring. An elderly sentry's duty was almost done. When he looked at Anna's face he did not seem at all surprised.

In the distance a lawyer's swirling robes disappeared down some steps. The scribe would not return until the following morning. Scribes did their jobs to the letter. They would not handle documents once they had left the premises. This was understood by the verger. 'You did that on purpose!' he hissed.

'I'll look after that,' said Micah, instructing the verger to hand him the wax tablet which had the details of Yeshuah's presentation. The verger thrust it in his hands and left in anger.

'Can it be altered?' asked Simeon.

'No,' said Micah. 'What's done is done. The verger will report any alterations. He's that type of man.'

'Will he go to Kedar?'

'I think not immediately. He will probably talk to his friends first. He will be scared of losing his position. They all are nowadays. But I will have to hand this tablet in first thing tomorrow.' He left them with a low bow.

'What do we do?' asked Yousef.

Flight

CALEB provided an answer to Yousef's question. 'First thing we do is leave the temple before that verger blabs.'

'Yes,' said Simeon, 'you had better disappear but remain outwardly calm. I can be more use here.'

'Come with us,' protested Caleb. Simeon shook his head and took Caleb aside to issue instructions. It was a lot to absorb. The boy was going to have to rise to the occasion.

'Tell me what is happening,' said Mary. 'I have a right to know.' Maybe she was tougher than she looked.

Simeon told her: 'Jerusalem is no place for the three of you. Follow Caleb.'

'Who's going to look after you?'

'Don't worry about that.'

The men would go separately. Anna offered to accompany Mary, for soldiers seldom stopped women. Yousef and Caleb would just look like two ordinary blokes.

There was always talk to be had in Jerusalem if you wanted. Simeon stopped at Huldah Gates and fell into conversation with the sentry. The pause was not entirely confected. Simeon was becoming short of breath, as if he had eaten something too fast. Sitting on this step for a while was welcome. The sentry recognised Simeon and humoured him by shooting the breeze. With the man's attention diverted, Caleb sauntered past with Yousef. Asked later, the sentry would report that he saw no accomplices.

After re-gathering some strength Simeon hobbled to his pitch, assumed his normal seat and fanned himself. Presently he spotted Lysander, who was delighted if surprised to find Simeon eager to chat. The neglected poet moaned at length about his latest literary disappointments. Simeon offered words of encouragement. Nothing was really worth trying, moaned Lysander. Simeon winced a little and clutched at his flank. 'Are you all right?' asked Lysander.

'Just a twinge of some sort,' he lied. 'Pulled muscle, perhaps.'

'I pulled a muscle once. Tell me what you think of this next poem . . .' Simeon's pain was almost anaesthetised.

Ezekiel trudged past with a barrow of almonds. He allowed Simeon to give him advice about not overdoing things. The graveyard was full of rich men: we brought nothing into this world and it was certain we could carry nothing out, that sort of thing. Ezekiel said it was a fine thing for Simeon to give others advice but he wasn't looking too bright. 'You need to take it more easily. How old are you now?'

'In some ways I have never felt younger,' said Simeon, despite these stabs of pain he was trying to ignore. And here came young Capillus, Tabitha's Roman beau. 'Hail, Capillus!' sang Simeon, long, high and tremulous.

'Simeon, you're singing again.'

'I am indeed.'

'But I thought ...'

'Things have changed.'

Capillus proposed a duet. 'There's a song about a lovesick bumblebee. Perhaps you know it.' Simeon nodded and he had little difficulty hitting the harmonies. Onlookers clapped as the duet ended. Out of one eye Simeon saw Anna and Mary slip out of the square down an alley. There was no sign of Yeshuah. Mary must have hidden him in the folds of her garment. Both women had veiled their faces and darted off almost like a caracal that Simeon recalled from long ago.

From his office overlooking Temple Square, Kedar heard the singing and moved to the balcony to see what was happening. Spotting Capillus, he lightened. Then he saw Simeon. The old fool. Why was he whooping it up and kicking his legs like a drunk? Kedar threw a couple of fat medjools into his mouth and half-drew a curtain for shade. Everyone knew Simeon didn't sing or, for that matter, drink too much nowadays. What was going on? Kedar sucked at a fleck of date skin in his lower teeth. Simeon was a throwback to the days before Herod's boom, when Judaea was a backwater. Fortune smiled now on initiative, aspirational men alive to the benefits of federalism. Power would belong to a technocratic elite that understood the facts of geo-politics unlike those nativists among the Pharisees and Zealots. Kedar snorted and returned to his desk. Simeon, for his part, was struggling to regain his breath. The duet had not been wise.

Although Kedar tried to focus on the temple's security budget, concentration eluded him. He sent for his aide. How were the street stop-checks going? Were there any reports of trouble? The aide knew of nothing amiss. Kedar's nose would not stop twitching.

Simeon calculated that it must be getting on for an hour since Yousef and Mary were smuggled away from the temple. He hoped Caleb was using the time well.

* * *

AT a shabby dwelling in Jerusalem's lower town, the verger's wife wrung her hands as she listened to her husband's story: the young couple with a baby, Bethlehem, old Simeon meddling. Damp straw and green wood smouldered in the hearth. The verger's wife had hoped to boil mutton stock but there was little chance of it reaching a decent heat on this fire.

'We're meant to report Bethlehem babies immediately,' said the verger.

'You did your job.'

'Not entirely. The report won't be submitted until tomorrow morning. That's what worries me.'

'We're better off keeping quiet.'

'I'll be in trouble if they hear about the delay.'

'Who's they?'

'The authorities.'

'You weren't in charge.'

'People in charge never get blamed.'

'Rabbi Micah told you what to do. He won't cause trouble for us. He'll be okay.'

'Micah! He'd never risk his neck. He's not that kind of man.'

This dank place was hardly much of a home. Maybe the verger could improve his lot. Though he normally kept his distance from Kedar there were times when you had to step forward. But what if Micah lied? What if he claimed the verger was a loafer who could still have made it to the scribe in time, had he not been lazy? Micah would be believed because he was a priest and priests had all the fancy words. Vergers, like lepers and Samaritans, were always given a kicking.

Kedar had favourites. One of the errand boys who reported a pickpocket was rewarded with promotion to the night watch. That boy was now on his way to being a full steward. He'd be on decent money then. Maybe the verger could pull off a similar trick. Then there was the reward. The palace had promised money for information about Bethlehem babies. Altar orderlies were bound by a code of discretion but you couldn't blame a working stiff for trying to get ahead in life. And they were still going to find out, so if he did nothing he'd look dozy, or complicit, and that would bring down a torrent of woes.

'Do what you think best,' said the verger's wife. 'But be careful, won't you? We don't want trouble.' As her husband fastened his tunic and departed, she stirred the dismal stockpot. Out of the water and onion rose a tangle of pale bones.

* * *

CALEB deposited Yousef at Simeon's rooms and hurried to the alley behind Onesimus's store. They were going to need some kid goats and he only knew of one place to find some at short notice. Benjamin listened intently to his request and jumped to action. Simeon's confidence in the two lads was well placed.

Benjamin was soon loading his cart with hay that would keep the goats content once he had collected them.

Onesimus was not pleased when Benjamin told him he was bunking off for the rest of the day but there comes a point when a father's complaints are ignored. Benjamin had been spoiled by his mother and there was no saving him. Of that Onesimus was certain as he turned back to his customers. 'Now then, Mrs Pappo, just those grapes was it for your good self?'

'Not the whole bunch,' said Mrs Pappo.

Back in the apartment Caleb pushed his arm deep into the cracked jug with the wide neck. Wrapped in wool he found the stash of coins. Mary arrived with Anna, the two of them not removing their veils until the door was shut. Noor and Reuben were already present. Quite a crowd.

'Were you followed?'

Anna: 'I don't think so but I wasn't looking round much. Didn't want to look suspicious.'

Mary rushed to Yousef and Caleb gave them a moment before asking Mary to hand her purple shawl to Noor. 'But it's the only one I have.'

'It's a beautiful colour,' said Noor.

'It's distinctive,' added Caleb. 'From a distance they might mistake Noor for you. If you wear it, Mary, you are more likely to be stopped.'

Noor and Reuben went off in search of Yousef's donkey. They found the little beast still tied to its trough in lower town. Reuben had persuaded Deborah to look after the tea stall in his absence. Onesimus was not at all pleased but there comes a point when a husband's complaints need to be ignored. Of that Deborah was certain.

In the cramped apartment Anna accidentally knocked a metal cup off the table. Leaning down to retrieve it, she spotted Simeon's low bedside shelf. Alongside his comb, candle, a small vial of incense and a ripening apple was a pottery figurine. Little longer than someone's thumb, it depicted a smiling, heavily breasted figure, elbows akimbo. Anna gently lifted the figurine. One of the elbows had at some point been broken. While the rest of the room talked, she ran the tip of one of her forefingers over the join. The discovery of the figurine disorientated her. Anna pondered all sorts of things in her heart.

'Put on these,' said Caleb, throwing Mary some spare clothes. He always kept a set at Simeon's for emergencies. Out on the roof terrace, Anna clutched the Judaean figurine. Some of Simeon's washing hung on a line. Its neatness gave her a pang. Maybe it would never have worked for them. Maybe he always had to be alone. But it hurt.

When Mary had changed into Caleb's spare tunic and bags, hair pushed inside a straw sun hat, she made a reasonably convincing boy. Caleb teased her about it. That at least drew a smile. Yousef was less happy when he was told he would have to leave Jerusalem on his own. 'No way, I'm not leaving Mary.'

'You've got to,' said Caleb. 'If you stay with her, you'll both be picked up and Yeshuah will be found. Any young couple will likely be searched.'

'Caleb's probably right,' said Mary.

'Start by taking the road to Jericho,' said Caleb. He issued further directions and made Yousef repeat them. He promised Yousef that Mary, or 'Avi' as she would be addressed, was going to be fine. They would set out once Benjamin returned. But when would that be?

Down at street level Benjamin clicked his teeth at Javelin as they clattered off to fetch the goats. The lad had to ask directions to Mrs Mizrahi's place. When people heard her name some rolled their eyes and a few wished Benjamin luck. 'She's that bad?' asked Benjamin.

'She's a feeder,' came the reply.

Once he found the Mizrahi house Benjamin explained his mission. Mrs Mizrahi watched him closely. She fully believed that Caleb had sent him to collect the kid goats and seemed happy with the money he gave her, which had come from the cracked jug in Simeon's room. She'd have sent the goats without payment, for she was devoted to her son. Yet she would not cease staring at Benjamin.

'Is there a problem?' he asked.

'You're thin.'

'Thank you.'

'It's not a compliment. If you're not careful, you'll fly away in the next wind.'

'Well, I really must fly because Caleb needs me back quickly.'

'Caleb's father was too thin. Look what happened to him.'

'What did happen to him?'

Mrs Mizrahi sucked her teeth and threw her head in the direction of the skies. 'May his memory be a blessing. He never ate. He never looked after himself. Do you eat?'

'All the time.'

'All the time? Then why are you so skinny? All the time? I don't believe it. There's more fat on a poplar tree. Girls like bulk, you know. Meat on the bone. I'll do you a plate of stew.'

'That's very kind,' said Benjamin, 'but I must hurry.'

'Too rushed to eat! That's what Mizrahi used to say. You sit down.'

She waddled to the pantry at the back of the house and there were sounds of pots and splashing water. By the time she returned, laden with stew and chopped fruit and bread and wine, Benajmin had gone, taking the kid goats with him and leaving the deposit money on the table. Mrs Mizrahi could hear his cart charging up the lane towards Deuteronomy Square. 'Boys!' she exclaimed, before sitting down to harpoon a juicy cube of nectarine which she proceeded to eat with much sucking of satisfied gums.

* * *

'YOU want to see Mr Kedar?'

'I do.'

'He's a busy man.'

'I know.'

'He's in a meeting.'

'It's important.'

'So is his meeting. There's a security alert.'

'That's why . . .' The guard's face was a portrait of obstinacy. 'I'll wait,' said the verger. 'If you don't mind.'

'It's not a question of what I mind or don't mind, sunshine. It's what the boss himself thinks. I wouldn't want to be in your sandals if you're wasting his time.' The verger waited on the floor outside Kedar's office.

For the sake of our heroes it was a blessing he was not shown at once into Kedar's private office. For the guard and the verger it was less fortunate. Despots have a lot going for them. They impose and collect taxes. They fill their granaries even when harvests are slight. But they do these things by creating fear and a by-product of fear is reluctance to interrupt the boss. For as long as Kedar's door remained closed the guard supposed the boss was busy with his aide. What he forgot was that the office had an interlinking door. The aide had long been back at his own desk, where he was composing limericks, while Kedar was in his own office having drunk a cup of hyssop and honey. He had drifted into a late-afternoon nap among the cushions and velvet throws of his day-bed.

* * *

REUBEN and Noor, in the purple shawl, were soon on their way, although the little donkey struggled to carry Noor. The pace was not going to be fast but if they could make a couple of miles it would help. If stopped, they would say they had fallen in love and were eloping for a few days. It was, without wishing to be indiscreet, a story neither of them particularly minded. It even made Reuben tingle a little. Noor found that Reuben's companionship fitted like a perfect pebble in the palm. The lines on their faces spoke of laughter and forgiveness. There was not enough forgiveness in Jerusalem.

The roadblocks had not entirely stopped and traffic was bad, as Benjamin himself was discovering on his way back up town with the goats. Drivers complained about the delays. Shopkeepers gesticulated at Herod's soldiers for ruining business for the afternoon. Reuben and Noor kept their patience. Reuben soothed the little donkey as they waited for the jams to ease. A platoon of Roman soldiers barged past, heading out of town. Noor squeezed Reuben's hand, partly for reassurance. In another fifty yards they would be at Damascus Gate. After that they should be able to pick up the pace a little.

* * *

'ENTER!'

'Mr Kedar, there's a verger wants to see you.'

'What about?'

'He won't say exactly but it's something to do with Bethlehem and one of today's presentation ceremonies.'

'Most of them cancelled, I thought. All right, show him in.'

The verger cringed. Kedar's room had a musky scent of orange and wax and mint. It was better than damp woodsmoke. 'Speak up, man!' Kedar told the shrivelling wretch. A short version of events was blurted out in terror. Then: 'Why was I not told this earlier?'

'We brought him to you at once, sir,' claimed the guard.

'I came as soon as my shift was finished,' claimed the verger.

Kedar shouted for his aide. Did anyone know where Rabbi Micah lived? 'We need answers and fast. Get on to it at once. Don't just stand there! We need to find this family.'

Micah was located at his barber's. The arrival of the search party made the barber jump and he nicked Micah's ear. It bled, as ears will. Micah explained that the registration tablet was in his locker at the temple and he was marched there while holding a cloth to his ear. The barber realised Micah had not paid for his haircut. He wondered if he would see him again.

For Simeon the afternoon acquired a sweetness unknown for decades. Though his eyes were dim they danced as guards ran out of Kedar's headquarters, red ants vacating a disturbed nest. He half-expected them to come and arrest him but they vanished down Deuteronomy Street. As they ran they passed a veiled old woman who walked serenely towards Simeon. He knew it was Anna from her gait, unchanged even with the years.

'I found this,' she said, opening her right hand. It was the figurine from Simeon's room. With her other hand she drew back the veil and Simeon could see that her eyes sparkled with tears. She leaned forward and kissed him, the gentlest of touches, her lips dry.

'She had a little accident, as you can see,' said Simeon.

'But you mended her.'

'The angel mended her.'

Anna touched the little charm to her heart. 'The angel mended us, too.'

* * *

'SORRY, bad traffic. And your mother wanted to give me something to eat.'

'That's Mum. I'll nip down there once you're rolling.'

Mary needed a push up on to the driving bench of Benjamin's cart. Caleb apologised for putting his hand where he oughtn't. 'Did the others get away safely?' asked Benjamin.

'Let's hope so. Yousef left half an hour ago. He's taking the new road then cutting across.'

'I'll stick to the old road. Shouldn't be as busy.' Benjamin finished fastening a box under the hay. He tied the goats to the back of the cart and jumped up beside Mary.

'You'll have cover until the city gates,' said Caleb. 'After that, you're on your own.'

'Not quite,' said Benjamin. 'As Uncle Simeon would say, God is with us.'

'If you say so.'

'Simeon is right,' said Mary.

* * *

KEDAR paced up and down. Micah's locker had been empty. The priest was as baffled as the soldiers were angry. They were not to know that Anna had removed the tablet. Micah was roughed up and soon it was not just his ear that was bleeding. Kedar left the downstairs wardroom where the priest was being held and returned to his office to question the verger once more.

'You're sure they were from Nazareth?'

'I think so.'

'You think so!'

'No, no, I'm sure. Definitely Nazareth. But I'm hopeless with names. Jacob and Miriam, or something like this. But I don't remember what the child was called. All I noticed was its eyes.'

'Useless!'

The verger wished he had listened to his wife.

'Send word to the northern gates and I want checkpoints on the Samaria road. We're looking for a couple with an infant. The father has a strong beard and the mother is in a purple shawl.'

'Yes, sir.' Staff scattered. Kedar reached a stressed hand into his dates jar. He looked out of the window just as Anna was kissing Simeon, and at that moment Kedar bit on the date stone. Kedar knew at once, from the loose grit in his mouth, that the tooth had shattered. He yelled in pain and his aide rushed into the room. 'My choof!' he mumbled, spitting out bits of broken enamel.

'Your choof, sir?'

'My bloody choof! Broke it on a date. Damnashun!'

'Bad luck, sir.'

'Ish not bad luck, ish . . .' In the square he now saw that Anna was helping Simeon to stand on his stool and that the old man was starting to sing. He didn't quite believe him capable of such a voice.

'Lord now lettest thou thy servant depart in peace, according to thy word.'

Kedar, wiping his mouth on a bloodied sleeve, said: 'Get him!'

'Do what, sir?'

'Him, down there. That interfering, bloody-minded old bugger Shimeon. Arresht him!'

'Arrest Simeon, sir?'

'Yesh!'

'What for?'

'DO IT!'

'We normally need a reason . . .' Kedar lifted the bowl of dates and threw it at his aide, who dodged it with commendably fast reaction and enquired: 'Shall we arrest the woman as well, sir?'

'Of coursh not. She'sh mad.'

'There's a lot of it about, sir.' Though he had never actually seen one, Kedar roared like a sea lion. 'On it, sir. On it right away.'

* * *

OVER Jerusalem flew a hawk as handsome as kept by any princeling. As it completed its slow circles its eyes saw soldiers fan through the crowded streets, heading for the city's gates. They had to push through a mass of humanity and its accompanying din of shouts, lowing cattle and wooden wheels. Once past the city walls, carts accelerated for all points of the compass, making up lost time. Now the hawk's circle brought it back over the upper town. At the royal palace a cold order prevailed, the king not yet having been told the news. In Deuteronomy Square, Deborah was running the tea stall. And as it glided towards Temple Square, and a thermal lifted its wings, the hawk saw a crowd draw round an ailing old man who was singing a song of rare force and beauty.

* * *

BENJAMIN'S cart was twenty yards from the Lions' Gate which would take them east out of the city. Mary had gone quiet. Benjamin rummaged in his bag and gave her a tin whistle.

'Play this.'

'I don't know how.'

'Few do. Blow into it and make some noise. It will stop you looking so frightened.'

They reached the checkpoint and a soldier asked: 'Where are you going?'

'Mount Scopus, if we ever get there. Picking up some apricots once we've delivered this hay and the goats en route.'

'I'll need to check the load.'

'Okay,' said Benjamin. Mary was blowing the tin whistle.

'That's a terrible noise,' said the soldier, walking towards the back of the cart. 'He needs lessons.'

'Try putting up with it for hours,' said Benjamin, following the soldier and scanning down the queue of traffic. He raised a hand in a gesture that had been agreed. 'Avi, give our friend here something patriotic. A march or something like that. Or maybe he'd prefer a love song for his girlfriend.' The soldier enjoyed the joke while Benjamin made a show of prodding the hay with the handle of his fork and offering the soldier a chance to do likewise.

'Balls to the emperor Augustus! A pox on all Romans and collaborators!' It was Caleb, shouting from the crowd like a Zealot. The soldier immediately lost interest in the hay cart and looked to see where the noise was coming from.

'Nuts to King Herod! Romans out of Judaea!'

'Arrest that man!' shouted a sergeant at the checkpoint.

The soldier sprinted off in pursuit of Caleb, who disappeared into the crowd. Now another, much louder voice cried: 'He's gone that way! Guards! Over here! He took my basket!' Only two people in Jerusalem could shout like that. One was Boaz the herald. The other: Mrs Mizrahi.

The checkpoint was deserted as its soldiers raced to Mrs Mizrahi to check that she was okay and to follow her directions which were, naturally, entirely misleading. The distraction was enough. Benjamin ceased prodding the hay – he had been careful to avoid Yeshuah's hidden cot – and hopped back up next to Mary. With a click of his tongue at Javelin, the little cart rolled forwards.

They were out of Jerusalem. It was a start – but not the end. Further trouble came at the junction of the new road. Another queue of traffic. Another check. And this one looked worse because the Judaean troops were being overseen by Romans. They were next in line to be checked when a clattering of hooves and chariot wheels came from behind. Angry shouts told the driver of the chariot to slow down and await his turn like everyone else. Only when they saw that the driver was a young Roman with a magnificent horse did they cease their complaints.

'Whoaaa, Sagitta.' The chariot threw up a cloud of dust as it halted.

'Cornelius!'

'Who's that?' The charioteer wiped the dust from his bronzed face. 'Benjamin! What are you doing here?'

'Trying to earn a living.'

'How commendable of you. Greetings, Officer.' The optio on the roadblock had come over, initially with a view to asking the idiot in the chariot what he thought he was playing at. Then he saw who it was.

'I might have known it would be a celebrity.'

'Sorry, Officer. Hope I haven't queue-barged. I was going to join the line like everyone else but Sagitta simply wouldn't stop. I expect I was speeding.'

'Probably thought you were at the hippodrome in Caesarea,' said the optio.

'Have you seen me there?'

'Only three times! Very good to meet you, sir.'

'Please, just Cornelius.' The other soldiers were now milling round, gawping at the famous speed-merchant and his chariot.

'I'd give you a race to the next bend but we're waiting to be checked,' said Benjamin.

'You old dog, any excuse!' roared Cornelius. 'Mind you, Javelin looks ready for action. I have always had a soft spot for this mule, Officer. Good afternoon, Lady Javelin.' Javelin ignored Cornelius but she bared her teeth at Sagitta. The thoroughbred remembered that bite to its tail and it neighed. Cornelius spotted Mary and added: 'And good afternoon to you, Mistress . . .'

'Master Avi,' said Benjamin rapidly. 'My cousin. He came along for the ride.'

While Cornelius did a double-take and goofed along to the laughter of the soldiers, a crying started. It came from the hay. Mary leapt down and hurried to the back of the cart where she grabbed hold of one of the kid goats. Without being seen, she dug her fingernails into the little goat's flank and it started bleating.

'You can see why they call them kids,' laughed Cornelius. 'For a moment . . . But, Optio, I fear we are holding you up.' This was reinforced by renewed grumbling from the long traffic jam. 'I can vouch for my friend Benjamin. He is a good friend of my aunt, Lady Zillah, who in turn is an intimate of Centurion Lucilius.'

'I'm sure that will be all right, sir. Privilege to make your acquaintance.'

'The privilege is all mine. All mine.'

'May we proceed?' asked Benjamin.

'We are looking forward to the race,' said the optio.

Mary, still holding one of the goats, was heaved back on to the driving bench and Benjamin nosed the cart out of the queue and followed Cornelius. Mary ensured that the goat kept up its bleats of protest, to which Javelin added some hee-hawing. What with the noise of the harnesses and the shouts of goodbye from the soldiers to Cornelius, Yeshuah's crying somehow went undetected. Clear of the roadblock, Benjamin and Cornelius put on a little show of a race for the soldiers, just as far as the next bend, and once they were beyond that Benjamin called whoa and brought the cart to a halt. But Cornelius had gone, off towards the horizon, his hair flowing in the wind, as golden as Sagitta's mane. And that night, once they had found their way safely to Isaac's Seat, and once they had been joined by Yousef who had cut through from the Roman road, Yousef asked Benjamin:

'Do you think your Roman friend knew?'

'That Avi was Mary? If you will permit me to say this, Cornelius has an eye for beauty.' Mary blushed. 'Cornelius is Zillah's nephew. And the Lady Zillah is an enigma.'

A Drape Billowing in the Wind

SIMEON, standing on his stool before a growing crowd, sang his song again and now one last time. Between each rendition and the next Anna explained to onlookers that Simeon had seen something remarkable. She spoke assuredly, without any melodrama.

It is a curse of the writer that music can never be captured in words. Melody is as elusive as angels' breath. Those who heard Simeon's song were struck by its lilt and instant catchiness; yet print, or at least the ink in this author's pen, is unequal to the task of describing it. The song had echoes of a temple chant and a medina's lament. It was lyrical and loving yet it possessed an urgency. Though Simeon's voice had started strongly, now his energy was fading. When he at first sang of his eyes seeing salvation, he had pointed to the very jellies in his grizzled head. He had beckoned the crowd in a gathering gesture when he mentioned Gentiles and Israel. He had stretched his neck for the high notes. Now he felt his heart flutter its protests.

Kedar's men pushed through the spectators, shouting at people to disperse. No one was budging just yet. Despite the pain in his chest, it needed one last go. One final push of volume. '*Lord, NOW lettest thou thy servant depart in peace.*'

Simeon fell from the stool. Anna half-caught him in her arms. The crowd gasped. A scuffle broke out between spectators and Kedar's guards. Someone's spear was snapped underfoot. 'Simeon's fallen.'

'Help the old man.'

'Stop pushing, won't you?'

Anna heard all this in a fog of slow motion. She lowered him to the ground. There was still a flicker of life but his ox-like heart was giving up the ghost. 'I love you, Simeon.'

One moment his eyes saw her and she knew they understood. Briefly it was as if his head was on her pillow half a century ago when she rose to stop a drape billowing in the wind and she looked back at him, drifting to sleep. The next moment his eyes were lifeless and the memory was gone. Around, all was again noise and brutishness.

'He's dead,' said Anna. A small, rough-handed woman, smelling faintly of woodsmoke, knelt beside her.

'Is that Mr Simeon?'

'Yes. Did you know him?'

'My husband did.'

It was an hour before Kedar's men allowed the body to be removed. Not having more than a handful of coins, Anna arranged for it to be taken to the Samaritans' cemetery, for that was cheapest. Adom the undertaker wound the body in a white sheet and two men carried it away. They were followed, at a distance, by an old, hobbling dog. Anna realised that she was still holding the little figurine in her hands. As she quietly kissed it the tears came. She wept and wept until they would flow no more. The verger's wife remained at her side, silent and uncomplicated, the first of many to be forgiven. Anna dried her cheeks, righted Simeon's tumbled stool and for the rest of her days, however long they were, told the world what he had seen, the light to lighten the Gentiles and the glory of God's people Israel.

Back in an English Town

THE 'Nunc Dimittis' ended with a long Amen. Under the cathedral's high roof its final note lingered and echoed before the choirmaster said: 'Lovely job, everyone. You can leave your folders here. There's time for a comfort break before we robe. Back in twelve minutes, please.' The choristers dispersed. Some chattered and one lay clerk hummed the tenor line as he sauntered down from the choirstalls and flicked on his mobile to check for messages. And yet he remembered to bow to the cross as he left the chancel.

That same cross was regaining its definition. The moment of blurring ceased. Had it only been a moment? Alex Symons blinked and shook his head and was not sure that he knew the answer to that question. He felt he had visited a different age and city, a time long before the invention of corduroy trousers – long, even, before the invention of slightly corpulent Englishmen. Yet here he sat in this cathedral pew wearing his trusty plum-coloured cords and his rain-damp coat, a faint taste of Rob's lemon cake still in his molars.

'Good evening.' It took him a moment or two to realise that a young man, hesitant and with a thatch of black hair, was talking to him. 'Will you be staying, sir?'

'I'm sorry?'

'For evensong. You're very welcome to stay. Perhaps you'd like a prayer book and pew sheet. The service doesn't last long.' It was as if the man understood that Symons's time was at a premium. Dying, one can become jealous of the hours.

'Oh. Right. Good idea. Yes, thank you.' A worn copy of the *Book of Common Prayer* settled comfortably into Symons's right hand. Inside its front cover a verger from long ago had written: 'Cathedral 1963'. The book was the same age as Symons.

The hand that wrote those words must now be long dead. Its neat, faded, fountain-pen script evoked an era of Sunday-best clothes and horn-rimmed spectacles, Alvis cars, Archbishop Ramsey, pork rissoles and junket. All were long gone, ground to dirt and dust, from fashion to ashes; yet this book's prayers remained, still salt after so many centuries, here in black ink on onion-skin paper. They shimmered in the minds of more people than modern bishops liked to admit. Bones crumbled but words endured, just like that Roman wall. Words had the power of a rushing, mighty wind. Words without end, Amen.

Out on the town's streets an ambulance siren could be heard snaking its way through the traffic. Some poor soul must be in mortal peril. Symons fell to realising that maybe six months was not such a bad settlement. There would be time, yet, for a few sun-dappled drives in his little

Mazda. He might persuade Anne to join him for a picnic and they could drive to the Brecon Beacons and lay the rug on that flat outcrop that looked west. Or was it east? He was never entirely sure. They could gaze at the British sky with its scudding clouds and they could console themselves that the same heavens, or something pretty similar, had been gazed at by lovers in most ancient of days, and that in every good marriage there would come a moment when one soul went ahead and the other was left behind to grieve. What could we do about it? Nothing.

The pew sheet explained that the canticle settings were Stanford in B flat. Symons recalled photographs of Charles Villiers Stanford with his walrus moustache and pince-nez glasses. Those snapshots made him look the crustiest of sorts yet with his music he had created the most vaulting fervour. Symons stayed for the service. The pieces were sung again, the choir now robed and combed. Attendance was slight but what did you expect at such an hour on such a day in such an era? Prayers were said for the people of the Middle East. All of them. Stanford's music and the testament of the Prophet Simeon wormed their balm into Alex Symons's soul. God being merciful, there was no sermon. Banal cadences and political platitudes would have shattered this peace. So long as the choir sang and the sempiternal prayers were intoned, Symons felt cocooned. After that, the present would slowly fizzle back into focus, at least for a few months more. This tightness in his chest, these fingernails and eyes, all eventually would dissolve. He might not last as long as those big new candles on the altar. So what? As Symons sat there in that English cathedral the border between life and dream was no thicker than the membrane in a boiled egg.

Only when the precentor sang the prayer about lightening our darkness amid the perils and dangers of this night did Symons remember he should have been home by now. Anne would be worrying. But as he was leaving the cathedral he felt something in his trouser pocket: it was the pen he had borrowed from Rob for the crossword. Returning it would not delay him long. Rain was still falling, though lighter than earlier. Cloisters was only a minute or so in the wrong direction. He walked back to the wine bar.

No one noticed when he slipped inside to return the pen. The place was humming with worldly mirth. Scilla was asking Rob what she should drink. 'The Pramnian wine isn't bad,' said Rob, and he rubbed his hands on his apron in a manner that gave Symons a jolt.

'I love Greece,' Scilla was saying. 'Such darling men. Did I tell you, I once posed for a Greek sculptor? Ravishing but not remotely heterosexual.' Scilla never changed. Not in a month of Sundays. Not in two thousand years. Her blazered boyfriend from earlier had disappeared and she was talking now to a suntanned, medallioned guy whom Symons recognised as a local builder. He was ordering platefuls of food and talking loudly about his current construction project. It was a government job and deadlines were tight.

Symons felt a lightness as he walked home. The pavement slabs glistened under the sodium-vapour street lights that were just starting to glow. Symons did something from childhood, which was to avoid walking on the lines. Would a bear not jump out and devour you if you trod on a line? Did not everyone know that for a fact? Not that any bear could frighten him now. The worst had happened. The doctors had delivered their damnedest. It would be harder for Anne, he knew that, but he was now reconciled to the inevitable.

'I'm home,' he said, hanging his coat and cap in the utility room where they could dry. Anne, in dressing gown and bedroom slippers, shuffled to the utility's doorway. The light from behind framed her and she looked as young as when he had first known her. She gave a rueful, loving look. Nothing was said. Nothing needed saying. He encompassed her in his arms and they knew the row was forgotten. There by the washing machine and the laundry racks they held each other a long time. After that, things felt a lot better.

For the first night in weeks, he slept soundly. His dreams were filled with the sounds and smells and sighs of a city whose walls stretched to the ends of the Earth. They were dreams with music, laughter, love and a slow certainty of where truth could be found. They also included a mule, bees, birds of prey and a loyal dog that walked in his shadow just as we can trail a Lord and master of our own.

Alex Symons made it to Christmas. A child was born: to Mia and Josh a son, in the city of . . . well, that's enough storytelling for one evening. All you need know is that the infant was fed on butter and honey and that he prospered. Somewhere in the top drawer of my desk at home a photograph exists of that babe, or one very like him, being held by his grandfather, who happened to be my brother. His end was near but in the picture he looks triumphant. He wears the certain, seraphic smile of one who has seen calamity dethroned and is now ready to sing at the gates of Paradise.

'*Nunc dimittis servum tuum, Domine.*'

FINIS